HARDING PROPER

HARDING PROPER

K.G. MONTGOMERY

Willow Park Press

ISBN 978-1-7332908-2-1

First printing January 2022

Cover design by Rowan Ridge Press. Cover © Willow Park Press

❀ Created with Vellum

To my husband and kids

1

CHARLOTTE

CHARLOTTE DEEMED the woman behind the bookstore counter as ninety percent *harmless*, ten percent a *threat*. Apparently, to the clerk, Charlotte wasn't worth even hollow pleasantries.

"You buy used books, right? I'm selling these," Charlotte said, forcing a casual tone as she hoisted a box onto the glass counter. In her mind, she rehearsed a prepared explanation for the sale—a lie that sounded plausible before she entered the bookstore. Now, confronted by the woman's impatience, she wasn't sure if her lie would stick.

The woman, *Alberta Sheppard* according to the worn nameplate, glared out over her reading glasses. Charlotte tried to appear casual and relaxed until the woman looked away. She studied the shop. There were several hand-written notes taped to the register— reminders—and a 1950's family picture hanging on the wall. A tiny, pencil-written caption read *Mom, Dad, and Berta*.

Berta eyed the box, raising an eyebrow.

"I'm selling everything," Charlotte said. "Gently used. Most are pristine."

"Did you steal them?" she asked.

"No . . . I'm selling the books because—"

"If you didn't steal them, then the reason doesn't matter," Berta said, her expression sagging along with the wrinkles on her face. She leaned over the box and ran her fingers along the spines while shooting quick glances at Charlotte, as if simultaneously judging the worth of both the books and their owner. "Our rates are one dollar for paperbacks, three for hard, and we don't buy family histories. Family stories don't sell."

Charlotte tightened her jaw, stifling a gut reaction to haggle over the poor buying prices. All she needed was a little gas money, not a confrontation. Plus, she couldn't waste time manipulating a stuffy, small-town clerk. "There isn't a family history in there," she mumbled, recalling how she'd burned it in a fire pit only days ago.

"Just saying." Berta continued to riffle, her motions quick and careless at first, then she slowed down as if her attention was catching on the titles.

Charlotte took a few steps from the counter, her heart racing and her palms sweaty. She put up a pseudo appearance of ease—a precaution for Berta's benefit. But the woman didn't glance up again, and Charlotte knew why. Even a stuffy old clerk, one who probably never left her shop, would notice the value in that box.

"Hope they work for you," Charlotte said. "I'd like to sell them all."

Berta nodded, her gaze wide-eyed and fixed.

Charlotte knew she'd won. She turned her back to the counter to take a deep breath out of view. The store was conveniently empty. She was the only customer in Sheppard's Used Books and Gifts, but there wasn't much room for a crowd anyway. The rows of shelves and end tables were covered in almost never-ending piles of aged books—mounds of teetering published works left to collect dust and add to the store's aroma of ink and wood polish. Charlotte expected to find a sense of nostalgia in such a small-town mom and pop bookstore, at least she assumed that was normal, but this place gave off an eerie waft of abandonment. She gazed around the ceiling, looking for security cameras. There weren't any to find. No one was watching her. Except Berta.

Berta cleared her throat. "Not sure how in-demand these titles will be for resale, but I'll take them all. The total is $54. They're in good condition so you get the full rate." She wrinkled the bridge of her nose as she counted out the bills from the register drawer.

"54?" Charlotte said, taming the heat building in her chest. She was getting ripped off. "That's . . . generous. Thank you." She took the cash from Berta's hand and flipped through the bills.

"It's all there. No need to question me, deary."

"Oh, I'm not," she said. *Re-adjusting: Bookstore Clerk—seventy percent harmless, thirty percent a threat.* "I just like to double check things. It's a habit, I guess."

"Fine. Anything else? If not, watch for ice when you leave." Berta drummed her fingernails on the counter.

Cracked nails. Bitten. Charlotte noted them. The clerk's cracked nails could've used a bit of polish to hide her habit, but Charlotte assumed Berta wasn't the kind of woman who bothered with vanity. Plus, Charlotte herself didn't care for such vain things. Polish was a luxury. It was for normal people. And Berta's cracked nails themselves didn't mean much, except perhaps the woman was having money troubles and bit her nails out of nerves. "No. I don't need anything else. That's it."

"Okay then. Have a nice day," Berta said. She slid the box off the counter and sat it on the floor without a second glance.

Charlotte hesitated for only moment, trying to sever any care she had for the box. Then she hurried out the door and ignored the chiming bell as it announced her exit. Winter air instantly stung at her face and hands, forcing a shiver down her spine that pricked like shattered glass. She pulled her jacket hood over her hair, tucked in a few escaping strands of rush-dyed brown, and shoved her hands inside her pockets. The bills crumpled in her fingers.

Fifty-four lousy dollars. It seemed like hardly anything, and certainly a fraction of what those books were worth from a collector. *Fifty-four pathetic dollars.* She stared down at the icy sidewalk and squeezed the bills until her fist ached, trying to rationalize how she'd just sold another part of her soul for practically nothing.

At least Pearl wasn't there to witness her belongings being treated like the unwanted scraps from a second-hand thrift store. Pearl couldn't have watched her precious books being pawned away for gas money. Although, selling them had been the plan all along. Her expression tightened. This was so much harder than she thought it would be.

"How are you doing today, miss?"

Charlotte glanced up and straightened herself.

A city police officer leaned against his parked patrol truck, the bold painted words *Harding Police* contrasting against the white door panel.

She forced the unconscious scowl off her face.

"Are you okay?" he repeated.

Heightened nerves swelled in Charlotte's chest and percolated up the back of her neck. She fought against the instinct to run.

Evaluating police officer—threat level unknown. The officer's tone sounded genuine, casual and polite, but she'd learned to be suspicious in spite of that. He had a good number of wrinkles near his eyes, and his graying brown hair was short and clean cut—practical. Probably around fifty years old. The name *Chief Walker* had been embroidered into his uniform, right below his left collarbone. She analyzed his casual posture and deemed the officer fifty percent *harmless* and fifty percent a *threat*—fifty percent due to the open ticket pad in his hand while he glanced at Pearl's ten-year-old Oldsmobile parked a space away.

"Is this your car?" he asked.

She bobbled a nod.

"Not from Northern Idaho, huh?" he said, pointing at the Utah plates.

"No."

"Okay." The officer stepped up on the curb and smashed the snow with his boots. "Then you're probably unaware of Harding's Main Street parking ordinance. It covers the old part of town . . . in Harding proper."

He pointed down to where she assumed a red-painted curb hid

under the snow. There weren't many cars parked along the road, and the tight strip of historic storefronts didn't possess the earmarks of an active shopping hotspot. *Sleepy* maybe, but not active. She assumed the officer's patrols were quiet ones.

The chief cleared his throat. "The space directly in front of each business is off limits. For emergency access if needed, you see? We're a small town, but even here we have traffic laws."

Charlotte couldn't tell if the man's sudden condescending tone was intentional or brought on by the cold. Perhaps both. She altered his percentages—*sixty percent a threat.*

"Sorry, I'll move," she said.

"Thanks for that."

Charlotte hurried to the driver's door and fumbled for the keys in the pocket of her jeans. Her cold fingers weren't cooperating fast enough. The officer walked along the side of her car, his gaze scanning the interior, and he tilted his head toward the rear license plate.

Seventy percent a threat.

"Looks like a full load," he said, motioning to the three boxes and two large duffle bags stacked on the backseat.

Charlotte prayed he didn't ask to look in the trunk.

"Where are you headed?" he asked instead.

She released a weighted breath. "University of Idaho," she lied. "I'm a student."

"In early December? You're a little late for fall semester."

Eighty percent a threat. "Going early for the next one," she said, realizing the impromptu statement didn't sound believable. She was a bit north of the university, not by much, but clearly wasn't on a logical route from the Utah border. "Just on my way to pick up a friend. Needed to stop, stretch my legs a bit, and get some gas. You know how road trips are . . . boring."

He eyed the car again.

"Uh, officer. It's real cold out here, and I need to get going. Sorry about the bad parking job. I'll remember the rule if I ever pass through again." She commanded her face to relax and smiled as if she held up a jug of laundry soap in a TV commercial—all fake, but forced to sell it. "I'm really sorry. Promise."

He paused, stared at her and the car for much too long, then nodded. "Yep, it is pretty chilly. And icy. Be careful and follow the speed limit."

"Of course," she said.

He pointed north. "The gas station is just a block up the street."

"Thanks." Charlotte slid into the driver's seat. She looked in her mirror while struggling with the keys and found him writing something down on his ticket pad. Perhaps her license plate number.

The car sputtered as she started the engine, barely revving to life as she pulled into the road. To keep her cover story, she headed one block north toward the gas station. In her rearview mirror, Charlotte glanced back at the officer as he climbed in his patrol truck. She expected more, but the cop just sat there . . . *no*, he leaned toward his mounted laptop. Perhaps he didn't care about her.

Re-adjusting. Police Officer—returning to fifty percent a threat.

The town's only gas station looked nearly abandoned under drifts of snow, except for the dozens of tire marks near the pumps. An Out of Order sign had been duct taped over the digital credit card slot, and by the frayed and faded condition of the edges, it must have been in place for a while.

Charlotte briefly made eye contact with the station clerk—a kid about sixteen who sat inside near the front window and held some kind of magazine. He didn't seem to care as she stepped out of the car and fiddled with the gas pump.

Gas station clerk—ninety percent harmless, ten percent a threat.

Charlotte gripped the precious fifty-four dollars in her pocket, calculating how much gasoline she could afford and still have money left for food. She stopped the pump at twenty dollars. Not quite full, but it would be enough to make it to the next town and leave Harding and its watchful police chief behind.

She entered the store and eyed the clerk as she approached the counter. To her relief, he didn't look up from his magazine. The cover read *Tech and Business*, and there was an image of geometric shapes in multiple colors. Charlotte thought the topic was an odd choice for a sixteen-year-old kid, but then again, maybe it was a ruse. Who knew what kinds of magazines he kept under the counter?

"Here," she said and placed a twenty dollar bill near him.

The kid swiped up the money and shoved it in the register. "Need a receipt?"

"No."

"Perfect. Have a nice day," he said.

Gas station clerk—one hundred percent annoying. Zero percent a threat.

Back inside the car, Charlotte glanced at the used bookstore. The officer's vehicle hadn't moved from its spot, and he wasn't doing much, merely shifting a little in his seat. She squinted. The one-block distance made it hard to see his face and impossible to read his lips.

The officer brought his arm toward his mouth, holding what could only be the hand-held end of his radio. He then reached for the mounted laptop again, all the while talking to someone.

Charlotte flipped forward. She bit her bottom lip. Perhaps the transaction at this used bookstore didn't justify the stop, even though she'd skipped nine of the twelve possibilities on her route north. Plus, Harding was the last store on the list—the final opportunity to get gas money without using her reserve funds. That money wasn't an option.

She started the engine. How long had she allowed herself to be in the town? She calculated distance from the freeway off ramp: *nine minutes into town under icy weather conditions. . . twelve minutes in the bookstore . . . another ten at the gas station . . . driving time . . .* it was too long. Too much attention. Too much notice. Pearl would never have allowed such carelessness, and would've upped the threat levels sooner. Pearl's voice played in Charlotte's mind from memory, "Reacting to threat levels keeps you safe, Charlotte. Assign everyone a threat level."

She grit her teeth. *Police officer—eighty percent a threat.* As she drove her car away from the gas station, the near-bald tires spun in the snow with each turn.

"One hundred percent control is a necessity. Anonymity is everything," she recited to herself, and proceeded to check her rearview mirror at least a dozen times in less than a minute.

The patrol truck pulled into the street at a crawl. Charlotte squinted at the mirror for a few more seconds, praying that the cop turned at the nearest corner. When he didn't, a wave of nausea filled her stomach. Getting stopped couldn't happen. Letting the car be searched wasn't an option. Charlotte suppressed the tingles of panic in her pedal foot.

In an instant, a strobe of red and blue lights filled Charlotte's mirrors and bounced against her face. Adrenaline surged through her body so fast she wondered if her chest would explode instead of breathe.

Police officer—one hundred percent a threat.

Charlotte pounded the gas pedal.

The tires spun in the snow before the small treads caught a bit of traction. She sped forward, searching for an escape route. *Five seconds . . . four . . . three . . . two . . .* Charlotte cranked the wheel at the next turn, and her body pressed against the driver's door. Her seat belt caught against her torso, the pressure digging into the skin at her neck, but the pain didn't register. She corrected the fishtail on instinct then checked her mirrors again, hoping the small-town cop wasn't experienced in high-speed chases. At least not as well as she was.

His vehicle fishtailed wild and quick, but evened out at just the right moment. Charlotte groaned and pressed harder on the pedal.

His sirens wailed. But what she heard was a garbled mess.

Harding—one hundred percent a threat.

Fifty . . . sixty . . . she reached a speed where the siren no longer wailed in her ears. Charlotte plowed past a stop sign at seventy miles per hour. She focused on an overpass in the distance and at the wide sign beyond its end that read *Leaving Harding. Thanks for the visit!* Her tires sailed over the snow in a juggernaut of speed, catching more air than ground. She hit eighty, then ninety. Charlotte white-knuckled the steering wheel as the Oldsmobile crossed onto the bridge. *This isn't logical. This is foolish. Re-calculating: Ninety miles an hour . . . bald tires . . . snow . . . black ice . . . police threat . . . fulfilling objective . . .*

She slammed on the brakes. *Outcome: one hundred percent . . .*

The steering wheel jolted in her fingers, pain surging through her wrists. The strobe of police lights cut across her mirror just as she collided with the edge of the bridge. A millisecond later, she glimpsed a flash of silver guardrail, and beyond it nothing but white as she gained air. Her body floated in her seat—weightless—lifting high with the car as if a bird soaring without a fear, all the while terror burned in her chest.

The car began to fall, G-forces fighting against her seatbelt and her limbs flapping helplessly. Boxes and duffle bags slammed against the roof. Her mind didn't react fast enough for even a scream.

The bottom of the Oldsmobile landed on powdered snow, metal groaning under the impact, then the car slid wild, crashing into a river of ice. Charlotte collided with the popping air bag, pain surging through her restrained body. For a mere three seconds, she breathed in the foul odor of stale air mingled with the stench of fresh starch powder before she lost consciousness—seconds before the frigid river water surrounded her ankles, and seconds before she could muster up the strength to free herself.

Charlotte's white winter turned to black.

2

THE TOWN

ALBERTA SHEPPARD KNEW she was finally going to be rich. And she deserved every penny.

She watched the young woman exit her family store, pretending not to care about the box sitting innocently near her feet. For about a half-minute or so, she stared at the glass door until deeming the wait long enough for normal common sense and regret to sink in, but the young woman didn't return. A smirk formed across Berta's lips. She shuffled behind the counter.

The box of books was heavy, but the sudden thrill of the new acquisition filled her with the strength of a woman half her age. She hoisted the box onto the back-office desk then hurried to the front of the store.

Through the glass display window, she spotted the young woman standing near Chief Walker's patrol truck. *Figures, that girl thinks she can park anywhere. Deserves to lose a few dollars.* Berta flipped the *open* sign in the window to *closed,* and glanced outside one last time before walking away. She couldn't baby anyone. If the young lady wasn't interested in doing a little research before selling collectable books, then Berta wasn't required to be her mother. Life was about loss, hard realities, disappointments, and not second chances. At least not today. Rebirth was a luxury too expensive for the average person to afford.

Besides, the young woman had been stiff and rigid. Not casual, and clearly hiding something. Berta huffed. The girl probably stole the books and wanted to unload them, trying to get some quick cash for drugs or something sinister like that. Illegal drugs were likely. Young people had no self-control. But, Berta had specifically asked if the books were stolen, and the young woman said *no*. End of discussion. Sheppard's Used Books was in the clear.

Berta shuffled to the office and slid the box near her computer, then sat in front of the monitor. She adjusted her reading glasses, though it didn't help much, and single-finger typed in the web address for The Treasured Book Auction—the only website besides Harding's community page that she bothered to learn the address. Everything else was unnecessary and too much of a hassle. Some days using the computer at all seemed a ridiculous pastime.

Except for today. *Today*, a young woman with a cardboard box and a hankering for illegal drugs had walked through her door.

Berta held a book by the spine and entered the information in the website's search slot—*The Adventures of Gilly Heel, Book One: Lost at Sea* by Ruthan Stanley 1st edition, printed in 1924. A picture of the book cover popped onto the screen, along with a description of the plot. Berta read the bottom-line result while holding her breath: *Estimated market value for a first edition of The Adventures of Gilly Heel is $200 for each original print in the ten book series.*

She covered her mouth. The complete series was in the box. Plus, there were many more collectable titles. Most she recognized but had never seen in person. There were millions of words in that box, and they probably totaled several thousand dollars in an online auction. Perhaps that teenager at the gas station could help her, Jan's boy, but she couldn't remember his name—Matthew or Michael or something—maybe he could sign her up for an online auction account. Teenagers knew all that technology stuff. She'd be willing to part with a tiny percentage of the profits if he'd keep quiet about it.

A faint sound of sirens filtered in from outside the bookstore.

Berta shuffled to the front door and peered through the glass. She couldn't see Chief Walker's patrol truck but figured he was pulling over a speeder. Harding wasn't a tourist town—it wasn't much of anything to anybody who hadn't grown up there—but that didn't stop the police chief from rightfully pulling over every car with an out-of-state license plate. She paused, recalling there were Utah plates on the young woman's car, and wondered if the traffic stop would lead back to her very legal transaction.

Berta threw on her sweater and headed outside. The sirens bounced in from every direction. She didn't remember hearing that much noise since the last Fourth of July when city council officials paraded around their new over-priced fire engine.

A patrol car whipped past the bookstore. Berta gripped her sweater for dear life then shook her head in disgust. In her opinion, the new deputy chief was too eager, and too ramped up and green at his job for anyone to take him seriously. After all, he wasn't from Harding.

Berta glanced up the road and spotted the teenager from the gas station, Jan's boy, standing near the pumps. He stood, mouth wide open, watching the deputy race by before he met Berta's stare. She waved and wondered if he would accept five percent of her online book profits or demand ten like any other greedy teenager.

Mason Trent heard the sirens blare and dropped his magazine on the counter. He stared out the window and looked past the gas pumps at the old grandma car in the road. The woman with the Utah plates didn't stand a chance against Chief Walker's patrol truck, but guessing which outsiders left Harding free and clear was a decent pastime. Well, as long as he was watching from afar.

He hurried to the pumps, the perfect vantage point to the end of the main street, and watched as the grandma car corrected a tailspin at the corner. Mason let out a chuckle. At least this outsider had fighting spirit. Not that he wished for a problem, but a car chase in Harding was rare. *Anything* happening in Harding was rare.

Chief Walker's truck cranked hard for the turn, barely holding its ground, but managed to clear the corner.

Seconds later, the new deputy raced past the gas station at full speed.

"Wait for it . . ." Mason mumbled, and leaned forward, watching the deputy crank right at the turn. "And . . ."

The front end of Deputy Franklin's car plowed into a snow pile, a wall of white avalanching on the front hood.

". . . there it is." Mason stuck his hands in his pockets.

The tires squealed, but the police car didn't move.

Mason tried to hide a smile. Yep, maybe the Utah woman had a chance. He stood there for a moment, watching the deputy's tires spin without traction, then a twinge of nerves stung through his skin. His smile faded. Ed, his lazy boss, was at home watching a football game instead of running the gas station and tow business. That left Mason as the only one with the tow truck. Which he'd hardly ever used alone.

He had a choice—get fired for slacking or force himself to interact with the Harding Police Department. And he couldn't help pay his mom's bills without a job.

So . . . Mason headed for the tow truck. He imagined the new deputy was probably cursing the mayor's name since an additional police SUV wasn't on the town's *financially important* list.

Neither were high school technology instructors.

Glancing down the street, he noticed Berta Sheppard waving at him from the front step of the bookstore. *Crazy old lady.*

By the time Mason forced the cold truck onto the road, the deputy's car was gone. He thought about going back. But guys from Georgia didn't know how to drive a car in the snow. The deputy was probably stuck farther down. Mason weighed his options.

He'd mastered various excuses over the years when it came to avoiding contact with Chief Walker. Perhaps one of those would work on Ed. Several stupid ideas filled his mind, and he mumbled them to himself. But in the end, he knew Ed wouldn't believe any of them. Mason headed for the corner.

Except for Crazy Berta, Main Street was empty. The cold weather kept everyone indoors, but it was still odd. Why didn't they think sirens and tire squeals were worth a look? Why didn't they care even a little? Instead, Harding people just gossiped about stuff they never witnessed.

He turned the corner and drove north, scanning the edges and side streets for Deputy Franklin's final slide. When Mason neared the bridge, he noticed red and blue lights tinting the snow. Franklin raced from his open driver's door and headed for the guardrail. Walker stood there too, shuffling his feet, then the chief bolted for the end of the bridge.

Mason rolled to a stop behind Deputy Franklin's car. The whole thing seemed different than the normal tourist pull-over. Something was off. He swallowed hard, harder than he remembered doing in a while, and stared ahead. The grandma car wasn't on the bridge, and Franklin leaned over the edge while speaking frantic words into his radio. A heaviness grew in Mason's stomach—a feeling of involuntary stress that he usually tried to avoid. He watched Chief Walker run across the bridge and slide down the embankment. This wasn't the simple entertainment Mason expected to find.

3

WALKER

CHIEF WALKER SLID to a halt at the edge of the broken guardrail. He scanned over the side, evaluating the half-submerged Oldsmobile. The whole scene felt surreal. About fifty feet from the bridge, thick tire marks cut into the heavy snow and trailed off for another twenty-five feet along the bank where the car had finally crashed head-first into the river. The back end stuck out in the air, the rear tires slowing to a stop. Even with the several layers of fresh snow to lighten the impact, the final slide into the icy water hadn't been cushy. *Why did she run?* he wondered. *No, don't waste time, just move.*

"Walker!" Deputy Franklin raced to his side.

Walker hadn't noticed Franklin arrive in the last few seconds, nor did he remember calling the tow truck that was stopping behind his deputy's car. He didn't have time to deal with either. *Get the girl.* Walker bolted for the edge of the bridge.

"Call it in!" he shouted over his shoulder. "And get the med bag from the car!"

Franklin's muffled words echoed over the radio, but Walker barely registered them. He jumped down the white slope and raced along the bank, his boots sinking deep into the uneven snow.

. . .

WHEN HE REACHED THE CAR, he braced one hand against the bumper and inched his way toward the water near the back door. The entire front half of the compartment was submerged.

Walker thought fast. The water was deathly cold, and the fire department had rescue suits. But they weren't enroute yet, and he could almost reach the front end. The seconds passing ramped up his adrenaline.

I'm an idiot.

Walker slid over the edge and lowered into the water. Sharp chills ached at his skin and sent shock waves to his spine. The river was shallow, maybe five feet at the most, but he prayed the car wouldn't shift. Through the glass, he could see the woman's brown hair floating in the water. She wasn't moving.

"Miss!" He pulled at the back door without success. "Franklin, get over here!" he shouted and sank deeper into the water until the surface touched the top of his vest.

He felt down for the driver's door handle. His seizing muscles barely gripped the chrome. He managed to tug with his body weight, but the water pressure wouldn't allow the door to open. Walker pounded his free hand on the glass, feeling the impact in his nearly-numb fingers. He knew his baton probably wouldn't work under water.

"Chief!" Franklin slid to a halt near the back tire. He dropped the med bag. "EMS is close. Here's a punch." He stretched to give him a small, hand-held tool.

Walker grabbed it and popped the sharp end against the driver's window. The tempered glass instantly shattered into a spider-web of fractures and spilled into the river.

"Chief," Franklin said. "I'm coming in."

"No, get the stuff ready," he said quickly.

Franklin riffled through the red bag, pulling out an AED and bag valve mask.

Walker took in a painful, labored breath, the waterline up to his chin. He leaned toward the open window until he could find the girl's shoulder. Then he tugged at her seat belt and sliced with the cutting end of the glass punch until the strap snapped loose. She floated free in his numb arms, sliding rough out of the vehicle. When he leaned away, he couldn't tell if his frozen grip held her tight enough and feared he'd lose her in the river.

"I can't hold her," he said. "I need you to pull her out."

"Come this way." Franklin stretched from the bank.

They flopped the girl onto the snow. Her face looked pale and lifeless despite the crimson blood dripping from her nose.

"She not breathing," Walker said.

"I found a pulse!" Franklin pushed the AED aside and grabbed the bag valve mask, putting it together.

Walker's whole body ached and tingled. He reached to double-check her pulse but found his fingers didn't want to work. "You'll have to give her air. My hands are stiff."

His adrenaline pushed through the sharp pain radiating in his muscles as raw feeling started coming back to his arms. How long had she been in the water while he ran toward her car? A minute? Maybe more? Probably less? It was hard to remember. His mind spun like a hamster wheel. Had the snow cushioned her impact enough? She had a pulse. That was something.

Franklin kept squeezing air into the young woman with the bag.

Walker pulled up on his duty belt, which now felt like 40 pounds of solid rock, and fumbled to straighten it around his wet uniform. Behind him, sirens echoed from the bridge. He glanced over his shoulder. A group of Harding firefighters and EMS personnel stumbled over the snow, all carrying duffle bags of equipment and supplies. Relief washed over him.

An EMT took over giving breaths with the BVM. Walker stumbled back on the bank, letting the team surround the girl. He rose to his feet. That's all he could do—watch and freeze and be exhausted—but he couldn't force himself to look away. Not until she was breathing.

Seconds passed that felt like hours. Then, she sputtered a breath on her own. The heart monitor registered her pulse, weak but there. Walker forced himself to calm down, but his whole body shivered.

"How long was she in the water?" a paramedic asked.

It took Walker a few seconds to make his brain focus on the question. "About a minute, I think. Not positive." The rest of what the woman said landed as background noise. Walker waited while they packed up the young patient on a backboard and carried her toward the bridge where the ambulance waited.

"You should go, too," Franklin said. "Don't worry, Stewart and Kemp are on their way from the station. They'll help me contain the scene. You're goin' get checked out at County Hospital."

"I'm fine."

"You look purple. Maybe you're fine, but you took an ice water bath. I'm pretty sure that much cold isn't good. Remember, it was you who told me not to dunk myself in near freezin' waters no matter how strong the polar swim urge. You said it on my first day here *after* pointing out that a guy from Georgia doesn't know how to survive an Idaho winter."

Walker stared down at his hands. They looked abnormally red and blotchy, and his wet clothes weighed like cement. The adrenaline must have been wearing off. The possibility of hypothermia wasn't new, but having it himself certainly was. "Okay. I'll go. But start a report. This license plate came back connected to a Utah missing persons case. St. George P.D. is looking for this car. After you pull the car out, clear it and have the thing towed to the station garage. We'll deal with it when I get back. Let St. George P.D. know we have the car and the driver."

Franklin scrunched his face. "Sounds good."

The ambulance drove away, lights flashing. A few firefighters and EMTs still lingered on the scene, waiting to help bring out the vehicle.

Walker glanced at the car again and groaned. "Searching that wet thing out here will be impossible. Stuff will get damaged."

"More than it already is?" Franklin glanced inside.

He took a deep breath. "Yeah, I know. But let's do our best."

"Yes, Chief."

Walker moved to the side of the car. He peered into the back seat that was exposed above the waterline, examining the scattered piles of boxes and bags floating inside. Objects and belongings were strung through the interior like confetti—soaked, ice-ridden, and smashed. It would take hours to sort through it all if the circumstances warranted. He ran his fingers along the back fender then stepped around to the trunk. It was amazing that the lid didn't break open on impact. The car was old. Perhaps the lock had been reinforced, or maybe even stuck in a closed position prior to the wreck.

"Chief Walker?" An EMT sat his bag on the ground. He reached over to check Walker's wrist pulse while another EMT examined his face. "So you were in the water for over a minute?" he asked.

"Yes. Not too long."

"Pretty risky in December temps though," he said. "Let's get you out of the wind and make sure you keep all your fingers. Gotta keep writing speeding tickets or the city will go broke."

Walker didn't laugh.

Deputy Franklin motioned for Mason Trent to come over from the tow truck. Walker noticed that the kid hung back, glancing between police, EMS, and the car, an uneasy expression on his face as if coming closer meant he was trespassing.

"Don't worry, Chief," Franklin said. "I'll take care of everything. Go to the hospital."

Walker hesitated.

"Chief," the EMT said, pointing him toward the bridge, "let's get you checked out and warmed up."

Walker took one last glance at the car, wanting to stay. The Oldsmobile belonged to a missing person. The driver evaded police. They had probable cause for a search. But it was tilted in a river, and under the circumstances, processing could wait. "Fine. Let's go. And Franklin, find her ID. Find out who she is."

4

CHARLOTTE

THE AMBULANCE SWAYED as it plowed over the snow, forcing a pseudo sensation of moving water around Charlotte's body. She tried to open her eyes, but the muscles in her face wouldn't cooperate. Maybe it was the breathing mask over her nose and mouth, or the collar around her neck, or the padding on her head, but her body pressed against the backboard as if weighted down with concrete. A feeling of confined helplessness flushed through her core—the panic hurting more than the pain. On the outside, Charlotte was still, but inside, she was screaming.

A woman's voice spoke somewhere over her head, but not to Charlotte, like she was talking on the phone. "We're incoming with a female patient. Car accident. Early twenties. Heart rate is 57. BP 106/54. Unknown medical history, unknown meds and allergies, GCS is ..."

The woman then uttered a rolling garble of details that Charlotte didn't comprehend. She tried to focus on the sounds, but her mind felt hazy, as if the voice was coming from some far-off place and it didn't apply to her.

". . . suspected facial and internal injuries. Fifteen minutes out from County."

Move, Charlotte thought, ordering her limbs. *Move. Get away.* Even if she could manage to shift, thick straps held her in place. Charlotte's lungs burned with each breath as if on fire, causing a surge of familiar fear. She wheezed in air and forced a groan—subtle, a bit guttural, but her voice came to life.

She felt a touch on her arm.

"Can you open your eyes?" the woman asked.

Out . . . I want out. Charlotte's lips didn't move. She groaned again.

"You were in a car accident. We're taking you to the hospital. What's your name?"

Cold.

"Can you tell me your name?"

Charlotte commanded her eyelids to move for the second time, but failed without even a flinch.

The paramedic repeated the request a few more times and squeezed Charlotte's hand.

The sensation of touch against her fingers snapped a flood of memories through the haze. The images, quick and solid, parade in her mind like a slideshow. *Charlotte* . . . Pearl's voice echoed within the memory . . . *Charlotte, take my hand . . . open your eyes . . . I've got you.* But it wasn't Pearl's aged and familiar hand that outstretched—through the darkness came flames and ash. Charlotte's body tensed against the backboard. Then the memory broke, and she listened to the siren.

"We're almost there. Hang on," the paramedic said.

The woman mumbled something into her radio about administering meds while a cold sensation flushed through the IV in Charlotte's arm. Everything seemed to slow down with the drug—the ambulance, the pain, the terror, and Charlotte's need to fight against the restraints. After that, each moment took on a life of its own without her interference. She was wheeled into a warm place. People shuffled around her gurney, adjusting her clothes, limbs, and head until the constant shiver she had felt in the ambulance subsided. Their voices sounded soft, distant, and calm as they tended to her.

In the minutes that followed, Charlotte faded in and out of

consciousness—unsure of the flow of events or who was near her. For the first time in years, she didn't detail her surroundings or analyze the threat levels. Instead, she allowed herself to feel safe. She allowed herself to trust. She had to.

5

WALKER

CHIEF WALKER FLUNG the curtain aside and glanced down the aisle of the emergency room. "Jan, what's the status of the woman from the accident?"

"Stable, last I heard. They took her upstairs for a few scans." The ER nurse wrapped a stethoscope around her neck and picked up Walker's chart. "Well, your temp, heart rate, and BP are all back to normal. I'll get a release from the doctor to make it official, but you can probably go." She began typing his vitals into a wall-mounted computer.

"Perfect." Walker hopped off the gurney and adjusted the scrubs Jan had forced him to wear. He shoved his wet uniform, coat, and Kevlar vest into a large plastic bag, then strapped on his duty belt. For a moment, he wondered how odd he must've looked in medical scrubs and a police duty belt, but he really didn't have time to care. He needed to contact the St. George Police Department. There was a spare uniform at the station. No need to go home to his empty house. He assumed Franklin had followed instructions about waiting to search the Oldsmobile, but then again . . . *new guy.*

Jan gathered up the blankets and towels on the gurney before turning to leave.

"Uh, Jan?" Walker asked. "Did you get the woman's name? Did she have anything on her? Stuff in her pockets? I need to open her investigation and report."

She shrugged and glanced over at the white board above the nurse's station. "She's listed as a Jane Doe, so that means no ID, but I wasn't on the team treating her. If you want to check for belongings, she was two curtains up. I don't think it's been cleared yet."

"Thanks, Jan. Will you tell me when she's stable enough to talk to us?"

"Sure. I'll tell Dr. Fielding you want to be kept in the loop. And let us know if you figure out who she is. I don't like calling someone 'Jane Doe'. That's only cool on TV."

"Right." Walker grabbed his plastic bag and headed two curtains over. The center space reserved for the gurney was empty, no patient, but nearby stood trays covered in used medical supplies, syringes, and half-empty IV bags. Pieces of blood-stained gauze littered the floor. Walker had seen worse in the aftermath of other accident victims, but he'd also seen better. At least the young woman was stable. That was good.

Two nurses stood near a small, wall-mounted table that held a computer monitor. He didn't recognize either staff member, and they both seemed too young to have graduated from high school, let alone from college. But these days, that's how everyone looked to him. One nurse typed on the keyboard while the other verbally cataloged the drug names and dosages given during treatment.

"Where's her stuff?" he asked.

The nurse reading labels stopped and eyed Walker's duty belt over his scrubs. "Are you a doctor or an officer?"

"Which answer gets you to cooperate?"

"Oh . . . you're a cop. Sorry."

Jan pulled the curtain against the wall. "Chief, they're new."

"I can tell."

"The patient's belongings should be in there." Jan pointed to a crumpled white plastic bag on the floor.

"It's empty," the nurse at the computer said without looking away from the screen. "Everything was cut off her. She came in with nothing else. No purse."

"Where are the clothes?" he asked.

The nurse pointed to a pile near the medical waste bin.

Walker retrieved a pair of rubber gloves from a box on the wall and visually examined the pieces of material. Most of the woman's jacket was intact, but little else. What remained of her shirt and jeans were cut into unrecognizable strips and stained with blood spatters. He studied the jacket next, recalling how the woman had kept her hands concealed when he first spoke to her on the bookstore sidewalk. Out of training and habit, he'd taken note of where she'd kept her hands during the interaction. Hands in pockets were never good. But it was winter, and she hadn't been wearing gloves.

He lifted the jacket just enough to noticed a few soaked dollar bills sticking out of the right pocket—a twenty, a ten, and four ones. The remaining pockets were empty.

"Jan, can you get me something to put these in?"

"Sure," she said. "We keep the correct bags in a supply closet just for you guys, but we don't need them much." She walked away for a moment and returned with a large bag. "She ran from you guys, right?"

"It's complicated."

She nodded. "Always is. Here you go."

"Thanks."

Jan held open the end of the bag as Walker placed the tattered remains of the woman's clothing inside. He taped it closed with medical tape and scribbled descriptions, the date, and his signature on the outsides. "Let me know when she wakes up."

"No problem," Jan said.

Walker carried his belongs and the evidence bag down the aisle of curtains towards the nurse's station, then beyond through the automatic doors into the waiting area of the emergency room.

Officer Stewart hurried in from the outside, his bony fingers fidgeting with his cell phone. "Ah, there you are," he said, a look of relief on his face. "Good thing you were easy to find. I figured your radio didn't work anymore, and I was about to call your cell number."

Walker stared at the skinny, twenty-four-year-old farm kid from Northern Idaho and wondered if he himself looked that young right out of the academy. Walker hardly remembered those days—no gray hair, a newlywed, and impervious to hardships—the poster child for bright-eyed and naivety. "My cell got drenched, too. It doesn't work."

"Oh, right. Let me see it," Stewart said.

Walker reached into the plastic bag and handed over the dead smartphone. "There's no use."

"Maybe, maybe not." Stewart popped open the casing, pulled the SIM card and the battery. "I'll let it dry. I've wanted to see if sticking a wet phone in rice actually works."

"Huh?"

"A bowl of rice. Uh . . . never mind. I'll take care of it for you."

Walker absent-mindedly nodded his head. "Fine. Let's just go. Did you and Kemp get my truck back to the station?"

"It's still at the bridge." Stewart cleared his throat and straightened himself. "The woman's car is being pulled out right now. Franklin said he'd pop the trunk at the scene to clear the vehicle, but nothing's been searched. He's going to tape it up for later. Pain in the butt getting that thing out of the river. The kid was fetching an extender for his tow cable when I left."

"What's his name again?" Walker asked.

"Who? The kid?"

"Yeah. I know he's Jan's boy, but remind me of his name. Man, I was just with her, should've asked."

"Mason. Sixteen, I think."

"Oh, right." Walker stared at the tiles as he walked. He hadn't said much to Jan aside from a causal, grumbled conversation regarding temperature readings and blotchy-red skin. Too distracted. He also hadn't realized her son was old enough to work at the gas station and tow cars. The only run-in he'd had with the boy occurred five years earlier after Mason led his friends on a mailbox bashing excursion on

Halloween night. Walker chuckled at the memory of four small-town eleven-year-olds in horror masks attempting to explain why a baseball bat was important to their costumes—and why the red mailbox paint on the Louisville slugger was actually fake blood smudges.

After sleeping one night in a jail cell and fixing ten mailboxes, Mason hadn't crossed Walker's path since. He assumed the kid was still scared of him. Maybe that was a good thing and kept the boy out of trouble. From what Jan mentioned five years earlier, she and Mason had a rough life before moving back to Harding. Jan grew up in town, moved away, and was now in her forties. She said they lived in Portland until Mason was eleven. Then they needed to start over. The reason for their move home wasn't common knowledge in Harding, but Walker knew the details. And it wasn't pretty. After the mailbox incident, he figured Mason Trent simply needed some time to feel normal. He gave the kid space. But Walker did enjoy saying hello to Jan whenever he got the chance.

"I'm at the curb," Stewart said. "Do you want me to get the emergency blanket from the trunk?" He motioned toward Walker's exposed arms.

"Nope. I'll be fine. But this needs to go inside." He held up the evidence bag.

On the street, Stewart's parking job resembled the aftermath of a high-speed chase—one tire over the curb, the trunk end sticking out into the ambulance bay.

"Anxious to get me?" Walker asked, sliding into the front passenger seat.

"Uh, yeah. Kemp said you went to the hospital. I didn't know your status. I was . . . hurrying."

Walker glanced at Stewart and relaxed. "Okay. Next time, slow down. Don't be careless. Trust the hospital staff to take care of things."

Stewart nodded and cleared his throat as if to speak, but didn't say anything. They drove away from the hospital. Walker decided to let the teaching moment stay simple and pass. His officer was young with fresh training. Experience in the field would age the kid a bit, just as it had for him. Stewart would learn to emotionally distance himself when needed, and the change would happen on its own.

"Head to the bridge," Walker said. "I'll drive my truck back."

"Yes, Chief." Stewart made a hard right at the corner.

6

MASON

MASON SPRINTED along the tow line, trying not to slip in the snow. Falling would make him look like an idiot, and chances were Deputy Franklin wasn't in a forgiving mood. The last thing Mason wanted was Franklin calling Ed and telling his boss that the teenager couldn't hack it as a tow man. Maybe police stuff would keep Franklin busy, but Mason didn't know his demeanor that well. He thought people from Georgia were supposed to be friendly—southern hospitality and all that. But Franklin must've missed the boat.

At least Walker was gone. That was something.

He fiddled with the tow controls on the back end of the truck.

"Hurry up!" Franklin shouted.

"Yah, yah," he mumbled to himself and slapped the red button. The tow pulled taut with a snap and groaned as it cranked in the steel line. The Oldsmobile wobbled, its back tires spinning at the sudden momentum. The car was a simple sedan but partially filled with water, and he'd never pulled this much weight before. In truth, he'd only towed two cars without Ed's supervision. If only his boss answered text messages during commercial breaks.

"Whoa! That's enough!" Franklin waved his hands.

Mason hit the halt button just as the car leveled out on the bank.

He waited while Officer Kemp snapped some scene photos and wondered how much trouble the driver would be in when she woke up. The woman didn't seem like the troublemaker-type when she bought gas. Running from police only worked on TV, not in real life, no matter how entertaining it was to watch from afar.

Franklin opened one of the side doors and leapt back as a flood of water drained onto the ground. He grabbed a few escaping belongings and tossed them back on the rear seat. Then he moved to the driver door, reaching low for the trunk release.

Mason absent-mindedly stretched a little taller to see, as if the extra two inches of height made a difference. He watched Franklin pace to the trunk, lean over and stare inside, and then stretch deep as he examined its contents without sifting through very much. Franklin wore gloves, but his body language said that he was too grossed out to touch anything.

"What's in it?" Mason shouted out of curiosity. But the deputy either didn't hear him or acted like he didn't care.

Franklin slammed the trunk. He placed small strips of police tape on the lid, and on all four doors at the bottom near the frame, although they didn't stick very well on the wet metal. He then pulled out a sharpie from his pocket and scribbled something on the tape. "Okay! Keep going!" He held up his hand, performing a twirling motion with his index finger.

It took another ten minutes to get the car to the bridge and about twenty to properly secure it on the back of the tow truck. The firefighters had left by then, and Franklin kept glancing at his watch.

"Hey," Mason asked. "What was inside the trunk? Pounds of drugs? A severed head?" He chuckled, but mostly out of nerves.

Franklin rolled his eyes. "Kid, you watch too much TV. I only checked to make sure there wasn't another person inside. Now, get that car back to the station garage. I'm following behind you. Don't get distracted."

"Distracted by what?" Mason asked.

"Kemp!" Franklin waved over Mason's head. "Go pick up Walker at the hospital."

"Stewart already left to do that," Officer Kemp said.

"Perfect. See you at the station." He turned back to Mason. "Are you sure you can drive this load, kid?"

"Of course."

"Hope so." Franklin walked away. "Don't want to call Ed if I don't have to."

Mason gripped the keys in his hand so tight his knuckles turned white, then he hopped into the tow truck's front seat.

7

WALKER

WALKER ADJUSTED the laces on his boots, his fingers working on autopilot while his thoughts were elsewhere. A fresh uniform, dry Kevlar, and a warm jacket—it all felt normal against his skin—unlike the scrubs which he tossed into the bottom of his locker before slamming the door.

"Chief? Are you in here?" Officer Stewart leaned into the locker room, obviously asking out of politeness since the tiny converted space was once used as a walk-in storage closet.

"Yes?" Walker looked up.

"The tow truck just finished unloading the car. Franklin said he spotted a wallet on the front seat."

"Good. Franklin needs to stay with the vehicle. I'll be there in a minute." Walker placed his old Kevlar vest on the bench and headed out the door toward dispatch. "I gotta check something."

"Okay." Stewart let the door smack shut behind him.

Before Walker made it down the hallway, an overpowering waft stung his nostrils. He flung open the metal fire door to the dispatch office and shielded his nose. "What's that stench?"

Kim, the twenty-something new hire, flipped around in her swivel chair and stared at him with a cocked eyebrow. "Stench? That's the smell of Christmas. It's festive."

"No, that's Christmas punching me in the face," he said, noticing the five or so baskets of cinnamon-doused pinecones spread around the room, as potent as stink bombs. "How do you breathe in here?"

"Chief . . . do you need something?" she asked, lowering the mic on her headset.

"Uh, yeah. Pull up the full report on the Oldsmobile."

"Sure." Kim slid away from the three oversized dispatch monitors and stopped at a fourth flat screen at the end of the counter. Her fingers chatter-typed against the keyboard.

Walker waited, the cinnamon aroma clearing his sinuses. His police station was normally anti-festive and practical by choice, and he liked the predictability. But things had recently changed. The dispatchers he'd worked with for the past thirty years had all retired or moved on, so he was training three new hires. They all seemed the same age—too young—just like Stewart and the new nurses at the hospital. When did he get so old? In truth, Kim's computer skills surpassed his own by a lot, but she had yet to memorize all the dispatch procedures and codes. Still, she was a hard worker. And that mattered.

"Here you go," she said. "Just as I read over your radio earlier . . . belongs to a woman in Utah who was reported missing."

"Can you print it for me?"

"You don't want to pull it up on a tablet? It's in the system."

"No."

"Okay," she said slowly and typed a few more keys.

Walker reached over to the printer and grabbed the stack of pages as they rolled out. "Thanks," he said. "Uh, Kim, ditch the pinecones."

She scrunched her face before adjusting her headset.

Cinnamon stench lingered in Walker's nostrils until he entered the station garage at the back of the building. The Oldsmobile had been towed through the large utility door and unloaded at the last spot in the row—just past the line of parked police vehicles. Stewart,

Franklin, and Kemp stood near the car's front end, right next to a plastic fold-out table. The evidence bag containing the woman's clothes sat on the table top, along with a few small belongings. Franklin leaned over them and typed on a tablet. As Walker neared, Stewart paced over to meet him. For a moment, Stewart's nose twitched, and he stared ahead without saying a word.

"It's not me," Walker said. "Kim brought strong pinecones today."

"Oh, right." Stewart nodded. "I wasn't going to say anything. In case you wanted to smell like Christmas."

"Here." He handed over the printed report. "Paraphrase these for me, please."

Stewart cleared his throat. "Missing persons report . . . Pearl Sanford, age seventy . . . no date of birth on the form . . . actually, no other info about her history . . . reported missing a couple days ago out of St. George, Utah, by a Mary Doone, listed as a neighbor."

"Not a relative?" Walker asked.

"Doesn't look like it." Stewart scanned the second page. "There's no listed relatives."

"Franklin," Walker said. "Did you call St. George P.D., yet?"

"Yep, I did." Franklin walked over holding the tablet in the crook of his arm, a smirk on his face. "Talked to a Chief Redding. I had to explain where Harding was located. He'd never been north of Boise. Go figure. He was surprised we found the car way up here. And that Pearl Sanford wasn't the one drivin' the thing. They're lookin' for her, but had no leads till now. He did say they found some suspicious evidence in her house. Didn't tell me what. And finding the car with someone else, they're real interested in the contents and what the driver has to say."

"Well, she can't talk at the moment. Any more details?" he asked.

"Redding didn't give me much more. He knows we have probable cause to do an initial search, but under the circumstances, he wanted the whole thing processed by our in-house techs immediately. He's worried the river water may damage evidence before the car's shipped to them. Said they want our crime scene people to process it.

Plus, send all forensic evidence to the State Crime Lab in Utah. The rest needs to be shipped back to them with the car. He'll start the paperwork."

Walker rubbed his temples. "Did you explain to Chief Redding that we're a small-town department, that we don't have our own in-house CSI techs or any detectives for that matter? We have to process crime scenes ourselves."

Franklin chuckled. "Not that Harding has many crime scenes."

"Yeah, well." Walker rolled his eyes. "Today it has a potential one, even if it's a car that smells like a wet dog. We'll do what we can, but sending stuff to the Utah Crime Lab instead of Idaho is going to take some time. The paperwork will be a nightmare. And an officer has to load this car and ship it down to Utah to preserve chain of custody."

Franklin raised his hand. "Is St. George warmer than Harding? Because, I volunteer."

"Let's not get ahead of ourselves," Walker said. "He's asking a lot."

"Yeah, but jokin' aside. I said we'd be right on it. And that you'd be contacting them personally."

Walker sighed and glanced at the floor. This is not what he had expected to do today. "Okay. You found a wallet in the car, right? Who's the driver?"

"You know, St. George is lucky most of this stuff didn't end up in the river." Franklin motioned to the few belongings that had been left on the table. A soaked, leather wallet lay open among them, a driver's license visible through the plastic ID slot. "So far no cash, credit cards, cell phone, or photos. Only a Utah driver's license with our driver's picture on it and the name Charlotte Sarah Evers. The address listed on the license comes back as a furniture store in St. George. No social security number. No other info. The Utah DMV people aren't sure it's really one of theirs. They'll get back to me. So not sure how real the name is."

"Okay," Walker said. "Well, she's definitely not seventy-year-old Pearl Sanford. Franklin, get me the number for the crime lab in Coeur d'Alene. If Redding wants techs to process it, they'll have to come from there. Let's work out what needs to happen next. And Kemp..."

Officer Kemp stopped taking pictures of the vehicle's damaged front end. "Yes, Chief?"

"Take the portable fingerprint scanner to the hospital. I want to confirm the identity of miss Charlotte Sarah Evers."

8

WALKER

WALKER STOOD under the open utility garage door, ignoring the cold sting in his fingers. "Thanks . . ." He hung up Stewart's cell phone and handed it back to him. "The St. George chief is going to call this cell number later today. When he does, find me. Turns out they have their hands full right now. Hold up at a pharmacy."

"Okay," Stewart said.

"Find something I can use while my cell phone dries."

"Right." Stewart walked to his patrol car.

Lost in thought, Walker stared at the fresh snowflakes falling on the cleared cement driveway. The snow was sticking again and would need to be four-wheeler plowed for a second time before the end of the day. Winter didn't wait for car accidents or missing person investigations, just snowed when it wanted. He zipped up the collar of his jacket, the left-over memory from his icy swim still forcing a shiver. No doubt the hospital staff would have used similar heated blankets on the young woman as they had on him. Depending on her injuries, she could have been awake by now. He needed answers . . . if she'd cooperate.

"Chief." Franklin came outside. "Are the State CSI folks here yet?"

Walker glanced down at his watch. "Not yet. We're lucky they could make the drive last minute and come out today."

"Calls from St. George P.D. probably helped. Man, does it ever stop snowing in Northern Idaho?"

"Yep," Walker said. "In summer. And even then, it's iffy."

"Funny. If it ever snowed in Georgia, everything would shut down."

"We don't have that luxury here."

"Nope . . ." Franklin trailed off and mumbled. "You don't have any luxuries here."

Walker turned away to hide his grin.

An SUV with the words *Idaho State Crime Scene Investigators* on the side panel pulled up in front of the garage. A woman with a pleasant demeanor and short, spiky black hair stepped out of the driver's seat.

"Chief Walker?" She held out her hand.

"Yes," he said.

"I'm Lee Parks, one of the field crime scene investigators from the lab in Coeur d'Alene." She motioned to another investigator who was already unloading equipment from the back of the SUV. "And that's my colleague Jake Martinez. We're going to get started. Show us the vehicle, and you know the drill—just observe."

Walker nodded.

"Do you have the proper paperwork?" she asked.

"Yep."

"Good."

Walker stepped back while Parks and Martinez began processing the car. They unsealed the doors and trunk, then started photographing the exterior.

"How long will this take?" he asked.

"Depends," Parks said. "A few hours maybe."

Walker pulled over a folding chair. "Take as long as you need."

WALKER GLANCED over Park's shoulder as she loaded sealed paper evidence bags into the cargo container of the SUV. Martinez packed up the camera and a handful of fingerprint kits and DNA sample bags. They meticulously labeled everything. Walker tried to hide how impressed he was with their attention to detail.

"You can search the contents of the car now," Parks said. "We'll get this other stuff to the state crime lab. Meanwhile, you guys have custody of the vehicle until it's handed off to St. George."

"Right," Walker said. He motioned for Franklin and the others to start searching through the rest of the car. He then pulled on a pair of rubber gloves and glanced at the back of the SUV. "You'll let me know if IAFIS gets a hit on the fingerprints? There's not a lot to go on here."

"Of course," Martinez said, gathering the bag holding the woman's clothes. He'd also bagged the thirty-five dollars found in her pocket. "Could take a while though. It all takes time."

"Sure." Walker headed inside the garage as his officers pulled out items and placed them on the table. The outsides of the duffle bags were destroyed from the river water, and smelled of silt on the outer fabric, but the bags had been reinforced with a water-proof lining. After unzipping each one, the dry contents were spread out on the table—cracked statues, pieces of broken dishware in frayed newsprint, knick-knacks made from metal and some from polished wood. There were numerous antique items with obvious monetary value, as if someone had raided the collectables cabinet of a senior citizen's home.

"What's in the trunk?" he called to Parks.

"More of the same," she said over her shoulder while typing on her tablet. "We photographed inside and took a few samples and fingerprints, but we didn't see anything else needing to go to the state crime lab."

Franklin moved to the back end of the car. "The tow truck kid expected a dead body or something." He blew out an exaggerated chuckle. "I cleared it at the scene. No dead body."

Walker glanced under the lid. Parks was right, more junk. He pulled out two crumbled boxes, both containing old books, and another duffle filled with clothes. There were a couple pairs of women's shoes, along with a pillow and a quilt. He emptied the contents until only a single box, one which had been tucked in the back, remained wedged against the rear seat.

"Maybe she was sleepin' in the car," Franklin said, inspecting the quilt. "It's a long drive from St. George to Harding."

"Maybe . . ." Walker placed the box on the table and opened the top flap. Underneath a single layer of books, he found fitted Styrofoam. "Hmm . . ."

"What is it?" Franklin asked without glancing over. "Was the kid right? Is it a severed head?"

"Not a head," he said, as he removed the top piece of Styrofoam. Inside he found an earth-toned, glazed ceramic container safely tucked in the protected form-fitted center. "It's an urn. As in, someone's ashes."

Franklin leaned over to get a better look. "Huh. So there was a dead body in the trunk. Tow truck kid will be thrilled."

"Parks, I guess we're not done." Walker pointed to the urn on the table.

Martinez hurried over with the camera.

"Man," Parks said. "Didn't expect ashes. I thought that was another box of books."

"Chief!" Kemp called. He stood near the trunk, holding his camera in one hand and the flap of the carpet lining with the other.

"What'd you find?" Walker asked.

"Something's shoved in the jack compartment," he said.

Both Walker and Franklin began ripping away the carpet liner above the back left tire mold, shifting the jack and tire iron.

"What's that underneath them?" Franklin asked, leaning closer. "Plastic?"

Walker moved the jack aside and pulled out a zipped gallon-sized freezer bag, the sides bulging from the over-stuffed contents. He quickly took it over to the table while Martinez snapped pictures of the items. There were three U.S. passports with various women's names and three corresponding driver's licenses—one from Utah, another from Nevada, and a third from Colorado—all with the same photo as the license for Charlotte Sarah Evers. He studied the names. "Rebecca Ilene Lee . . . Megan Sue Fosters . . . Elizabeth May Collier."

"So which one is real?" Franklin asked.

"I don't know." Walker handed the IDs over to Parks. "We need to run them and find out."

In the bottom of the freezer bag, he found a half-size manila envelope filled with both American and Canadian cash. There wasn't much in Canadian money, maybe a couple hundred dollars, but the banded American bills numbered in the thousands. He placed the money stacks on the table while both Martinez and Kemp shot photos of the new items.

"Looks like thirty grand in American bills," Franklin said, staring at the stacks. "What are you thinking, Chief?"

"Still don't know. Wait . . ." Walker slid out a final object from the bottom of the plastic bag, this one so small and light-weight that he almost missed it. "A wrist watch? Get this, Martinez." Holding it in his rubber glove, Walker held the small watch for a photo. The once gold metal was nearly black—aged and perhaps tarnished or warped or something of the kind. It looked as if the watch had been dropped in a camp fire. He couldn't tell for sure, but the thing had been beaten up.

"Why steal a tarnished broken watch?" Franklin asked. "It's junk."

Walker and Kemp stared at him.

"What? I'm just statin' what's obvious. This fake Charlotte lady stole the missin' woman's car and a bunch of her stuff. Probably killed the old lady before she left."

"That's just guessing," Walker said.

Franklin shrugged. "Like I said, just statin' the obvious."

"And what about the ashes in the trunk?" he asked with a raised eyebrow.

"She stole those, too. To sell them at a pawn shop."

"Stealing ashes for financial profit? Franklin, that's enough," Walker said. He sat the IDs and passports on the table along with the money and wrist watch. "Write it up. When she's released from the hospital, I want the process started to send her back to St. George. And Franklin, St. George P.D. will probably request all this evidence from us, so I want it ready and stored with proper procedure. Preserve the chain of custody. No slip ups."

"Got it." Franklin's cell phone rang from his duty belt. "Hello? Hey, Stewart, what'd you find? Oh . . ." He held out the phone and cocked his head. "Stewart says he'll only report to you."

Walker took the cell phone. "Yeah?"

"Chief, the woman is in and out, not all the way awake. I can't ask her questions yet. The doctor said he'd call you at the end of his shift with a status update. But Jane Doe is stable. Her injuries are listed as moderate. But they can't tell me more than that. I'm not a doctor, but I'm guessing pain meds are making her sleep."

"Stewart, we're calling her Charlotte Evers. That name's most likely false, but it's better than Jane Doe."

"Okay, Chief. Well, I fingerprinted Charlotte Evers. Nothing came up in the system."

Walker sighed. Things kept getting better and better. He was going to need more caffeine. "Okay. Get the prints to the CSI people, then wait at the hospital. Maybe she'll wake up enough to tell you her real name and where to find the owner of the car."

"Right, Chief."

He hung up and handed the phone back to Franklin.

Parks bagged the false IDs and passports, then she bagged the money. "Chief, we'll process these at the state lab, and we can take a sample of the ashes, but there won't be any DNA to analyze, I'm afraid. The fingerprints will go through IAFIS, but the FBI field office could process the facial recognition along with the fingerprints faster than our lab. We'll send that stuff to them."

Walker nodded. "Right, that'll work. Keep me updated on your progress."

"I will," she said. "Since this involves an active missing persons case, we'll process as fast as possible, but Chief, it'll still take a little while."

"Yeah. Martinez said that earlier. It's understandable. Thanks for coming out here." He placed the urn and wrist watch with the other items on the table. "Franklin, you and Kemp finish cataloging this stuff and box it up. Seal the car when you're done. Keep working on the case report. I'll be back. Call over the radio if you need me."

"Where are you going?" Franklin asked.

"I need to build a timeline. And that means questioning the one person in Harding who's guaranteed to give me the run-around. I'm going to the bookstore."

Franklin snorted and raised an eyebrow. "Radio if you need backup."

9

BERTA

BERTA SHEPPARD STOOD behind the *closed* sign hanging against her bookstore's window and watched as Chief Walker parked his patrol truck at the curb. Her muscles tensed with a slight panic. Without waiting for him, she hurried to the back office, placed the *Gilly Heel* collection with the other books, and slid the box into the shadow under her desk. She then rolled the office chair in front of it before stepping back to verify the box was concealed.

The books were a legal purchase. The young woman wanted to sell, and Berta wanted to buy. Nothing wrong with keeping them safe, and nothing wrong with paying the young woman ordinary rates for a fortune in books—or at least Berta told herself as much. And she knew she was right.

The entrance bell chimed.

"Berta?" Chief Walker's voice echoed from the main room.

"Coming," she said, giving the word a forced, sing-songy tone.

Walker stood near the counter, his cheeks and nose flushed pink from the cold and his eyes looking tired. She wondered how long he'd keep being Harding's police chief before realizing it was finally time to retire. She was twenty years older than him, but running a bookstore was different than being a cop. She wasn't protecting the public. A police chief, on the other hand, needed to be on his toes. The community expected nothing less.

His late wife Marie never let him work long hours at the station. Before she got sick a decade ago, Terry Walker seemed to balance his time better. And after her death, Berta noticed he was different. Kept to himself. Didn't socialize. Neither did she, but the police chief was a public figure. She wondered if Terry really cared about Harding anymore. Remembering the mischief he pulled as a teenager, she wondered if he every truly cared at all.

"How are you, Berta?" he asked.

"Fine. Can I help you, Terry?" Berta shuffled over and stood behind the counter. She busied her hands by straightening insignificant odds and ends near the register. "Do you need something to read? Perhaps a crime novel or a western? A really short one maybe . . . a novella . . . with over-sized print . . . a simple, quick read?"

Walker raised an eyebrow. "No, thank you. I'm not here as a customer."

"Well, I'm only guessing what type of books you like . . . if you read at all. I don't know for sure because in the thirty years I've owned this store, you've never bothered to buy a book. Perhaps you'd rather use that Amazon jungle website the young people talk about." She studied his face.

"Berta, tell me about the woman who came into your store earlier today. She was young, college age, Caucasian, brown hair, small build, about 5'2' or 5'3" maybe."

"Wow. That's a lot of detail. Are you expecting me to identify her in a line up? As far as I can remember, she didn't rob me—"

"Berta," he said. "I'm not implying anything about the woman. I simply need to know what she did in your store." Chief Walker rested his hands on his duty belt.

She hesitated, fiddling with a clicky pen. "Well, let me think." The chief was only doing his job, and she knew it, but she was also trying to do hers. It took extra funds to keep the store open the last few years. Utility companies kept upping their greed levels. And Harding wasn't the wealth of intellectual prowess it once was before the latest generation discovered the internet. How was she supposed to compete with the TV games, or the online games, or whatever else the young Harding kids did for fun? Whatever it was, reading wasn't it.

"Berta?" he repeated.

"Oh, right. Well, she came in to the store . . . didn't do much before leaving."

"Didn't do much?"

"Yes." Berta began wiping the register with a rag, her gaze away from his stare. She needed to give him something, and in general, she didn't prefer lying. Well, only when it was necessary. "I bought a couple used books from her. Gave her cash. Then she left."

"I need to see the books," he said.

"Okay, but the young woman told me they weren't stolen. Didn't see a problem. Innocent purchase on my part."

His face tightened, the wrinkles intensifying between his eyebrows. "I still need to see them."

"Fine. I'll be right back." Berta walked into the office and stood by the desk. She rubbed her temples and wondered how much utility money she was giving up by handing over the box of books—money that would power and heat the store for months. And help her with the property tax she owed. Her mind raced. About a minute passed before she was able to roll away the chair, retrieve two books from the box—ones not belonging to the valuable *Gilly Heel* collection—and return to the counter.

"Did you get lost?" he asked.

Berta wrinkled her nose, resulting in a slight slip of her reading glasses. She readjusted. "I had to make sure I pulled the right ones. Here you go."

Walker took the two aged books in his hands and examined them, flipping through the pages and checking the bindings. "How much did you give her?"

"Not a lot. I can't remember exactly."

"I found thirty-five dollars in her pocket. Does that sound about right?"

Berta straightened up. "In her pocket? What happened today?"

"She . . ." he hesitated for a moment. "Her car ended up in the river."

An instant shock filled Berta's stomach. "Is she alright?"

"Not sure yet. Haven't heard from the hospital." Walker tucked the books under his arm. "If you don't mind, I need to hang onto these. But I'll send Kemp over later with a paper for you to sign."

She nodded.

"Anything else? Maybe something she said or did that you can remember?"

Berta swallowed hard. She glanced toward the back office, then eyed the rows of packed bookshelves and the empty aisle ways in between them. The young woman had been her only customer that day. And no one had come in the bookstore the day before. Solitude was her new normal. "No. That's it."

"Okay, thanks."

She waited for him to leave, holding still as she listened to his truck door and the engine hum as he drove away. After a moment of staring at the counter, her thoughts heavy, Berta walked to the back office and pulled out the box. She crouched on the floor, leaning close, staring at the piles but not focusing on them. *Bad things happen. I can't control what trouble that girl got herself into after she left my store. She's not my problem.* Berta repeated the words again, trying to imprint them in her mind, to make truth out of uncertainty. *Sell the books. Do it for the store, and for Mom and Dad who built the business from nothing. You own them. Now, get up.* She stood, ignoring the familiar ache in her joints as she straightened. After a quick finger-brush through her short, gray curls, Berta grabbed *Gilly Heel* from the stack. Her plans needed to change. Letting the gas station kid be a part of her clandestine book sale wasn't an option any more. Too risky. She now needed to figure out how to sign up for an auction website by herself. Out of habit, Berta thumbed through the opening pages of the book. The paper smelled wonderful.

As she reveled in the printed sheets, inked writing caught her attention and required a back track to the title page. An inscription had been penned in black ink where the author would have autographed the book.

To my sweet Pearl,

The little one who reminds me to be brave, strong, and to fill life with lasting adventures, even at my old age. Of all my written creations, this one reminds me of you.

With love,

Grandfather

Also known to the dull, insipid adults as Ruthan Stanley

The breath fell from Berta's chest. The book was signed—personalized as a present to the author's granddaughter, whomever she was. Berta's thoughts raced with possibilities. The woman who came into the store that morning was too young to be Ruthan Stanley's grandchild. From what she knew of Stanley, his grandchild would be in her golden years. Most likely in her seventies or even eighties, perhaps the same age as Berta herself. But maybe, just maybe, the young woman could tell her how to find this *Pearl* person. With any luck, the books might be worth a finder's fee. *If* she could give the collection back to the author's family—a reward more lucrative than any auction. She didn't know how to do that online stuff anyway, but collecting a large reward . . . that she could do with gusto. In an instant, Berta Sheppard made a new plan, one that involved paying a visit to the hospital.

10

MASON

MASON SAT in the driver's seat of his mother's truck and watched the county hospital's emergency bay. He fiddled with the keys still hanging in the ignition, all the while hoping to see her emerge each time the automatic doors opened. Several medical personnel exited the building, even a few members of the public, but not his mom. As usual, she was taking too long after the end of her shift.

He glanced at the time on his cell phone—6:11 P.M. She should have been waiting by the door. Mason blew air into his fist, hoping to warm his fingers enough to type. Incoherent texts wouldn't do him much good. Mom refused to answer nonsense, even if it made perfect sense to him and everyone else on the planet. She wanted proper English. *Almost finished?* he typed.

No immediate answer.

He repeated the message in variations of *I'm freezing* and *Any time now* and *It's against the law to leave a kid alone in the car.*

Still nothing.

Another minute passed. He resisted the urge to turn on the engine and fire up the heater. Idling used too much gasoline in the fourteen-year-old Ford, and his mom didn't want anything wasted. Filling the tank meant spending real money, but zipping up the coat he already owned didn't cost anything. At least this time wasn't one of her twelve-hour shifts ending at three in the morning. He hated those nights.

After another minute watching his warm breath swirl in the chilled air, Mason couldn't take the cold any longer. He grabbed the keys and headed across the parking lot. Inside, instant heat flushed his face.

"Jan's son! How are ya?" An ER medical assistant waved at him through the half-wall of plex over the check-in desk.

"It's Mason, and I'm good. Just need to pick up my mom." He smiled at her, choosing not to mention that he'd already introduced himself at least a dozen times before.

"Haven't seen Jan come out yet. Head on back."

"Okay, thanks." Mason cleared the double fire doors and scanned down the aisle. Most of the curtains were open. A handful of medical staff stood around the nurse's station, chatting amongst themselves. Obviously, it was a slow night. He walked over to the counter where a nurse in pediatric scrubs typed on the computer. "Do you know where Jan Trent is? I'm her son," he said.

She glanced at him. "Uh, not sure. I think her shift is over. Try texting her."

"Thanks. I didn't think of that," he muttered under his breath and pulled out his phone to send another message. *Mom, where are you?*

"Hey," the nurse said over her shoulder. "Tess, take the Jane Doe off the board. I think she went upstairs a couple hours ago. Someone forgot to erase her name."

A brunette in purple scrubs reached up with a foam eraser. "When are they going to give us a flat screen for the list instead of a white board and dry erase markers? This method is so ancient."

The other nurse chuckled. "As soon as you pay for it."

"Yah, right."

They continued chatting as if Mason wasn't there. He ignored their conversation on neglectful boyfriends and instead watched the words disappear with each eraser swipe. *Jane Doe. Accident victim . . .* The rest was cleaned before he could read it, but Mason guessed who had been labeled as the Jane Doe. He wondered if the crash could be labeled an *accident* when the woman caused her own car to sail into a river. Maybe an *inevitable* accident, if there was such a thing. Still, the day hadn't been dull.

His phone beeped.

Mason, I'm checking on a patient for Chief Walker. I'll be there in a minute.

Fine, he texted. *I'll be the starving one in the waiting room who's asleep in an unnatural and upright position. Sorry if I drool on the floor.*

Not funny. Just wait patiently.

Mason wandered to the waiting room and slumped down in a chair. He didn't bother glancing at the check-in desk. The medical assistant probably forgot his name the second he walked away. Instead, he pulled up his coat hood and tried to zone out. His mom was doing her best, and he knew it. It just sucked waiting in a hospital.

He scrolled over her texts again . . . *checking on a patient for Chief Walker*. Mason thought about his latest close-call at the bridge. Avoiding Chief Walker was getting harder and harder, especially now that Mason worked at the gas station. Although, he couldn't decide which was stronger—his need to avoid Walker or his annoyance at having to deal with Deputy Franklin in order to do so. It was a toss-up.

"Mason?"

His mom tapped him on the shoulder.

"Hey," he said.

"Why are you slumped in this corner chair with your hood covering your face like that? You look like a druggie."

"Mom, it's just a hood. And don't say that too loud." He scanned the waiting room, thinking he should've just frozen in the car.

"Nevermind." She rubbed her eyes. "Let's go home. I took an extra shift tomorrow. I've got to get a lot of sleep tonight or I'll be exhausted."

"How long is this one?" Mason asked.

"Only eight hours, like today. You can drop me off before school."

He nodded. "Sure."

"Hey," she said, motioning toward the automatic doors. "You drive. I need to make a call to Chief Walker on the way. And don't worry, it's not about mailboxes."

"Funny, Mom. How long are you going to tease me about that?"

"I'm your mother. I love you. So . . . forever."

He rolled his eyes. "Uh, perfect."

11

WALKER

THE CHIEF SHIFTED in his office chair, leaned back, and rubbed his forehead in a pressing swipe. If only the motion could have taken away the wrinkles and worry lines. Although, he knew he'd earned every single one of those age marks. Walker glanced at his wrist watch: 6:11 P.M.

Stewart's cell phone sat quiet on a mounding pile of paperwork on the desk while he waited for St. George P.D. to call him back. Another hour-worth of unfinished case reports presented on his computer screen, all needing his approval. He drummed his fingers against the wooden desk and simply stared at the phone, then at his watch again. "Forget this nonsense."

He picked up his office landline and dialed the St. George phone number which Stewart had written on a bright pink sticky note.

"This is Chief Redding," a low voice said on the other end.

"Good evening. This is Chief Terrance Walker from the Harding Police Department."

"Harding? Oh, right. Up in Idaho."

"Yes." Walker leaned forward in his chair. "Looking to touch base with you on this car we've got in our custody."

"Sorry, I didn't get back to you earlier," Redding said. "I left instructions for one of my detectives to call an Officer Stewart up there, but we've been so busy today. I apologize that the phone call didn't happen. But let me pull up the case you're interested in."

Walker listened to the sound of typing on a keyboard. "Well, it's actually your missing persons case. We just found the woman's car. We're processing it."

"Right, right. I'll be straight with you, Chief. Between the hold-up at the pharmacy and a multi-vehicle crash on I-15, we haven't been able to look at this case since you guys called. So, you're positive about the VIN number?" Redding asked.

"Yes, but someone else was in possession of the vehicle. Don't have a confirmed ID yet." Walker cleared his throat and shifted in his chair. "What info do you guys have so far?"

"Well, it says here that Pearl Sanford was reported missing yesterday by a neighbor . . . a Mary Doone, who claims she noticed Sanford's dog loose in the neighborhood. In Doone's statement, she said that she tried to return the animal several times in a two-day period, but no one ever answered at the residence. She thought things seemed off and called us. Doone said it was strange that the lady wasn't home. Said the lady never left her house."

"Never left the house? How is that possible?" Walker asked.

"The neighbor reported that she doesn't know the woman very well. Sanford has lived there less than a year. Doone once had to tell her the dog barked too much. Said Sanford told her that she has no family, only the dog. A delivery truck from the local grocery store drops off food to her. Doone never noticed any visitors."

"What did you find that suggests she's missing and not on vacation?"

"Well, let me see here." Redding mumbled for a moment as if he scrolled down the page. "Ah, here we go. My officers found the home's back door wide open, and they entered the premises. The master bedroom was in disarray. Our crime scene guys went over it today. They're not done, but so far they reported there's some belongings still there, such as clothes, etc. But nothing personal with her name or picture on it. No medications or papers. No blood, no sign of a struggle, but it's obvious that a few cabinets and bookshelves have been riffled through. Dust marks suggest items are missing, but hard to say what kind without the owner. There was a portable fire pit on the back patio. Looks like it was used recently. The whole scene is suspicious. Her car was gone from the garage, of course. But once again, too early to know if something went wrong in the house or if the woman simply drove off. That's possible with the elderly."

Walker glanced down at his own printed report. "But she was only seventy. A little early for dementia."

"Hard to say. I'm not a doctor. We couldn't find a DMV photo, so we found a business security camera image of the lady and put it on the local news in case someone spots her wandering around. Trouble is, now that her car turned up in Idaho, there's more to it."

"Yeah, sounds like it."

"And there was no sign of Pearl in the car? Another passenger?"

Walker rubbed his forehead again. "No. Just the driver . . . a young woman. Tried to do a traffic stop. She fled. The car ended up in a river. She's in the hospital. Belongings in the car look like keepsakes and may be the missing items from Pearl Sanford's home. We also found fake IDs for the young woman, thirty grand in cash, and an urn."

"An urn?" Redding asked.

"With ashes. Did Pearl Sanford own an urn?"

"No idea. But this sounds like a burglary. Will you send us the car photos and evidence report? We'll get to them as soon as we can."

Walker let out a heavy breath, then compressed his grip on the phone. "Chief, I've got a young woman at County Hospital who's getting arrested for fleeing when she's well enough to be released. I'd like to know if I'm booking her in county lock-up or shipping her back to you."

"I'll let you know."

He shook his head, trying to control the heat building in his core. "I hope soon. Time matters. There's a missing woman to find."

"Yes, there is." Redding's voice tightened, obviously annoyed. "I've got an alert out to find her. Chief, I don't know if you guys are busy in

Harding, but don't let the doctors on the golf course and the senior picnics fool you about St. George. We aren't sitting on our hands down here. The suspect in today's pharmacy hold up was on his way north from Las Vegas and insisted on stealing his daily fix of prescription narcotics at one of our local businesses. I've got a pharmacist and a tech in the hospital, an unidentified accomplice to locate, and a community that needs to feel safe again. And yes, of course, I've already got a detective assigned to Pearl Sanford's case. His name is Peterson. I'll have him contact you tomorrow with instructions regarding the vehicle, and we're adding the driver as a person of interest."

"Fine. We'll assist where we can."

"Great. I appreciate your cooperation. Thank you, Chief."

"Yep." Walker hung up the phone and tried to let the tension leave his muscles. "Stewart, come here a minute," he said into his radio.

Moments later, Officer Stewart came into the room and motioned to his cell phone on the chief's desk. "Did St. George call?"

"No, I called them."

"How'd it go?"

"It was . . . really pleasant," Walker said, smacking his palm on the desk. He handed the cell phone back to Stewart. "Does my cell phone work yet?"

"Uh, no, Chief. It's been drying all day but doesn't look good. I think I can put your SIM card into another phone if the card dries okay. Maybe into a pre-paid cell until you get a better one. The drugstore sells a few."

"Fine. Will you help me with that?"

"Sure. I'll bring an extra phone tomorrow morning."

"Thanks. Go home. You're off shift."

"Right." Stewart nodded.

Walker half-expected the kid to salute before he left the office. "See ya tomorrow."

"Yes, Chief."

He waited for Stewart to leave then stared at the work he needed to finish. Putting in another late night at the station wasn't a big deal. His house was empty anyway.

The office landline rang.

"This is Chief Walker," he answered.

"Chief, this is Jan from the hospital."

"Jan, I've known you since forever. You grew up in Harding. Call me Terry."

"Okay, Terry. No, wait . . . that feels weird. Not official enough for this call. Chief, Dr. Fielding asked me to call you with a status update for the Jane Doe. She sustained minor injuries. Her condition is stable."

"Okay," he said. "Can she be discharged?"

"Not yet."

"Is she awake?"

"No. The doctor said you could come by tomorrow and talk to her then."

"Thanks, Jan."

"Yep. No problem, Chief."

"Oh, and Jan," Walker said. "Tell your son he did well today with the tow truck. I'm surprised he's old enough to drive one. But, uh . . . yeah."

"Thanks, I'll tell him. Bye, Chief." She hung up.

Walker sat back. He strummed his fingers on the desk, this time ignoring the paperwork. Tomorrow he would get answers. Questioning persons of interest wasn't new to him, even in a small town. When confronted, they all reacted in a handful of predictable ways—some got quiet, some got loud, a few broke easily, and others always told lies. He needed to find out what kind of person Charlotte Sarah Evers was.

12

CHARLOTTE

A FRESH DRY erase marker squeaked along the surface of a small whiteboard. Charlotte lifted her eyelids just enough to notice a stream of dim morning light along the wall and a nurse in purple scrubs writing a name under the board's RN space. She proceeded to add another name as the patient's listed CNA. The woman wore a hospital ID badge around her neck, which swung loose as she shuffled over to the computer.

Charlotte pretended to be asleep. She controlled her breathing until it settled back into a deep, steady rhythm. A blood pressure cuff hummed to life on her right bicep, squeezing hard and forcing her to resist the urge to wince. Everything hurt—her chest, her ribs, every breath and every swallow. The feeling of helplessness annoyed her.

After the cuff released, the nurse typed away on the keyboard, her nails clicking on the plastic keys. She then adjusted the oxygen and pulse monitor on Charlotte's index finger.

More typing.

Charlotte analyzed the sound of the women's rubber-soled shoes on the hard floor, noticing how often they would stick to small spots of left-over disinfectant cleaner. *Two . . . three . . . four.* The nurse fiddled with the I.V. line and touched the over-head monitor, all the while Charlotte tracked the woman's steps.

Just leave, she ordered the nurse in her mind. *Just go.*

Another thirty seconds passed before the nurse actually left her alone. Charlotte opened her eyes and quickly evaluated the room—hospital bed, two chairs under a far window, a closed door leading to a bathroom, numerous medical supplies and equipment, sink, exit to the hallway . . . and the absence of handcuffs or restraints.

Her surroundings looked standard, therefore, despite the circumstances, she deemed the room itself twenty percent a *threat.* Assessing the staff would be far more complicated.

The whiteboard listed her name as Jane Doe. She raised an eyebrow in amazement, though it hurt to do so. Retaining her anonymity was ideal, priceless even, and since no cops stood in her room, perhaps the Evers identity was still intact.

She pulled herself into a sitting position using her right arm, the good one, to support most of her weight. Charlotte examined the rest of the whiteboard, breathing hard and ignoring the pain as she glanced up. The board didn't give any indication of the date and time or what had happened. Perhaps the computer would. The last images she remembered included a stuffy bookstore, a cop, and a city sign. The rest was a blur.

Assessing—*sharp radiating pain from the left collar bone . . . probably a hairline fracture or bruised tissue.* She searched her memory for survival details she'd learned over the years. The clavicle, a.k.a. the collar bone, could snap with minimal pressure, as in from wearing a seat belt restraint during an accident. It didn't take much to break, between five to ten pounds of pressure in just the right unlucky spot. Healing would require immobilization for a while, less time if the tissues were simply bruised. Either way, the injury was painful. Charlotte didn't dare remove the tight sling supporting her left arm and shoulder, but instead decided to pull the oxygen tube from her nose. She hesitated before removing the I.V., bracing herself for the quick pain that would accompany taking it out.

Continue assessment—hurts to breathe, lungs burning, chest aches. Bruised ribs maybe? Not sure. Sore throat . . . a likely result from intubation or some other kind of tube. Must have needed help to breathe. Headache, minor laceration to bridge of nose and tenderness under the eyes . . . possible injuries from a deployed airbag. Calculating—likely probability of a vehicle accident at fifty percent. No, wait . . . one hundred percent. Her head felt foggy. She needed pain meds, but decided clarity had to come first.

Charlotte stopped short, an instant wave of panic filling her. She had no idea what happened to her car. Or to the urn, or to her Go Bag.

She ripped out the I.V. needle, medical tape and all, from the top of her hand. Stabbing pain surged through her nerves. She grit her jaw and ignored the blood oozing from her skin as she slid off the BP cuff. Then she glanced down and hesitated. Removing the heart monitor from her finger would be a problem. She eyed the vitals screen above the bed. It beeped and flashed, sending readings to a nurse's station somewhere outside her room. Hopefully they weren't watching that closely.

Charlotte leaned over till her feet rested on the floor, and she stood upright. Her movements slowed. Instant vertigo swirled the room. She gripped the bed and held on while her head pounded as if a jack hammer pressed against her skull.

Seven feet away, the door handle clicked.

Charlotte lunged back into the bed, a surge of pain radiating through her entire body. She flopped the blanket over her blood-smeared hand and tried to lean back without screaming. The heart monitor beeped wildly.

When she looked up, a woman stood at the door. She wore a heavy-knit sweater and reading glasses perched in the short gray curls on the top of her head. Her wrinkled face seemed familiar, but Charlotte couldn't place it.

"Are you alright?" the woman asked.

She didn't reply.

"I suppose no one is completely alright when they crash their car in a river."

Charlotte sucked in a weighted breath. Her thoughts raced. *A river? The urn is under water.*

13

BERTA

Berta entered the hospital room, hoping the nurses would stay busy somewhere else.

The young woman shuffled in the bed, her face wincing as she fiddled with the blankets. Berta waited a moment for the girl to settle. The room felt unnecessarily warm for a December morning. She wondered how much money the hospital wasted by keeping the rooms in the mid-seventies. Berta wrinkled her nose at the waste.

She stared at the young woman's bruised and puffy face. Her injuries looked terrible.

Their gazes met.

"Are you alright?" Berta asked.

The young woman said nothing.

"I suppose no one is completely alright when they crash their car in a river," she said, forcing a casual smile.

The young woman's face tightened. Worry lines formed on her forehead.

Berta regretted the statement. Too much, too soon. "What's your name, deary?"

Still nothing.

"I'm Berta Sheppard. I own the used bookstore you visited

yesterday. Do you remember me?" She studied the young woman's body language, searching for a hint of recognition.

"What do you want?" the young woman asked.

"Just to check on you. Heard there was a scary accident at the bridge. What's your name?"

Berta tried to appear harmless and concerned as she formed her facial expressions, her aim to appear as a loving grandmother. A few awkward moments passed before the young lady glanced at the whiteboard on the wall, then at the open door leading to the hallway.

"I'm Charlotte," she said after nearly a minute of silence.

"That's a beautiful name." Berta took a step forward. "I brought something that I want to ask you about." She pulled *Gilly Heel, Book One* from her purse. "This book is interesting. You see, I enjoy discovering little known facts behind the books I sell. Mainly so I can tell the new owners the book's history. It adds to the sentimental value. That way I can treasure the book while it's in my possession. It's a thing I do." Berta held still and waited.

Charlotte glanced at the book then back up at Berta. She didn't speak.

Perhaps Berta's voice wasn't sweet enough. "I noticed," she continued, flipping open to the title page, "that it's signed to a person named Pearl. Did you know her?"

"That name is not important."

"Where did you get the book? How long did you have it?"

Charlotte stiffened in the bed, leaning back farther into her pillow. Her gaze went again from Berta's face to the open door.

"Are you expecting someone?" Berta asked, feeling frustrated.

"No. But I'm in a lot of pain. Can you leave now?"

"Of course, I can. Just tell me more about this book and I'll go. Was it a gift? Or did you come by it through more clandestine means?"

"What?"

Berta slouched, her impatience taking over. "You know exactly what I mean, Charlotte. Yesterday, in my store you said, point blank, that you didn't steal the books. But they are worth a lot of money, too much for someone like you to buy, and I doubt you knew the author Ruthan Stanley."

Charlotte's mouth dropped open. She pushed her head against the pillow, closing her eyes tight for a moment.

"Come on, deary. You ran from the police. We both know you stole the books. Tell me from whom, and I'll leave the hospital and never speak of this conversation to anyone. Unburden yourself. The truth can be our little secret."

The young woman's expression hardened, a look that chilled Berta to her core.

"You don't know what secrets are," Charlotte said. "They're not freeing."

"So, you *did* lie to me."

"Accept your lie and leave."

Berta stepped closer. "Not until you tell me who Pearl is and how to find her."

The sound of utility boots on the tile floor filtered in from the hallway.

"Leave me alone," Charlotte said. She closed her eyes again, turning her head away.

"Fine . . . for the moment." Berta stowed the book in her purse before she reached the doorway.

Chief Walker nearly ran into her.

"Berta," he said. "What are you doing here?"

She motioned him back into the hallway, her gaze bouncing from the ceiling to the hall and then at his concerned face—buying time. "Terry, the young lady is sleeping. Under heavy medication if you ask me. I wanted to make sure she was alright, but I'll have to visit later."

"She's still out?" Walker moved into the doorway, glanced toward the bed for a moment, then returned to Berta. "Did she wake up at all while you were in there?"

"Nope. Didn't say anything. I guess the poor girl isn't ready to join the world yet."

He rubbed his forehead. "Okay, thanks. You should go. I don't want you talking to her."

She took a few steps toward the nurse's station, pretending to leave, then flipped around. "If she's still asleep, you don't have to wait here. Terry, I'm sure you have a lot to do at the station before you can return my books. I could wait here for you."

"The books are evidence, Berta."

"Not forever, I hope. I paid for them."

Walker raised an eyebrow.

She hesitated to give up a chance to talk to Charlotte, but his stern expression didn't change. "Have a nice day, Terry." Berta scurried down the hallway until she rounded the corner, taking one last glance at him from the edge. She watched Walker peer inside the room for a moment, then pull a chair from the nurse's station and place it outside the door. He spoke into his radio and sat down.

Stubborn man. Berta tightened her jaw and headed for the elevator. The rest of her conversation with Charlotte the Liar would have to wait.

14

CHARLOTTE

From outside, the conversation between Berta Sheppard and the man in the hallway entered Charlotte's room as a rolling muffle of words—bits and pieces that she needed to assemble—but the tone was obvious. Sweet Berta was lying.

Charlotte maintained her allusion of sleep, resisting the urge to discover who owned the male voice on the receiving end of Berta's lies. Eleven seconds into the conversation, the man wearing heavy, loud boots stepped into her doorway and hovered briefly before returning to the hall. Charlotte's bruised face flushed as she imagined the man studying her at-rest expression. She hated the scrutiny, feeling like a caged animal at the zoo.

Approximately ten seconds later, a high-pitched squeak of chair-legs on the linoleum floor told Charlotte that the man wasn't leaving. The sound stopped just outside her open doorway.

His lowered voice carried inside her room. "Dispatch, Bravo-One."

"Go ahead, Chief."

"I'll be 10-20 at County Hospital."

His voice spoke into what she concluded to be a police radio. The echoing clicks and static—such familiar sounds—caused her heart to race.

The subtle static broke. "The hospital, Chief? Um . . . copy, Bravo-One."

Charlotte opened her eyes. She heard the man sigh, then shuffle around a bit in his chair. Velcro ripped.

"Damn cell phone," he said under his breath. "Ah, here we go."

Charlotte figured he was using his phone.

"Hey, Kim, so that was me checking in. My location is the hospital . . . just log it as . . . yes, I'm fine. I'm just waiting for Charlotte Evers to . . . affirmative. I'm simply checking in and telling you I'm on duty now. Kim, I need you to learn all the 10 codes that we use. It's important. The schedule and procedure list are taped near your screen."

Charlotte heard the man groan. He paced outside the door.

"Fine. Send Kemp to County."

"Kim," the officer's voice elevated. "No, not the jail. Send Officer Kemp over to County Hospital to switch places with me. Thanks."

Charlotte listened to the chief plop down on the foam-cushioned chair. The next few seconds were quiet, then she heard him sigh . . . again.

She pulled herself up, trying hard not to create any noise as she moved. Her body ached, the soreness deep and unforgiving. Each breath stung at her insides. Gritting her teeth, she managed to reach the supply cabinet near the sink.

Charlotte found a stash of Band-Aids in a drawer and, using her teeth, stripped off the paper and applied one over the drip of blood from the I.V. hole in her right hand. For twelve seconds, Charlotte counted the shifting sounds from the officer while she simultaneously calculated her escape chances. The officer knew her Evers alias. Which meant the urn and her Go Bag were probably at the police station, a retrieval problem by itself, but her first objective needed to be getting outside the hospital. She studied the *In Case of Fire* escape plan attached to the wall. *Five doors over . . . left-hand side . . . stairwell leading three floors down to ground level.*

"Chief Walker, you're here early." A woman stopped outside the door.

Charlotte thinned her body against the wall and tried to control her breathing.

"Jan, thought you only worked the ER," he said.

"I do. Just came up to check on the Jane Doe for you, but I see you beat me to it."

"I wanted to be here when she woke up. Hasn't happened yet." He stood, and his chair squeaked. "Is there a chance I can talk to Dr. Fielding about her status? When she'll be released?"

"Sure. Come over to the nurse's station. We'll page him, or at least get him on his cell."

"Thanks, Jan."

Charlotte waited for their footsteps to fade, then she peered into the hallway. Jan, the nurse, sat behind the desk and held the stationary phone to her ear while looking at the floor. The officer, Walker, stood with his back to her room, his forearms leaning on the tall counter over the desk. Something about Walker seemed familiar to Charlotte. She searched her memory and retrieved a fuzzy image of a Harding police vehicle and, after another five seconds of focus, she recalled his face from their conversation near the bookstore.

"Sorry, Chief," Jan said. "Someone should be sitting at the desk all the time. But some of the med staff is new."

"There's a lot of that going around. All three of my dispatchers are new."

She smiled. "Most of the new ones want to move to bigger hospitals. Can't take rural living, I guess. I'll just call the doctor's cell and leave a message. Might be faster than waiting for him to do rounds."

Walker tapped his fingers on the counter. "Let's just call and see if he answers."

Jan started typing numbers and launched into a rambling chat about giving a message to her son—something about tow trucks.

Charlotte saw her opportunity. She stepped lightly, but calculating, out into the hallway and hurried along the wall toward the stairs. All the while, her gaze never left the nurse's station as she counted the passing doorways. *One ... two ... three ...*

When she reached the fire doors, two nurses emerged from a nearby room—a woman and a man. They chatted and laughed as they headed for the desk. Charlotte pressed the bar on the door as stealth as possible then slid out through a two-foot-wide opening. Pain shot through her bruised collarbone as she twisted the handle, avoiding a loud *click* as the heavy door closed. She listened for the discovery of her absence. Nothing came. She slouched over in relief. Even this little amount of freedom felt good.

Charlotte glanced around the stairwell. It sounded vacant except for her own gasps for air. With luck, the time was too early in the morning for a busy crowd moving in the hospital. She rested her back on the wall, using it to brace herself. In an instant, a wave of vertigo attacked her head. Charlotte took in a few deep aching breaths, waiting for the pounding of her pulse to stop. The room seemed to spin forever, too long for her dazed mind to count the seconds.

Keep moving. Charlotte leaned her good arm against the handrail and descended the stairs only a few steps at a time. Her skull pounded in rhythm alongside the blood vessels throbbing in her shoulder. In that moment, she regretted not pushing the morphine button on the I.V. drip right before ripping it from her vein.

Second floor . . . keep going. She fought the pressing heaviness taking over her head. *Almost . . . first floor.* On her left, she found a door leading to the hospital's interior, and to her right stood an exterior exit. The words *ground level* and accompanying fire code sign displayed the escape route to the parking lot using a bold red line. Charlotte channeled her last ounce of strength and pressed on the fire door. A chill of December air stung at her face.

15

WALKER

"Dr. Fielding will be up in a minute," Jan said.

Walker nodded and headed for his chair. "I'll wait." He glanced at his watch—8:07 a.m.

"I'll see ya later, Chief. I'm late for my ER shift." She headed down the hall toward the elevator.

"Yep. Thanks," he called. Walker turned his back to the chair, intending to sit, but a sudden, continuous alarm squealed from both the nurse's station and inside Charlotte Evers' room. Two nurses hurried to the desk.

"Number six. The vitals aren't reading anymore." The nurse pushed past him.

Walker bolted into Charlotte Evers' room. The bed was empty. Blood spatters dotted the white sheets, and an I.V. tube hung loose against the stand.

"Where is she?" The nurse flung open the bathroom door. "She ripped out her IV! Call security."

The other nurse sprinted back to their desk and picked up the landline. "Why would she leave?"

Walker huffed, scanning the hallway. He dismissed the direction Jan left by—she would have seen Evers leaving—instead he ran down the hall toward the stairs, checking inside each room as he passed. "Dispatch, Bravo-One."

"Go ahead, Bravo-One," Kim answered.

"What's the location of Bravo-Three?"

"Bravo-Three is . . . ten minutes out."

"Coordinate with hospital security and the sheriff's department," he ordered. "Our person of interest left her location without being discharged. She may be outside the building."

"Copy."

Walker reached the stairs and flung open the fire door. The space was empty, so he stood still and listened.

A door slammed in the lower stairwell.

Walker raced down a level and onto the second floor, his adrenaline slamming the fire door into the wall. A handful of medical staff and a man in a wheelchair startled instantly.

"Did you see a woman in a hospital gown?" he panted. "Dark hair, arm in a sling?"

They shook their heads in unison, still clearly confused.

Walker hurried back into the stairwell. When he reached the ground floor, he glanced between both doors. Evers wouldn't risk being seen in the hospital, and the air felt cooler on the bottom landing than near the stairs. He popped open the exterior door.

Winter air stung at his skin, but Walker dismissed the distraction. In the dim light, he scanned the area for movement and began searching. The parking lot wasn't full of cars, but there were enough vehicles to hide behind in order to reach the main road. "Dispatch, Bravo-One. I'm 10-20 in the west parking lot. Update hospital security."

"Copy," Kim responded.

A set of small, light-weight footprints led away in the fresh layer of snow. Walker figured Evers' feet were still bare, and wearing only a hospital gown wouldn't keep her protected against the December temperatures. She was injured and running away, with no indication whether or not she'd found something to use as a weapon. Nothing about the situation felt good. He followed the prints to a nearby parked SUV, then searched around the vehicle, all the while keeping his adrenaline in check. He didn't see anyone.

The radio crackled with Kemp's voice and dispatch responding. He was in the parking lot, and hospital security was searching the building.

Walker lowered the volume on his radio.

The footprints blended into the dozens of impressions left by morning visitors and hospital staff. Finding Evers' tracks in the mess wasn't possible. He crouched low, scanning under the cars as he moved, expecting to find her nearby. There was no way she'd make it far in the snow.

16

MASON

MASON GLANCED at his watch—8:10 a.m. He jogged to his mom's Ford truck parked at the end of the hospital parking lot while cradling the orange juice and warm breakfast burrito he'd picked up at the cafeteria. They had one car. So, he was his mom's ride every morning. School started in five minutes, too soon to get to the high school before the first bell, but a tardy seemed reasonable compared to eating cornflakes for the eleventh day in a row.

He hopped into the driver's seat and unwrapped the burrito's top half while the truck engine warmed. As he took his first bite, Mason noticed a flash of movement in the rearview mirror. An inch of brown hair pressed against the outside of the cab's back window. He squinted, then glanced back, his heart rate speeding up. The hair was definitely attached to a head. Someone was in the back of his truck. He dropped the burrito on the dash.

"Hey!" Mason said, hopping out. He stared down at a woman attempting to hide in the truck's bed. She wore a hospital gown and an arm sling, her skin blotched with red patches as she shivered in the cold. To him, everything about the woman implied *bar fight gone wrong*, but he knew better. Mason recognized her face despite the cut on her nose and bruises under her eyes. "What the hell are you doing in my truck?"

"Freezing," she managed to say.

"Why aren't you in the hospital? It's right there!"

The woman slid out of the tailgate while wincing and panting for air, then she climbed into the truck's passenger seat.

"No!" he shouted, leaning inside. "Go to the hospital!"

"I can't. Get in and shut the door."

He raised an eyebrow. "Are you threatening me? Is this a carjacking? Where's your gun?"

"I don't have any weapons. Just please shut the door. I need the heater to work."

Mason watched her cower near the weak-blowing heater vent. He guessed she was older than him, in her twenties, but her injuries aged her appearance considerably. She looked helpless, not the kind of body language he expected from someone stealing his truck. Not that anyone would want to steal such a piece of junk anyway. She seemed more *lost and hurt* than *grand theft auto*.

"Okay." He climbed in and shut the door.

"Thank you." She turned the heater up all the way. "Can you drive, please?"

"No way."

Her face flinching in pain. "Can I at least have your coat?"

"You want my stuff, too? I don't understand what's happening here. You don't have a gun, which is good, and you don't seem to be stealing my truck, which is also good, but I know you're the Utah woman who crashed her car into the river. I'm pretty sure that the cops are charging you with a bunch of stuff. You're going to jail."

"How do you know I'm from Utah? And how do you know I crashed my car?" she asked. Her words slurred as she spoke, her lips quivering against the cold.

Mason wondered what his mom would do in this situation. He considered texting her. The hospital did lose patients occasionally, but not in the parking lot and not literally. "I'm the gas station clerk." He handed over his coat. "You bought gas there yesterday. Before running from Chief Walker, remember? I also towed your car to the police garage. That's how I know stuff."

She laid the coat over her body and tucked her legs underneath. "You look familiar, but I don't remember why. That's strange for me. Maybe I have a concussion."

"Probably." He wrinkled his nose. "Concussions are the worst. Maybe you should, I don't know, see a doctor about that. There's a ton of them over there." He pointed to the hospital. "No doctors in my truck."

She scanned the parking lot, her forehead tensing. "What's your name?"

"Um," he said, hesitating. "Look, my mom's a nurse. I'll text her to come get you. No one will ever know you were out here. We'll make this easy."

"Tim. You seem like a Tim."

"Tim? Are you kidding me? My name is Mason. I don't even look like a Tim."

"Mason, I'm Charlotte. Now we're friends. Friends help each other, and I need your help. Do you see those men by the building?"

He glanced up and squinted at the distance. His adrenaline spiked, a flash of heat filling his face and ears. Police officers and hospital security staff searched around the parked vehicles in a sweeping pattern, heading toward Mason's part of the lot. That was the last thing he wanted, for his first interaction with Walker in five years to be about *aiding and abetting a felon*. Or was it *harboring a fugitive*? His mind raced too fast to think straight. This kind of thing never worked out in TV shows. He was going to get screwed for sure.

"Yeah, I see them," he said. "Chief Walker and the other cops. Hard to miss. They're searching for you?"

"Yes. But I can't let them find me."

"Maybe they should, but . . . I don't want them finding you in my truck."

She slouched her back, obvious worry tightening her face. "Then drive, please."

"Like they won't notice a truck leaving when the rest of the lot is quiet. Lady, just go back inside before you pass out."

"Have you ever been afraid of them before, Mason?" She looked him in the eyes, her body visually shivering underneath his coat.

Afraid? Mason thought of his night in jail as an eleven-year-old. His friends were the only other people locked in the cell, and in hind sight, he was in no real danger. The whole thing had been a stunt constructed by Walker to teach them a lesson, and he knew it. But still, he hated the memory. He hated the fear he felt that night, hiding tears with his sleeve as he wondered if his father felt that scared in prison. Even though Mason knew his father deserved to be there.

"Have you ever been really afraid?" she repeated.

"Maybe."

"Well, I'm terrified of them finding me," Charlotte whispered. "The police are an unpredictability." Tears welled up in her eyes. "I need your help. They can't find me. It'll get bad."

"Why? What did you do wrong?"

"It's complicated. I wish they'd stop looking for me."

"What in the crap does that even mean? Of course, there's cops looking for you. Escaped fugitive in a hospital gown, remember?"

She glanced back toward the officers. "Not them. They're not the ones."

"What? Again, what in the crap does that mean?"

She winced. "My head hurts."

"That's what concussions do." He rolled his eyes.

"You towed my car?"

"Yeah," he said. "To the police garage in Harding."

"Do you know what happened to all the stuff inside?"

"They have it, I guess." He shrugged.

"I need some things from the trunk. Then I'll go and you'll never see me again. Can you help me get my stuff?"

"No way. That's crazy."

"Please, Mason," she said. Her voice quivered with each word. The cold was obviously getting to her again. "I just need a little help. That's all."

He stared at Charlotte's face. She looked and sounded frail. Plus, something about the woman's expression reminded him of his mother—a look that meant she was at her breaking point and just needed him to understand. His mom had that tortured look too often, usually after her nursing shifts . . . and the day his father went to prison. Mason remembered that same expression the morning his mom picked him up after the night of mailbox bashing. She said only thirteen words in the car ride home before a long day of silence: *Mason, don't grow up to be like your dad. I couldn't bear it.*

"Mason?"

He glanced at the officers again. Walker was among them, getting closer. Mason crouched in his seat, panic pounding his heartbeat into his ears. "Look," he said, speaking fast. "Let's be clear. I'm not afraid of the police. I'm only avoiding the chief. That's not the same thing. It's different, because . . . because I say it is. And it's complicated. And it's different than whatever crazy reasons *you* have for avoiding them. I'm not going to hide you or drive you across state lines or whatever else you're planning. That's nuts. But if you leave my truck before they find you in it, and go back inside the hospital right now and stay there, I promise that I'll find a way to check on your stuff at the garage."

She grabbed her temples, her face wincing with sudden pain. Tears ran down her bruised face.

"Charlotte, you need a doctor, and I don't need the police finding you passed out in my car. Go back inside, and I'll help you a little bit. That's my deal. Take it or leave it."

Her breathing shallowed and sped up. "Okay. It's an urn and a plastic bag of documents and other stuff. And a watch. The rest I don't care about."

"An urn?"

"Yes. Thank you, Mason. I can trust you. I know it—one hundred percent harmless." She smiled through another stream of tears, but it looked forced and desperate. Then Charlotte climbed out of the truck before he could respond, leaving his coat on the seat.

Mason sat still and watched her wander toward the building. He was *one hundred percent harmless*? What in the hell did that mean? He slapped his forehead. *You're an idiot.* He replayed the conversation in his mind, trying to convince himself it hadn't really happened. That he didn't just involve himself in a mess that his mom wouldn't understand. Not again.

Mason collected himself and watched Charlotte slow down between two SUV's parked a row away, bracing herself against their sides.

Dread tied his stomach in a knot. *This is crazy. She's not getting there fast enough. It's too cold.* In the elements, he knew her injuries and the thin hospital gown were Charlotte's enemies more than the police.

Charlotte leaned her head against one of the vehicles, then she paused, slouched, and began to fall into the light layer of snow. Her body crashed down helpless and didn't move.

Mason's instincts kicked in. He jumped out of the trunk and ran around the front end, scanning the parking lot as he raced straight for Charlotte. The others were close, but not close enough. "Hey!" he shouted, waving his arms. "Over here!" Mason slid to Charlotte's side. She was breathing, but her skin felt like ice.

Chief Walker and Officer Kemp were the first to reach them.

"Mason, back up!" Walker said.

"She's really cold. She needs help!" He tried to lift her.

Without hesitating, Walker and Kemp scooped Charlotte up and headed for the building.

"Get a gurney!" Walker shouted ahead. "Mason, don't leave."

One of the hospital security officers radioed to someone inside. The crowd seemed to follow Walker in a flock. All except Mason. He stood in the spot where Charlotte fell, holding still in the winter air but without noticing the cold anymore. He simply panted and watched the crowd move, his hands shaking. In that moment, his only concern was how quick Walker entered the building and in turn, making sure Charlotte got help. At least *half* of the help she needed. The other half was contingent upon him fulfilling his promise. And standing there, his pulse racing, Mason's mind felt numb.

17

WALKER

WALKER KNEW the odd feeling weighing on his mind wasn't déjà vu, although he wished it was that simple and dreamlike. But the familiarity of the moment wasn't that elusive. As he stood at the foot of the ER gurney, a single instance in his life played out for the second time—watching the pale face of Charlotte Evers as medical personal tried to pull her from the frozen grip of hyperthermia. Only in this reliving, he didn't see her as an innocent victim. This time, uneasiness filled him fueled by dozens of unanswered questions.

"Step back, please," an ER physician instructed. A med team surrounded the gurney, attempting to warm Charlotte enough to wake her. They covered her body in heated blankets and reinserted a fresh I.V. line.

He stepped toward the aisle. "I'll be out front. Get me when she's settled back in her own room. I need to cuff her to the hospital bed."

The doctor half-smiled, as if she couldn't tell if he was serious or joking.

He wasn't sure either. This whole situation pissed him off. So, he stepped away and headed for the waiting room.

Stewart, Kemp, and Franklin stood by the open fire doors dividing the ER from the waiting room. They became quiet as he approached.

"Chief," Stewart said. "Is she going to be okay?"

"Yeah, I think. But we can't talk to her right now." He motioned to the security staff waiting near the front desk. "When the woman is in her room, use restraints. Not heavy, just enough that she can't run away again. I'll post someone at her room. Thanks, guys." Walker waited for the officers to walk down the hall before he turned back.

"So, what's really going on?" Franklin asked.

"The St. George woman, Pearl Sanford, is still missing as of my phone call last night. Chief Redding said they're looking into it, but so far, they had no other leads until the Oldsmobile showed up in Harding."

"I was right." Franklin's eyes grew wide. "Evers did it."

Walker held up his hand. "We don't know what she did or what 'it' is. But between Evers and the St. George Police Department, I'm tired of this yo-yo game I'm getting played. Time for some straight answers. Kemp, I'm assigning you to Evers. Stay in the hospital, right next to her bedside if necessary, but the moment she's up and alert, you ask her to identify herself. The second thing you do is call me."

"Right." Kemp headed through the aisle of curtains.

"Franklin, is the car sealed up and ready to transfer to St. George?" Walker asked.

"Not sure."

"Well, find out."

"Okay. Guess there's nothin' left to do here anyway," Franklin said and turned away.

Walker relaxed his fists, attempting to release the anger he had been holding on to. He glanced at his watch. It was still morning, but he physically felt as if an entire day had played out. He was tired, drained, and frustrated.

"Here," Stewart said, handing him a non-descript smartphone. "I put your SIM card into a prepaid cell. Uses your same number. I left a message with St. George P.D. to call you when they have new info."

"Thanks, kid." Walker slipped the phone in his pocket.

"Just don't swim with this one," Stewart said, smiling.

Walker snickered. "Stewart."

"Yes, Chief."

"Go back on patrol."

"Right." He saluted, but with a smirk on his face.

Walker waited while his greenie officer left through the outer door. Then when Stewart was out of sight, he turned his attention to his next, and vital, task at hand. Franklin was wrong. Maybe not regarding Evers' involvement in Pearl Sanford's disappearance, but about insisting there was nothing left to do at the hospital. Walker stared across the waiting room to where Mason Trent sat slouched over in a chair, and he braced himself for an awkward conversation.

18

MASON

MASON MADE it into the ER waiting room before his adrenaline fizzled into nothing. He stumbled over to a chair and plopped down. The events of the morning, combined with the lack of breakfast, drained every ounce of energy from his body.

He glanced toward the ER. The fire doors were open—unusual, but nothing about the morning fit "normal" anyway. A group of police officers stood in the hall. He couldn't hear what they were saying, but at that moment he didn't care. Instead, he texted his mom: *I'm in the waiting room. Can't leave. Found the missing patient in the truck. Don't worry. She's in the hospital now.*

Mason tucked his phone inside the pocket of his jeans, realizing he'd left his coat in the truck. He didn't like sitting there without a hood, without a way to hide his face from the world. Looking like a druggie wouldn't be bad at that moment. People would leave him alone at the very least. He leaned forward on his elbows and stared down at his shoes. Maybe if he looked sick, no one would talk to him. *Sick* wasn't far from the truth anyway.

A minute later his mom rushed to his side. "Are you alright?" She had *the look*. The one he'd seen on her face many times before. The one he'd just seen on Charlotte's face. Only his mom had a touch of *scared* mixed in with it.

His stomach turned. Mason focused on the uneven weave of his shoe laces in order to keep from freaking out.

"Are you okay?" she repeated.

"I'm fine."

Jan sat down next to him, placing her hand on his back. "I heard she ran away. There was a hospital-wide alert. Did she try to steal the truck?"

"No. Only hide, I think. No sane person would ever steal that truck."

"What if she's not sane?"

"Mom, I think she's just scared, not crazy or dangerous."

She hugged him tight. "I'm glad you're okay. You're my world, you know?"

Mason didn't pull away after a few seconds like he usually did. This time, he let Mom get the hug she needed to feel better. "Nothing happened, Mom. Really. The cops want me to hang around for a minute, that's all."

"Okay." She leaned back into her chair, obviously planting herself for the wait.

He glanced over at his mother's face, noticing how her expression morphed from fake relief to serious again, as if her thoughts turned heavy. "Mom, it was no big deal. The lady didn't even talk to me. I'm good. Really."

She smiled, though the worry line on her forehead didn't disappear. "I know you're okay. You're not a kid anymore. Children grow. Mothers have a hard time remembering that sometimes. And let's face it, we've both been through enough reality for one lifetime. I should have protected you better."

He shifted in his chair. "You couldn't have babysat me this morning. I'm sixteen, you know."

"I wasn't talking about this morning. At least, not only. I'm just grateful nothing happened today."

Mason watched her eyes water and felt a sudden sense of guilt. There was only a handful of moments in his life when he remembered lying to his mother. He didn't want this to be one of them. "Mom, the lady did say a few things to me. Not change-the-world stuff, but . . ."

His attention broke from her face and focused near the fire doors. Walker stood in the group of officers. One by one, they spoke to him before heading in opposite directions.

"Well, what did she say?" Mom shifted to block his view. "Tell me."

He watched Officer Stewart pass by on his way outside. That left Walker alone, standing only fifty feet away and staring right in Mason's direction.

"Um, nothing. Just that she's scared. I guess we're all nervous about something, right?"

"Mason?"

"Yeah?" He couldn't think of what else to say. His mind went blank. Instead, Mason sat helpless as Chief Walker paced over to him. *This is going to be awkward. And suck.*

"Hey, Jan," Walker said.

"Chief." She leaned forward in her chair.

"I need to ask Mason a few questions. Should only take a minute."

"Okay," she said.

Mason stared low at Walker's shoes as the man sat down in the chair directly opposite him. The fact that the chief remembered his name wasn't a good sign. Mason wanted to be forgotten.

"So you found the woman in the parking lot, huh?" Walker asked.

Mason raised his head and nodded.

"Did she say anything to you?"

"About what?"

"How about her name?"

Jan waved her hand. "Chief, he found her in our truck. Maybe she was trying to steal it. She said she was scared, that's it."

"Is that true?" Walker leaned forward, resting his elbows on his knees.

84

"No," Mason said. "I mean, no she wasn't trying the steal the truck. Just get warm because the engine was running."

Jan's pager went off. "Crap, I gotta get back to the ER. Still on shift." She stood up but kept her hand on Mason's shoulder.

"I only have a few more questions, Jan," Walker said. "Then Mason can go back to school. Is it okay if I ask them without you?"

She hesitated a moment while glancing at her pager again. "I guess that's fine. Mason, text me when you get to school."

"Sure." Mason watched her leave the room, willing her to stay and failing, before he glanced back at Walker. The man's expression looked firm, but after a few seconds it softened a little. He wondered if the chief saw him as a normal young man or as a scared, troubled eleven-year-old—one with a father in prison for making a meth lab in his basement. Even though Mason's dad was arrested and sentenced in Portland right before Jan and Mason moved to Harding, he suspected that Chief Walker knew their family history. Harding was a small town—secrets always surfaced.

"Mason, how are you doing right now?" Walker asked.

The question caught him off guard. "Today, or in general?"

"Both."

"I'm . . ." He didn't know how to answer without spilling too much of his actual mood. "Fine, I guess."

"What happened this morning must have surprised you."

"Maybe. I found the lady in my truck, but that was about it. She just . . . needed help."

"Okay. Brave of you to get her some. It would have taken us too long to find her where she fell."

Mason leaned back in his chair. He noticed a look in Walker's eyes, and something in his expression—bit of compassion perhaps? Real or fake? It was hard to know for certain. "Yep."

"You did a good thing . . . helping her . . . and us."

Mason was confused. The conversation wasn't going the way he'd always imagined in his head—no asking if Mason was keeping himself out of trouble or heading down the same path as his dad. There was no obvious disappointments or stereotypes or labels being tossed in his lap, but then again, he couldn't read Walker's face more than knowing he was serious. He simply couldn't tell what the man was thinking. After five years of avoiding this moment, Mason felt uneasy, but not the sheer dread he expected.

"I suppose it was a good thing," Mason said. For a moment, he considered telling Walker the full details of his conversation with Charlotte—her request for help, the urn, and the plastic bag of documents—all of it. The impulse surprised him. Sharing the information would certainly clear his mind. He'd be free to walk away.

"Did she tell you anything? Maybe her name?"

"Charlotte. And she's afraid of the police. Terrified actually."

"Why?"

"I don't know that."

"Anything else, Mason? It's really important."

He recalled the image of Charlotte's pleading face when she asked for his help, asking him to believe her, and saying she trusted him. A sudden sense of betrayal rooted in his stomach. Whatever he decided to say in this moment, whomever he sided with, Mason was choosing to lie to someone. Maybe Charlotte was a liar, too. Or maybe not. Perhaps she didn't do anything wrong as she professed. Maybe, just maybe, there was much more to her than all the Harding people assumed. She wasn't the only one with a painful history and the need to hide a complicated past. Mason knew what that felt like —lonely.

But he'd never tell Walker all that. He needed more time to think.

"Mason?" Walker said.

"There wasn't much else, Chief. I asked her to go back to the hospital. She did. When she passed out, that's when I got your attention."

Walker stared at him for a moment, as if studying Mason's face.

An instant flush of nerves filled Mason's head and chest. His mind flashed on all the stupid crime shows he'd watched on TV where the interrogator "stared down" a perp, the overhead light bulb sweating the guy into submission. In the reality, it was nothing like on television. At least, not in Harding.

"Okay, Mason," Walker said. "Thanks. Let me know if you remember anything else." He stood from his chair and headed for the ER.

The conversation was over. Mason sucked in a much-needed calming breath and gripped his head, staring down at his shoes. Maybe he really was going to be sick.

19

BERTA

BERTA TILTED her head toward the rearview mirror of her Buick sedan, attempting to appear as if she were checking her makeup. As if she wore any in the first place. Berta didn't have time for such vanity. Instead, her actual attention focused on the front entry door of the Harding police station. She made a mental note every time someone entered or exited the building in the ten minutes she sat there while innocently "checking her make-up" and not-so-innocently formulating a plan. Kemp had left in a hurry right after she arrived, and so had the new guy—Deputy Franklin. It was just as well. She didn't want to talk to them anyway. Berta wasn't sure what was so important that justified speeding away in their patrol cars with lights flashing.

Maybe their absence would work to her advantage. She headed across the parking lot and entered the building, keeping her stride and posture business-like but not harsh. She needed to play this just right. Option #1: Bend the truth a little. Option #2: Out-right lie. Either way, she didn't have time for any nonsense. And she'd grown up in the town, any misbehavior on her part would be forgiven. That was her small-town birthright.

Inside, much to her annoyance, no one sat behind the high-countered reception desk, and the chairs in the tiny waiting area were also empty. She stifled the urge to drum her fingernails on the counter and instead searched for a customer bell. If the Harding Police Department insisted on inconveniencing the public, the least they could do was have a bell to ring. That was civil.

"Um . . . can I help you?" A young man, maybe eighteen years old by the look of his acne, entered the room from the back hallway. He wore casual clothes and an uneasy smile.

"Do you work here?" Berta asked.

"Yes. Well, no."

"Which is it?" she said. She had no time for his shenanigans.

"I'm a volunteer," the kid said. "Criminal Justice Student. Or at least I will be in the fall. The chief lets me help out sometimes. Look, Bob the receptionist is in the bathroom. All the cops are on a call at the hospital. So . . . I'm Jed. Can I help you? Or like, . . . try to?"

Berta tightened her lips, annoyed by Jed's innocent and somewhat vacant expression, then she relaxed. *A volunteer. That's perfect. Option #1.* "Yes, Jed. I think you can help me. You see, I need some information. The woman who was in the car crash yesterday morning, she came into my store and left a couple books. I'm trying to find the original owner so I can return them. It's a surprise. Kind of a secret project. So, Jed, I need to know more about the woman from the crash. Do you know anything about her?"

Jed rubbed his chin. "I don't know anything. But . . . yesterday was awesome. The CSI team came and did stuff with the car. They took all this evidence. I wasn't allowed to be in the room, you know, liability and whatever, but it was cool. Although it took, like, forever. Not quick like on TV. I guess DNA and fingerprints take, like, months to process. Sad, 'cause it's a crazy mystery what happened to that missing lady."

"What missing lady?" Berta asked.

"Um," Jed said, scratching his head. "I can't remember her name. Like I said, I'm not allowed in the room much."

"Do you know how to find her name?" Berta tried to sound sweet and non-threatening, but by the distant stare on Jed's face she knew theatrics weren't necessary as long as she remained pleasant.

"Bob'll be back in a minute," Jed said. "He can help you."

"That's great." Berta flashed a loving grandmother smile. "But you're helping me just fine, and I'm in a terrible hurry. Can you find the name of the missing woman for me? It's very important. The Chief already knows I'm looking into it. So it's okay to tell me."

Jed hesitated for a moment, then his expression brightened. "I'll look in the chief's office. Hang on."

Berta waited until he left the room before she sat down in one of the chairs. She smiled to herself, amazed at how the direct approach had worked. All she needed was a cooperative and distractible mind. Not one like Charlotte the Liar. Berta had no hope of ever getting any information out of that girl.

The glass door swung open. Berta stared up in alarm, afraid to find Terry or Deputy Franklin standing there, but it wasn't them. The young man from the gas station, Jan's boy, stood in the doorway. He wiped his sneakers on the rug while looking down, barely acknowledging Berta with a mere awkward nod.

The kid wore a dark coat with a hood covering his disheveled hair. Berta gripped the straps of her purse a little tighter, wondering if he knew how much he resembled a drug dealer. Under the circumstances, it now seemed silly to think she once wondered if he'd help her with an online auction. Tech savvy or not, the kid had to be unreliable.

He searched the counter. She figured he was looking for a bell.

"Oh, hey," Jed said when he returned to the room. In his hand, he held a stack of papers. "Can I help you?"

"Uh, yeah. I'm Mason, the guy who towed the car here yesterday. I guess I left a tow cable here by mistake. Can I go get it from the garage?"

"Um, a cable?"

"Yep," Mason said. "Well, more like a tow hook that attaches to a tow cable. It's complicated. My boss will kill me if I don't get it back."

Jed nodded. "I think you need, like, an escort person or something. Bob'll be back. Hang on." Jed held up the papers and motioned to Berta.

She hurried over to the counter.

"You know what, man," Mason said. "I'm in a hurry and I know right where it is so . . ." He moved toward the back hallway.

Berta huffed and reached for the papers. "Yes, yes, go away, tow truck kid. I'm in a terrible hurry, too. Jed, let's find that name." She could tell by the look on Jed's face that he felt torn in two directions.

"Okay," Jed said.

Mason disappeared down the hallway. Berta didn't give him a second thought. Instead she glanced over the printout stack in Jed's hands, pages that resembled some kind of police report. She wasn't really sure. On the bottom of the first page, she found an active case update written by a Detective Peterson. The report stated a woman named Pearl Sanford was missing from St. George, and that the Oldsmobile had belonged to her.

Pearl. Berta tried to hide her excitement at the discovery. She wrote down what she could in a notebook from her purse. Jed shifted a bit, staring down the hall, then back at the papers.

"Is that all you needed?" he asked in a hurry.

"Yes. You've been very helpful. I'll let the chief know how professional you were."

Jed grinned and scratched his chin. "Maybe someday I'll be chief of this place. I've got big plans."

"I can see that happening," Berta lied with a full smile. She hurried out the glass door before Jed could engage her in a full-on philosophical discussion about his life and where it was or was not heading.

She slid into the driver's seat of her car. The second part of the plan involved returning to the bookstore and using the computer, if the dumb thing would cooperate. There was no way she was going to involve Mason-the-gas-station-kid in any of her plans now. It was research on the internet. How hard could it be? Plus, now she had a name—Pearl Sanford out of St. George. Someone needed to report

Pearl missing, which meant someone was looking for her. Berta imagined the family would be grateful to have Pearl's prized books back in their possession. And, she imagined, they would be ready to pay a hefty reward to do so.

20

MASON

MASON STROLLED DOWN the hallway without glancing behind him, relieved to be putting distance between himself, the-crazy-bookstore-lady, and the gullible guy at the front desk. But he had no idea where he was going. Avoiding Chief Walker for five years meant avoiding the police station, and until towing the Oldsmobile to the garage, he didn't expect to ever again enter the building. At least not voluntarily.

The maze of hallways looked different than what his memory had stored as a freaked-out eleven-year-old. He tried several doors before finding the correct one. It was surprising how many times he encountered the aroma of scented Christmas pinecones. Strange how a police station could smell so much like an old lady's house.

He stepped inside the station garage and let the door gently close behind him. No one guarded the massive space, although he wasn't sure why he expected someone to keep watch. The two garage doors were closed and locked in place, plus the only way to access the room was from inside the station past Jed as security-watch-dog. Yes, the system was flawed. But at that moment, Mason wasn't complaining.

He headed past the stalls where two out-of-service patrol vehicles had been parked and found the Oldsmobile right where he left it—at the far end of the row. From his coat pocket, he retrieved a spare tow hook that he'd swiped from work before heading to the police station. Just in case—as a backup plan. It took most of the day before he decided to keep his deal with Charlotte, planning to do only the minimum required, but he wasn't crazy. Just stupidly curious.

Mason gripped the hook in his hand then glanced inside the car's windows, noticing both loose and bagged items on the seats. The opening for the driver's side window had been taped with clear plastic. He moved toward the rear end and knelt down by the trunk. Two pieces of evidence tape extended from the trunk lid to the bumper. One piece had been cut. The other was intact. And by the look of the pieces, Mason guessed the car had been searched then resealed. The fresh tape had vehicle info, signatures, and dates all written in black marker.

Mason leaned back on his heels and groaned. There was no way to open the trunk or access the bags on the back seat without altering the tape. Someone, at some point, would notice tampering.

The inner station door flung open. Mason nearly fell back onto the floor behind the car. He held his breath for a moment, listening to the sound of utility boots on cement. He wanted to run or hide, but there wasn't enough time. The footsteps stopped near the Oldsmobile. A wave of panic radiated through his whole body.

"Hey, kid. What are ya doin'?"

Mason stared up at Deputy Franklin. "I . . . I . . ."

"Aren't you supposed to be in school?" Franklin asked, overshadowing him. "How come you're in here?" He eyed the car, then around the room, and then Mason again.

"Well . . ." Mason stared at Franklin's shoes. His mind was blank.

"Stand up, kid."

He fumbled to his feet.

"How come you're in here? It's a simple question." Franklin folded his arms and leaned back on his heels, a scowl forming on his face. "Waitin' for an explanation."

"Uh . . ."

"Hey, what ya got there?" Franklin pointed to the tow hook in Mason's hand.

Duh. I'm an idiot. "Tow hook," Mason said, mentally kicking himself for forgetting his own escape plan. "I left it attached to the car by accident. You know, when I towed it here. Don't want to get into trouble for losing another one. Came back to get it."

"How did that thing stay on the . . . wait. Did Bob let ya in unescorted?"

Mason shook his head.

"Jed then . . ." Franklin tightened his upper lip. "I knew that kid was too spacey. If it were me, I wouldn't allow volunteers. They can't be trusted with responsibility."

Mason raised an eyebrow. "Well, he wasn't being lazy. I was in a hurry and Jed was helping the lady from the bookstore."

"Berta Sheppard was here?"

"Yeah."

"Huh," Franklin said, scrunching his nose. "I guess Jed has been through enough punishment already. A scoldin' and a conversation with that lady are about the same thing."

Mason tried to laugh at the poor joke, but what came out of his mouth sounded more like an awkward goose squawk.

Franklin stared at him. "So, you got the hook now. Better be goin' to school." He motioned toward the door.

"Right." Mason followed Franklin, but couldn't help glancing back at the Oldsmobile as they walked away.

"Oh, by the way," Franklin added puffing up, "you'll like this. So we searched the trunk and didn't find the severed head you expected, but . . . there was an urn full of ashes. Turns out there was a dead body in the trunk after all."

"Whoa. That's crazy." Mason tried to sound casual. "And kinda awesome. Different for Harding anyway. Not boring. So what happened to the urn? And . . . what else did you find? Must have been some weird stuff, right?"

"Yeah. Some is bagged up and sealed. Can't show you anything, of course. Official police business." Franklin gripped his duty belt. "The CSI team took the good stuff to the State Crime Lab. It'll be a while before we know anything more. The car is getting shipped away as soon as I make the arrangements. So . . . life will get back to normal. Back to boring."

"What about the lady at the hospital?" Mason asked.

"We can book her in Harding for failure to stop, evading, and what not. But I'm thinkin' St. George P.D. will want her down there. They have a crime to solve."

"A crime?"

"Yep. A missing persons case. And this woman, she's involved somehow." He tapped his temple. "And I've got it all figured out."

"So what happened?" Mason asked.

"Can't talk about it, kid. Once again, official police business and you ain't official."

They headed down the hallway.

"Don't worry about making sense of things," Franklin said. "Stick to improving your tow truck skills. Heaven knows you need the practice. Besides, what's entertainment today is yesterday's tall tales. It'll go back to borin' in no time."

"Right," Mason said with a forced chuckle, though his true mood didn't match. In truth, he felt sick inside. He didn't make eye contact with Jed as he headed past the front desk. The kid was going to get it for letting Mason wander, and Franklin would make Jed's day miserable. Mason's guilt couldn't change that. Still . . .

"Hey," Mason said to Jed. "Thanks." He held up the tow hook.

"No problem. Boss trouble would suck."

"Any trouble sucks," Mason said, nodding.

Franklin held open the glass door. "Hey, kid, next time don't forget stuff."

"Okay." Mason walked back to his truck and tossed the tow hook into the front passenger seat. For a moment, he sat still, gripping the steering wheel, and waited for his adrenaline to subside. He hated the sunken feeling that getting caught in the wrong place had left rooted in his stomach. The nerves ate at him. He only had one objective in his mission, and he'd failed. He felt useless. And he felt like a wimp. Charlotte would be disappointed.

Another thought popped in his head, just as quick and urgent.

Franklin said Charlotte was involved in a disappearance. She trusted Mason, but could he trust her? Full trust was a slippery thing. What else had she lied about? The ashes were probably gone, along with the bag of documents that Charlotte wanted. They could have been on their way to the State Crime Lab or locked up at the station, either way, Mason didn't have access. But he'd tried his best to get them. He could tell her that. Then he'd be free to walk away—promise fulfilled.

21

WALKER

"STILL NO SIGN OF PEARL SANFORD?" Walker asked into his cell phone. He entered the third-floor hallway and headed toward Charlotte Evers' hospital room.

"None," Chief Redding said. "Our news coverage yielded a few false sightings, but we're still treating her disappearance as suspicious. Search and Rescue and other agencies are on alert in surrounding areas. Detective Peterson will handle transferring the Evers woman and the car back to St. George. In the meantime, I'd like to see her initial statement. Then if you could keep her in custody, we'd appreciate it."

"We're working on that," Walker said. He glanced at his wrist watch—3:30 p.m. "Not sure when the hospital will release her."

"Okay, Chief. Sounds good. Peterson will be in touch."

"Thanks." Walker hung up and hurried down the hospital corridor.

Kemp stood just outside Evers' room. "Chief, she's woken up a couple times, but she's been too groggy to say anything. Thought I'd let you know anyway."

"Thanks. I'll switch you. Head back."

Kemp nodded. He walked toward the elevators.

Walker sat in the chair placed inside Charlotte Evers' room. Last time sitting in the hallway proved to be a mistake, and he wouldn't let her escape again. Not that she was in any position to get away. He glanced at the fabric Velcro wrist restraints tying Evers to the bed rail, and then at her sleeping face—the rest of her body had been cocooned under warming blankets. Evers' color had improved over the lifeless pale hue that he'd seen on her twice before. Despite the few minor facial marks left from the car crash, and the obvious soreness she would experience from being moved around like a rag doll, she looked . . . like a survivor.

He sat for a time and stared at the floor—going over a dozen or so unanswered questions in his mind. When he glanced up again, the wall clock read 3:45 p.m., and he noticed another change in the room.

Charlotte Evers' eyes were open.

"Hello," he said out of habit, rising to his feet.

She blinked several times, as if adjusting to her situation, then tugged at the wrist restraints.

"Do you remember me?" he asked, choosing his words carefully.

Evers simply stared at him.

"My name is Chief Walker. You met me before your car accident. That was yesterday. A lot has happened since then. And a lot of people are worried about you. What's your name?"

She pulled on the wrist straps once more before letting out a light groan. Every movement looked labored, and Evers winced a bit when she inhaled.

"I'll tell the nurse you're awake. Just need to know your name so we can inform them at the nurse's station. They've been calling you Jane Doe."

"Charlotte," she said. The word sounded heavy. She leaned back against the pillow and closed her eyes, more worry lines forming on her brow.

"What's your last name?"

A nurse walked in the room. "Ah, you're awake again."

"It hurts," Charlotte mumbled.

"What does?" the nurse asked.

"Everything."

"Okay. The doctor left an order for a pain med when you woke up. I'll bring you a dose." She headed for the door.

"No, don't leave," Charlotte said to the nurse, her voice shaking. She looked at Chief Walker, specifically at his chest as if she was only seeing his uniform, the worry deepening on her face.

"Oh, no stress," the nurse said. "The chief will keep you company. He's the one who saved you, did you know? He pulled you from that car in the river. Nothing bad will happen to you." She left the room.

Charlotte stared up at Walker's face, at his eyes.

He felt a flush of uneasiness, as if embarrassment, frustration, and awkwardness all collided into a perfect storm in his gut. Why did the nurse have to give Charlotte Evers a promise that he wasn't sure he could keep? Bad things happened all the time. "What's your name?" he asked again.

She didn't respond, simply glanced at the window then scanned the room before settling her gaze at the door.

The nurse returned, and in under twenty seconds, Charlotte had taken the pain medicine through her I.V. line and the nurse left again.

"Charlotte?" He stepped forward, softening the tone of his voice. He couldn't ask her any real questions, but maybe he could still get her name. People were required by law to identify themselves to a police officer. The rest would have to wait. "What's your full name? Do you remember?"

Her eyelids drooped a little, and she rested her head on the pillow.

"What did your parents name you?" Walker asked.

"It doesn't matter anymore." Her words began to slur together. The medicine was kicking in.

Walker knew the conversation was about to end. "Did they call you Charlotte Evers? Or was it . . ." He pulled a small flip notebook from his pocket where he'd written the ID info they'd found in the car. ". . . Rebecca or Megan or Elizabeth? Do those names sound familiar?"

She tilted her head and closed her eyes for several seconds before opening them again. "They're not real. Those people aren't real. My mother . . ." Her eyes watered. "She called me Charlotte. Charlotte the Great. But she can't anymore. She's gone. And I'm not supposed to be Charlotte anymore, but I couldn't help it. I couldn't let go of Charlotte. She was so mad at me when she found out I kept my name." She closed her eyes.

Walker moved to the end of the bed, his curiosity taking over. Charlotte's last sentence barely came out audible, mostly a quiet slur of mumbles.

"Who?" he asked. "Who didn't want you to be Charlotte anymore? Your mother?"

Charlotte opened her eyes a sliver. "No, not Mom. Pearl was mad." Her breathing slowed. "But I told her it was okay this one time. Just once. And she could be 'Pearl'. Just this once."

Walker knew the pain killer was talking now and he needed to walk away, but he couldn't help himself. He just stood there and listened.

"She's gone too," Charlotte said, emotion and sleepiness winning. "She burned. Just like Mom. Pearl burned. I did it."

Walker took a step back. Everything felt heavy—the moment, the room, the words.

Charlotte's face softened as the young woman relaxed into a heavy, drug-induced slumber, and he wondered if she looked as innocent when she burned Pearl Sanford. The pain medicine could have caused confusion, but he knew better. The shock and sick in his gut told him as much—something bad had happened.

Walker stepped into the hallway and pulled out his cell phone, steadying his mind and muscles as he straightened up. The line rang twice.

"This is Chief Redding."

"Hello, this is Chief Walker again. I just spoke with the woman caught driving Pearl Sanford's car."

"Did she give you her real name?" Redding asked.

"Sort of. Her first name is Charlotte, but no solid answer on her surname. But . . . here's the thing . . ." Walker glanced down the hallway toward the elevators, briefly listening for anyone nearby in the side halls. He lowered his voice, still reeling from the weight of his next words. "It wasn't an official statement. She was rambling before she fell asleep after being given pain killer. None of it is useable. But she said Pearl was gone. That she *burned*. Charlotte said that she did it. Again, Chief, the young woman was out of it, but I think the missing persons case is looking more like a homicide investigation."

Redding let out a sigh. "Okay. I was hoping Sanford would turn up somewhere like a bus stop or a park bench—dressed in a robe, curlers in her hair, confused as hell. That's how it goes sometimes. That's how you hope it goes anyway."

"Guess we're not that lucky," Walker said.

"As soon as Charlotte Evers is alert, try to get an official statement. And when she can travel, pack her up and ship her down here. Make sure she knows her right to an attorney. Make sure this is handled within normal procedure. Detective Peterson will need to interview her soon. He has a full load right now, but I'll try to shift his workload to get this case coordinated with him and a detective in homicide. Thanks for the quick update."

"Yep."

Walker ended the call. He turned back and leaned against the door frame of Charlotte's room, studying her face while the sick feeling still pitted in his stomach. His instincts had been wrong, and what was worse, Franklin's suspicions were right. There was deceit behind Charlotte's soft sleeping eyes—perhaps even violence. His own instincts hadn't flagged such possibilities when he dragged her from the river, or when he carried her frozen, lifeless body in from the snow. She needed to live. It was that simple. And he needed answers and to do his job. Again, simple.

But Charlotte Evers wasn't making things easy. Walker's mind ran wild with possible scenarios. What if Charlotte was lying, or at least she was good at deception, and Pearl Sanford was dead somewhere? People were innocent till proven guilty, but that didn't mean his gut instinct wasn't valued. He knew it was only a matter of time before all the gruesome facts came to light. At least she'd be out of his town soon.

Walker stepped away from the room and combed his hand through his hair, frustration roasting inside him. He headed for the fire doors. His mind raced, thoughts spinning at a hundred miles an hour. What time was it? He needed to check in with his officers—update them, get organized, give orders, be normal. The woman was restrained, drugged, asleep, and the nurses and hospital security could watch her for a while. But mostly, Chief Walker needed a breather. If only for a moment.

22

CHARLOTTE

THE CNA LEFT Charlotte's room. She was alone again. The voices of the security officers in the hall blended into a steady rhythm of casual conversation. She wasn't sure what they were talking about. Something about fishing. The longer they chatted, the more distant they sounded. Charlotte sat up the best she could, despite the wrist restraints. She was feeling better, but she couldn't let them know that. Wellness meant she could be booked into the jail.

The wall clock read 7:18 p.m. How long had she been asleep?

Someone entered her room in a hurry. Charlotte jumped back, adrenaline spiking in her body. She tried to lay down, but couldn't do it fast enough.

The teenager stared at her.

It took Charlotte a few second to remember him. The boy looked tired and a little pink-in-the-cheeks from the December evening winds outside the hospital. His hands were casually tucked in his pockets, but the rest of his body language betrayed him. The kid was jittery, staring at the floor and only briefly glancing at Charlotte as he spoke.

"Hey," he said.

"Hi, Mason." She hoped that was his name. Most of their

conversation in the truck jumbled together in her memory, but the critical details were intact.

He glanced at the floor again.

"Mason, it's a relief to see you. I'm feeling better. Went back to the hospital just like you asked. You saved me."

He nodded without looking up.

Charlotte swallowed hard, choosing her words carefully. "Did you do what you promised? What happened?"

Mason leaned back and looked out the doorway for a few seconds. "We don't have a lot of time to talk. Security is distracted. My mom will be off shift soon. I'm supposed to be working at the gas station. I get that you've had a couple terrible days here, but some of us have to keep living a normal life, you know?"

This time, she was the one who nodded, surprised by his sudden burst of conversation. "I know," she mumbled.

"I kept my promise. I went to the police station, but the car's been taped up as evidence or something and your stuff is gone."

Gone. The word pounded into her brain. Charlotte's world seemed to crash in on itself. The moment slowed, and her heart felt like it would break in two . . . if she could keep breathing at all. "Gone where?"

"Not sure. Some stuff is sealed in the car. Some may be in the station evidence locker." He shrugged. "But a bunch was taken to the crime lab. Point is, I can't get to any of it. But you need to know, I tried. I really did. You just have to let all that stuff go. Move on. Leave this in the past."

"From experience," she said, ". . . that is easy to say, but not even close to being easy to do. Kid, you try running away from the past and see how long you endure before your mind goes crazy."

"Is that what you are . . . *crazy*?"

She tugged at the wrist restraints. "I can't afford to be crazy."

Mason shifted farther away from her hospital bed, leaning his back against the wall, all the while keeping his hands in his pockets. "Just so you know," he said. "I'm not an idiot. Running from the past isn't that foreign to me. I know all about it. And my mom knows about it, too. But you're wrong. It's not the running away part that's the worst. It's the trying to be normal afterward that sucks."

"You're right. It does."

"Charlotte, the deputy said someone is missing and you're involved. Said you know what happened."

She breathed deep, her headache returning. "I didn't hurt anyone if that's what you're wondering."

"I was . . . wondering. And I had to check. Cuz, sometimes people don't know how much they're hurting others. They just don't see it." He shifted toward the doorway. "*That* I know from experience."

"So, that's it," she said, studying his face, ". . . that's why you and your mom ran away? Someone hurt you?"

Mason gripped his hand on the door frame and glanced down at the floor. "We didn't run away. We left someone behind. There's a difference. And I can't help you anymore."

"Wait." She didn't know whether it was while he searched the police station or if their conversation itself had been the turning point, but at some moment she had lost him. Lost his help. Charlotte felt alone again.

Evaluating: Current situation—One hundred percent a threat.

"Mason, please do one last thing for me before you go. I know you don't want to help, that you don't trust me. I don't blame you. But we're more alike than you think. We're both trying to be okay. Undo the wrist restraints and I'll slip out. Leave Harding. This town can go back to normal. You said it yourself, it's the trying to live a normal life after running that sucks. Let me make it easier for everyone. I'll disappear. Normal will come back."

"That's not enough," he said. "Things are really messed up now. And *normal* doesn't exist anyway."

She stared at the window, calculating outcomes, analyzing probabilities, doing what she knew best—surviving. Then, she sighed deeply, years of past stress taking their toll. She was going to have to give up a bit of her anonymity. "Then I'll trade my freedom for an answer. A piece of truth." She waited for his reaction, but he didn't speak. "Okay. I didn't hurt the missing woman, Mason. Her name was

Pearl Sanford, although it wasn't always. She was my grandmother. She saved me. And protected me. Then she died. I couldn't bury her properly. No tribute. No obituary. I bribed a mortuary assistant to cremate her body without a paperwork trail. Then I left without telling anyone of her death. I did all this because that was the plan. That is what she asked me to do."

"She asked you? Why can't you just tell the police?"

"I have my reasons."

Mason snorted. "You have more secrets, you mean. More lies. That story could be a lie."

"It's not. The police think I've done something awful. Their minds are made up without knowing the full story. I didn't get the luxury of leaving someone behind. I had to run. I'm not done running."

She noticed how Mason shifted forward on his feet, all the while he stared at her face for a long minute in silence. Boisterous laughter filtered in from the hallway, the security staff and the nurses chatting about Christmas parties and spiking eggnog. Both their words and their voices sounded so loud and yet, so distant. All Charlotte could do was watch Mason, analyze him, and hope she was being taken seriously. She wasn't used to telling people the truth and expressing how she was really feeling. That vulnerability was scary. But for some reason, telling him the truth wasn't. Whatever happened, Charlotte felt lighter letting go of a couple secrets.

"I've been hurt, too." Charlotte studied his eyes, trying to grasp what he was thinking, but she couldn't read him. So, she gave up. "I'm still trying to find my *normal* again. But I don't think I have one."

Mason glanced up at the ceiling and closed his eyes. The look on his face was heavy.

She slumped back against the pillow.

Mason whipped his hand from the door frame and hurried to her side. He ripped the Velcro strap holding her right wrist until it was free. Then he turned around and headed for the door, glancing at the nurse's station as he left. Just as Mason rounded the doorway, he reached up and pulled the fire alarm.

Then he ran.

CHARLOTTE BLENDED with the crowd exiting through the fire doors on the lower level. For the second time in days, the winter air outside the hospital stung at her face, and every breath was a reminder to be cautious with her sore body.

Flashing flood lights and buzzing alarms added to the confusion, a distraction she welcomed as people around her complained about the noise. She clung to the wool coat she'd found in a room a few doors down from her own—one used by an elderly woman whose bag of personal belongings Charlotte grabbed off a chair as she headed for the stairwell. The elderly woman's shoes and clothing size was slightly larger than Charlotte's body, but that didn't matter as much as how convenient the dark and neutral-toned clothes allowed her to slip into the general population of exiting visitors. She pulled the fake-fur lined hood over her hair.

Outside, people wandered to their cars, but mostly they stood at the far end of the parking lot to watch the fire trucks stop outside the building's entrance.

She hurried past the first few rows of cars and spotted Mason standing near his truck at the far end of the lot. He bent over to rest his hands on his knees, his body showing signs of fatigue. Charlotte assumed he had sprinted the entire way from her room to his truck. The kid probably wasn't used to the adrenaline rush.

Charlotte stepped away from the crowd and braced herself against a large van. It wouldn't take long for the nurses and security staff to run through their fire procedures. After the initial alarm, one of the security officers had checked on her for a few seconds and failed to notice how her right hand was concealed under the blanket. After that, it hadn't taken much to free herself and slip away in the chaos. But soon, if not already, they would notice her absence.

She considered her options, formulating the logical steps needed to leave the area. Transportation was the first priority. Then funds. Then heading North. The original plan could still work.

"I'm okay, Mom."

Charlotte singled out Mason's voice through the commotion. He straightened up while talking on his cell phone.

"I'm in the lot. I came to get you, but this is crazy." He held up his free hand to cover his other ear. "What? I can't hear you. Did you say you're staying longer? What? I said, you are staying longer, right? Helping to evacuate?"

Charlotte hated using him again, especially after he'd wanted to walk away. But stealing a car wouldn't get her very far without a fake license plate. She moved behind the cars until she reached his truck.

Mason didn't seem to notice her. "Mom, don't worry about me. I don't see any smoke. Things are okay. I'll go to work and be back in an hour to get you. Is that good?"

Charlotte climbed into the truck's back bed, this time taking precautions to conceal her body in the space behind the cab so both the night and her dark clothing would hide her.

She held tight to the truck's side wall as Mason pulled out of the parking lot and headed north on the main road. Wind whipped at her hair, her bare fingers turning pink as she held down the loose strands. She calculated the time it took Mason to reach the outskirts of Harding's township and breathed easier when the flashing lights and sirens from the hospital fire alarm faded into the distance.

They pulled onto main street, right into the old part of town—Harding proper. Mason slid the truck in an unplowed parking stall beside the gas station. He sat in the cab for a moment with the engine running. Charlotte waited, wincing at the pain of her sore left shoulder.

Finally, Mason turned off the engine and headed inside the gas station. Charlotte released a warm breath into the frosted air, then sucked in another along with the first sense of relief and freedom she'd had in two days. She refocused and scanned over the lot, hoping to find some kind of mechanic shop attached to the business. Quick fixes on a spare car would get her out of town, and no one would notice the missing vehicle until she reached Canada. The bigger problem would be getting over the border without a passport. Or any money. But she had a plan for that.

The back lot was mostly bare. She groaned. There was no mechanic shop. No spare cars, merely a conspicuous and slow-moving tow truck and Mason's Ford. She couldn't take either. Charlotte stood near the building, calculating and analyzing. Her mind raced.

Then . . . she saw it. Light filtered through the front window of Sheppard's Bookstore where the woman, Berta Sheppard, peered through the glass. Berta gripped one hand on the *closed* sign and the other she pressed on the window; her silhouetted face so close to the slick surface that Charlotte imagined the woman was squinting to see out. As she traced Berta's focal point, sharp panic surged up Charlotte's spine.

Their gazes met. Berta was watching her.

23

BERTA

BERTA GLANCED at the desk clock near her keyboard. It was after 7:30 p.m.—the time she'd planned to go home. She squinted at the tiny lettering on her computer monitor, then manually adjusted the view percentage until the words were enlarged and readable through her glasses. That was one of the few things she knew how to manage on the screen. That, and web searches. But it had taken hours for her to navigate as far into the internet as she had gotten. There were too many window screens open at once. Berta was about to hit her breaking point.

She continued scrolling down the chat forum in the St. George community page, just as she had done for the last hour. Before finding the forum, she had clicked through the comment sections of the local news stations, the St. George P.D. page, and something called *Senior Living in the Red Rocks* where retired citizens mostly complained about dog parks and broken air conditioners.

To Berta, as she sat in the tiny back office of her parent's dying family business, complaining about dog parks seemed beyond shallow. The bookstore required every penny from every book she'd ever sold just to try to cover the yearly property taxes, never allowing her to build up a nest egg let alone retire to a place like St. George.

Berta knew she'd be putting her every breath into this place until the day it all killed her.

Someone with the user name *BeatTheHeat101* caught her attention, posting how the missing woman on the news looked similar to a homeless person who frequented a local park. But, thirty minutes later, the same user changed his mind. Berta commented where she could, asking people what they knew about the missing woman and her family. Nothing had been too promising, mostly gossip, until someone with the username *FamilyIsLife* replied to Berta's question.

She stared at the enlarged text. There was no profile photo attached to the user name.

FamilyIsLife: *Did you know her personally? Are you a friend? You seem to care a lot about what happens to this lady.*

Sheppard'sBooks: *Not a friend. Just hoping to find a family member. Personal business. Do you know her?*

FamilyIsLife: *Yes. I'm a neighbor. Sad she's missing. Lots of gossip here. I guess her car is gone too. No one really knows her personally. It's weird.*

Berta shifted closer to the monitor, her excitement taking over. Finally, someone who possessed useful information.

Sheppard'sBooks: *Do you know how to contact Pearl Sanford's next of kin? I have some items of hers that I'd like to return to the family.*

It wasn't far from the truth. Berta did want to return the books, but she also wanted a reward for their recovery. A hefty one. The bookstore needed a new roof.

FamilyIsLife: *Hope I can help. I'll make some calls and see what I can do. Maybe we can meet.*

Sheppard'sBooks: *I can't.*

FamilyIsLife: *It might be easier to help you if we meet in person.*

Berta scowled at the suggestion. This person was nosy.

Sheppard'sBooks: *Not possible. Too far a drive from Idaho. I'm two days away at least. Plus can't leave my business. But I'll keep checking here for your next message. It's very important I find the next of kin.*

FamilyIsLife: *So glad someone cares. I'll help.*

Berta ended the conversation with a *thank you* and one of those pseudo-smiley faces made of a colon and half a parenthesis, one that she'd seen others in the forum use at the end of their sentences. The combination looked ridiculous, but she was trying to appear casual and blend in. She didn't need any of the other commenters suspecting her motives.

She glanced at the clock again, realizing she'd been too distracted to change the *open* sign in the front window. Not that customers were breaking down the door to buy books after store hours, anyway. In truth, there had only been one other person by the store that day, and she was pretty sure the Harding City employee reading the water meter wasn't interested in the complete collection of Tolstoy's works. Although to be fair, he could have been. But she knew better.

Berta walked to the front of the store and flipped off the interior lights near the counter and bookshelves, leaving a single glow from the office doorway to light her way back. She stood near the massive glass window for a moment. Moonlight illuminated the strips of fresh December snow that powdered on the tree branches outside. Half-shoveled mounds of white clumps and blue salt piled near the curb, the footprints from Charlotte and Chief Walker long since scrapped away. Berta locked the door, a motion she'd done thousands of times, then she turned the *closed* side outward.

Half a block up Main Street, she noticed the head lights of Mason Trent's truck. As soon as he pulled in, Ed's monstrous 350 pulled out. Obviously, the boss was heading home for the day. Berta snickered as Ed drove by the bookstore. She didn't understand why he would leave at a reasonable time but keep paying an employee to stay a couple extra hours beyond the flow of customers. The residents of Harding knew to buy their gas before seven, and the kid just sat at the cashier counter till nine o'clock without anything to do. It was a bad business move. Such a waste of money.

Berta watched the kid enter the building, remembering how jittery and nervous he acted that morning at the police station. He'd looked like a drug dealer, with his hood pulled up and his hands buried in his jacket pockets. Why wasn't he aware of the impression he gave off? What was he trying to hide under that hood?

Movement near the station startled her, Berta nearly forgetting that she still clutched the *closed* sign in her hand. She squinted through the glass. Someone shifted in the shadows, a tall figure, but hunched forward and slow moving with each step. The woman's dark hair escaped her hood in the wind, forcing her to grasp the strands away from her face. Berta instantly recognized Charlotte the Liar's pale skin and chilled, blotched red lips in the moonlight. For a moment, the sight forced her to recall one of the hundreds of fairy tales in her bookstore—poor Snow White, lost in the woods, hiding from the wicked queen. Only Charlotte wasn't so innocent. To Berta, she was more like Goldilocks—leaving destruction in her wake.

Their gazes met. A surge of adrenaline nearly knocked Berta backward. She stepped away from the glass and waited, fighting to control her nerves as Charlotte crossed the street and stood outside the entry door.

Charlotte knocked on the glass. "I need to talk to you," she said, her words muffled by the cold and the barrier between them.

"About what?" Berta took a step forward. "I tried to talk to you at the hospital, deary. I tried to give you a chance to answer my questions, but you lied to me."

"How do you know I lied? How do you know that I didn't simply hold back part of the truth?"

"I guess I don't."

"Can I come in? I'm ready to make a deal with you."

"Why now? And how did you leave the hospital without doing it in handcuffs?"

"Ms. Sheppard," Charlotte said, her tone deepening. "You're right about one thing. Those books are worth a lot of money. And if you want to know if it's safe to sell them, I will deal for that information. Now, let me in."

Berta unlocked the door.

They moved toward the back office, but not before Berta checked the street for any witnesses once Charlotte entered the building. When she was satisfied their visit would stay secret, Berta invited Charlotte to sit in the office chair. She turned off the computer monitor as she scooted herself against the wall. Her visitor didn't need to know Berta's involvement in the St. George community page.

"Okay," Berta said. "You're inside. Tell me how you got those books. Did you steal them?"

"No."

Berta groaned and wrung her hands. "How can I believe you? If you stole the books, I can't sell or auction them off. Harding P.D. won't let me. The books will be evidence. If you didn't steal them, there's no logical reason why you'd give away a collection worth two grand for a mere fifty-four dollars at a used bookstore. Like I said, it isn't logical. So . . . what's your deal?"

Charlotte leaned forward in the chair. "I'll level with you."

"About time, deary."

"I need to get out of this town. Because of the accident, I lost my money, my ID, and my plan to keep heading north while staying off the grid. I propose that we help each other. You lend me your car and—"

Berta snorted. "Why in the world—"

"You give me your car for one week, don't report that it's missing or who has it, and I will have your car towed back here. An envelope with ten thousand dollars will be in the glove box."

Berta sat on the edge of the desk. She eyed Charlotte, her reading glasses falling loose from her hair and swinging on the chain round her neck. She barely noticed, the words *ten thousand* ringing in her brain like a boxing bell. "If you don't have any money, how do you have ten thousand dollars?" she asked.

"I don't have any money *here*," Charlotte said, emphasizing the last word.

"North? As in . . . Canada. How are you planning to cross the border without an ID, passport, or a visa?"

"I have my ways."

Berta shook her head, her gaze on the dark computer monitor. "You certainly do, missy." She stood and paced near the closed door. "Well . . . I have my ways, too. This isn't enough."

"After one week, when your car comes back, I will leave a paper alongside the money—a note with beneficial information. When I told you on the first day that I didn't steal the box of books, I meant it. They were given to me with instructions to sell them and the other items in my car as I needed travel money."

"Did Pearl Sanford herself give you the books?"

"Yes."

"Why?"

Charlotte glanced at the floor for a moment, then at the closed door. "Because I'm her granddaughter. Ruthan Stanley was Pearl's grandfather. He left the books to her along with a sizable inheritance. When she died, they came into my possession. I was her only living relative. You want to contact her family, correct? Well, I'm it. And I'm offering you a ten-thousand-dollar reward, plus the profit that box of books will fetch from a private buyer. That should be in the thousands. Just . . . lend me your car and give me a week."

"And if I do, what will be on the note attached to the money order?"

"The name and contact information of another small-town book collector. He's like you only, he won't pay fifty-four dollars. This guy will buy the collections from you in a heartbeat. He'll do it at full value, and he'll do it quietly."

Berta bit her bottom lip, pacing along the far wall twice before turning back. Her mind spun at the options, the possibilities, and the consequences to consider. The two thousand from the book sales would pay that year's property taxes, even have some leftovers for a few electric bills. But in time, it would all run out. It always did. Ten grand, on the other hand, . . . plus more . . . how many years could she keep the bookstore going for that much? If she stretched every penny, if she sold more books while Charlotte's money paid to keep the lights on and the doors open, would it be enough to see her through? Berta glanced over at the clock on the desk. She ignored the time, instead looking at the small bronze plaque under the face. The inscription read *Sheppard's Books—Harding City Chamber of Commerce Business of the Year 1949*. On the wall above the desk hung a picture of her father and mother holding that very clock. They stood near the mayor and police chief, surrounded by other Harding business owners during a chamber of commerce banquet. Her parents grinned for the photo as they each held a side of the award. That image had been printed in the local newspaper. Berta never could get rid of the silly thing, even though in its old age the clock mechanism lost seconds of time. She simply kept correcting the hands. "If the collector wants them so badly, why haven't you sold him these books yourself?" she asked.

Charlotte stood. "Because I can never in my life go back to that town. I can never contact any of those people."

"Why not?"

"I have my reasons."

"You mean, you have more secrets, deary."

Charlotte opened the door wide, letting the office light flood into the dark bookstore and stretch her silhouette across the room. "Yes, I do," she said.

Berta peered at the towering book shelves and empty aisleways, at the mounds of published words, and at the thousands of stories that no one in this town was likely to ever read again. She wondered how her own story would sound, if someone were to read about her life. Would she be remembered or forgotten? Would she become like one of the old books shoved in the back of a shelf somewhere—left to rot? Left to die? What would happen to all the other stories when she was gone?

"What's your answer, Berta?" Charlotte asked. "Do we have a deal?"

"I'll tell you in the morning."

"Wait—"

"Listen, young lady. If you want to take my car and drive through Harding, you have to look like me and that means starting with short hair and gray dye. The drug store is closed till morning. That will give me time to think this mess through properly, and you can sleep on my couch until then."

"Staying longer is risky. Every minute—"

"Yah, yah. I get it. Well, that's the way it is. I've lived here all my life. People know my car here. If you're on the road and don't look like Berta Sheppard, you'll get caught. That means no money for me. So . . . let's do this right."

"So . . . that's a deal?"

Berta tightened her lips. She needed more time. There had to be another next-of-kin. Charlotte couldn't be the only one. Perhaps *FamilyIsLife* could still help her online. She wasn't naive, and she needed a plan B if Charlotte's plan A backfired. "I said *in the morning*. Things always look different in the light."

"Fine."

"My car is out back. Let's go." Berta grabbed her purse and keys. She led the way to the back wall, opening the fire door and checking the lock before heading to her twelve-year-old Buick LeSabre. The faded and scratched paint job had once been red, cranberry she thought, though it was too long ago to care about such a detail. She noticed how Charlotte studied the tires and exterior of the car as they get closer.

"Don't tell me it's not good enough for you," Berta said, fighting a sneer.

"It's perfect. One hundred percent."

Berta unlocked the driver's door. "Deary, nothing is perfect."

24

MASON

MASON DRUMMED his fingers on the counter, his leg bouncing in rapid fire as he leaned forward on the stool. Soon after arriving at the gas station, the extra adrenaline in his body tanked. He'd felt numb, drained even, and began second-guessing his actions. The numbness soon morphed into a heightened state of nerves. He couldn't sit still. What had he been thinking? Pulling the fire alarm at a hospital? He was such an idiot.

Not surprising, not a single person had gotten fuel in the twenty or so minutes he'd sat at the counter. He glanced at his cell phone again, feeling as if the slow passing seconds were pounding into his brain. It was eight o'clock. He only needed to hold it together for an hour, then he could go home and try to feel safe.

Mason took a deep breath.

A text came through.

Mom: *I'll be late. Fire was a false alarm. They cleared the building. Things are still crazy. Shelly from Peds is giving me a ride when things calm down.*

Mason: *Ok.*

He slipped the phone into his pocket, his fingers shaking. Hospital security and the fire department cleared the building faster than he thought possible. Pulling the alarm had been an impulsive move, but under the circumstances he didn't have a plan beyond telling Charlotte her belongings were gone. He hadn't thought he needed one.

But it was done. The distraction no doubt gave Charlotte time to get out of Harding, and also gave her a chance to return the town to an uneventful sense of normalcy. When daylight came tomorrow, life would seem different. His life would get back to normal, too.

Then again . . .

Mason paced behind the counter. He thought of his mom, and how pissed off she'd be when she found out what he'd done. A sudden, pitting wave of nausea took hold of Mason's stomach. Why hadn't he thought of her in that moment before he pulled the alarm? Instead, all he considered was the expression he saw on Charlotte's face, in her eyes—helplessness—a feeling he remembered well from his life with his dad. Right before the police took his dad away in handcuffs. Mason remembered the heartbreak nearly engulfing him as the paramedics separated them and put him in the ambulance—a poor little boy sickened from the meth lab in the basement. Dying from the chemicals. His mother had left her shift to meet the ambulance in the emergency room, devastated to discover that her ex-husband had been keeping a selfish secret. His mom had cried many times after that. And a lot of adults had told Mason what to think and how to feel.

But Mason didn't know how to describe what he felt. And he *did* learn a hard lesson that day. Life can suck. And somebody ends up cleaning up the mess.

He swallowed hard, praying that Chief Walker wouldn't figure out Mason's own secret—that he understood and pitied Charlotte enough to help her escape. Tomorrow, the mess would go away. The thought should've given him comfort, but instead Mason ran to the back bathroom and threw up.

Minutes later, he closed the gas station early, not thinking once about what Ed would say the next day. Mason headed home, driving the near empty streets on autopilot instead of using conscious thought. When he entered the driveway, their tiny farmhouse looked more like a dark, uninviting rental house than the home they'd lived in for the last five years. Snow drifted against the peeling wooden slats, and the burned-out porch light darkened the steps just as it had for the last two winters. Mason shivered during the long walk to the front door.

Once inside, he hurried into the darkened bathroom and threw up for the second time.

25

WALKER

"WE SET up the last road block, Chief," Stewart said through the phone. "But there's no one out here to stop."

"I know. But stay alert. I'll be back out there soon. Right after I check in with hospital security and the county sheriff," Walker said, leaning both elbows on his kitchen table.

"No, Chief. We're switching in the morning, remember? That was the plan."

"Plans change. She could get pretty far in one night. And it's winter. I'll be back out." Walker ended the call and set the phone down next to his sandwich plate. He rubbed the tired from his eyes, feeling the late hour for the first time. Even with the urgency of the situation, he didn't handle one o'clock in the morning the way he did twenty years ago. He couldn't sleep knowing Charlotte Evers was out of custody, and he couldn't function at one hundred percent effort without rest and caffeine. His officers were conducting searches in shifts while coordinating with other agencies. They'd follow his instructions, and he'd prepared them enough to handle things in his absence. But still, being away required a lot of trust on his part and sleep didn't mesh with worry.

He bit into his ham and cheese sandwich. At least there wasn't anyone around for him to disturb. A single ceiling light lit the kitchen and shined on the backdoor where he'd let himself in at around eleven o'clock. Walker had kept the rest of his house in darkness. After Marie passed away, he didn't see a reason to leave the lights on for a bunch of empty rooms. His heart still ached every time he thought of her. The absence was heavier than his neglected home. For a while, his son's family would stop by, keeping the house from going dormant. But new jobs and new lives out of state led to change. Now, he only kept one light on at a time.

An email came through on his cell phone: *Chief, this is Mark from hospital security. We looked through all the footage. Found your POI leaving her room. There's another person involved. Here's the video clip from the camera in the hallway.*

Walker opened the video attachment. The pixels were a bit grainy and the camera separated out the frames in a semi-quick but awkward fashion. He squinted at the small screen, trying to study the chunky movements of the security staff and nurses around the hallway desk. They grouped near the nurse's station, their backs to Charlotte's door. Then someone in a dark hoodie entered Evers' room. The person's hands were concealed in his jacket pockets, and his gaze looked low so the camera didn't fully capture his face.

Several minutes passed in the video.

The person in the dark hoodie returned to the hallway. He reached up and grabbed the wall. No, not the wall. Walker looked closer. The person grabbed the fire alarm. Then he ran.

The next couple minutes consisted of the staff and security checking on Evers and hurrying about from room to room. Their movements were in obvious confusion, until their emergency drill-training kicked in. Amid the chaos, the camera caught Charlotte Evers leaving her doorway and running down the hall. She entered a room near the fire escape, then came out wearing a set of dark clothing. Ten seconds later, Evers was down the stairs without anyone noticing her absence.

Walker leaned back in his chair. He rubbed his forehead. If only he had been there. If only he hadn't trusted the security staff to watch her while he took a breather. If only he hadn't needed a break in the first place.

The video clip ended after Evers disappeared through the fire doors. Walker dragged the footage back to an earlier minute, where the person in the dark hood stood outside the room. He replayed that section a few times, then studied the part where the person pulled the fire alarm. The individual was male, young, that was obvious. But his walk and build, the human characteristics that a dark hoodie couldn't conceal, had a familiarity to them. Walker paused the image one last time and stared at the person who helped Charlotte Evers escape from her restraints.

A sunken feeling hit his stomach stronger than the tiredness in his eyes or the lack of caffeine in his body. "No, not him," he said under his breath. "Not Mason Trent."

———

WALKER STOOD outside the Trent's rental house. A chill ran through his body, the December wind whipping through the dark porch. Stewart waited in silence at his side.

The front door flung open.

"Chief Walker, is that you?" Jan wore her pajamas and stood in the doorway, her hair wild from sleep and makeup smeared. "Crap. It's one-thirty in the morning. And it's freakin' cold. What are you two doing here right now?" She rubbed the sleep from her eyes.

"Can we come in?" he asked.

"What's wrong?"

"I need to talk to Mason."

Jan groaned. "At one-thirty? You're kiddin' me."

"I wish I was," he said, noticing how her face scrunched in disbelief. "Look, Jan. You and I go way back. Your roots are in this town. It doesn't matter that you were gone for a while. As far as I'm concerned, you and your son are Harding people. That means something. But . . . I still need to do my job no matter who it involves.

There were some issues at the hospital earlier. I need to talk to Mason about them."

She straightened up, her posture tightening. "Is he in trouble?"

"Right now, I just need some information."

She hesitated for a moment, then stepped aside. "Okay. Come in."

Walker stood in the living room with Stewart while Jan turned on a few lights. She went down to wake up Mason. A few minutes later, he stumbled into the room, his eyes bloodshot and his face pale.

"Are you alright?" Walker asked him.

Mason nodded.

"I need to show you something." Walker held up his cell phone so Mason and Jan could see the image on the screen. The video was paused at a certain frame, just as the person in the hoodie stood outside Evers' room.

Mason glanced at it, then looked at the floor.

"I know it's you," Walker said. "I had to watch the footage a few times to make sure. In truth, I didn't want it to be you, kid. Well, . . . now we have to talk. Have a seat." He motioned to the couch.

All four of them sat down, Walker taking the chair across from Mason.

"What's going on?" Jan asked. Her eyes narrowed on the chief.

He glanced at his phone, wishing he didn't have to shatter the peacefulness of her night. "The fire alarm wasn't a tech glitch like the hospital announced. Someone set it off. This person in the hoodie." He held up the screen again. "What I don't know, and what I came here to find out, is why Mason pulled it."

"No, he couldn't have," she said. "That's ridiculous." She studied the cell phone image. Then Jan glared at her son. "Did you do that?"

Mason leaned forward, staring at the floor while he gripped his stomach. He breathed so heavy that Walker worried the kid might pass out.

"Tell the truth, honey." Jan put her hand on his shoulder. "Please, just tell the truth."

"It was me," he said, saying his answer more to the floor than to those in the room.

Walker slipped the phone into his pocket. He steadied himself, trying not to reveal his disappointment. "And you talked to Charlotte Evers before you pulled the alarm?"

Mason nodded.

"Do you know where she is?"

"Not exactly."

"Okay." Walker stood. "Jan, I'd like you and Mason to come down to the station. I need a full statement from him."

"Do we need a lawyer?" she asked.

"You do whatever you think is best. I'm trying to understand what's going on. I'd like to be at the station and be formal about this. Mason interacted with a person of interest in a missing persons case. We'd like to ask him some questions about that and about what happened after."

Jan sighed. "Okay, I guess we'll go with you."

He waited by the door as Mason and Jan took a few minutes to go get dressed. He hated this part of the job—bringing disappointing news to a parent. At least Mason was *alive*, even if he wasn't *well*.

Walker stepped aside while Mason slipped on his coat. The kid could handle stress, at least Walker hoped as much. Any kid who lived in a meth house, nearly died, and was brave enough to start over could handle himself. Still, Walker wondered if Mason's persona was more of the scared eleven-year-old who got caught smashing mailboxes, or the sixteen-year-old in the hoodie who helped a POI escape custody. How much was Mason like his father?

They headed out the door. He would know in about fifteen minutes.

26

MASON

T<small>HE TAP WATER TASTED TERRIBLE</small>, but under the circumstances, Mason felt like he didn't deserve anything purified and bottled. He gulped down a swallow, his mouth dry from all the talking. Normally, he would have chosen to be tight-lipped, but his mom hadn't been too happy when she found out there was more to his encounter with Charlotte than the simple conversation in the truck. He hated it when Mom was hurting. And he was causing it this time. Maybe that was why Mason was now word-vomiting the truth like he'd eaten bad meat.

"That's everything you remember?" Walker asked. The chief stared at him from the other side of his desk.

Mason expected this moment to be more intimidating than the simple questions he'd been asked in the hospital waiting room, but Walker's calm demeanor had surprised him. The environment wasn't the scenario he expected—no poorly-lit interrogation room with a single table and a two-way mirror. For the second time, and much to his relief, fake television wasn't real life, and Walker had directed him to a padded seat in his office. Jan sat next to her son the entire time.

Walker rubbed his chin. "So, Evers said that she's afraid of police.

Can't be caught. And the ashes are from her dead grandmother—Pearl Sanford?"

Mason nodded. "But Sanford isn't the lady's last name. Not really."

"Okay," Walker said, standing from his chair. He held out a legal pad. "Here. Write it all down for me. In an official statement. Thank you for cooperating."

Mason took the notepad.

"Jan." Walker motioned her toward the door. "Can I speak to you in the hall for a minute?"

After his mom left the room, Mason leaned over a corner of Walker's desk and wrote down everything he'd told the chief—the entire truth. It took over fifteen minutes. Several times he stopped to recall both his and Charlotte's words with exactness. Or at least, remember their conversations the best he could. Somehow the truth became easier to release the further he got in the story. He included everything—their meeting at the gas station, the conversation in the truck, his visit to the police station, and their final words in Charlotte's hospital room.

He read over his completed written statement five times. In hind sight, he knew his shaky handwriting would be hard for Walker to decipher. But then again, the letter became more legible as he unloaded his dealings with Charlotte Evers. The truth was easier to handle than maintaining the secrets, and although he was pretty sure everyone was either disappointed or pissed at him, he somehow felt a little lighter. Less weighted.

Jan returned to the room. Her face was red and puffy from crying, and she dabbed at her nose with a tissue. Mason slouched forward. His peaceful release instantly faded.

"You're going to stay here tonight, honey," Jan said.

Mason stood. "What?"

"They think Charlotte Evers is still in the area somewhere. It's possible that she'll contact you for more help and they don't want you in danger. Neither do I. You're all I have—"

"Mom, Charlotte's not dangerous."

She put her arm around his shoulders. "In the morning, I'm calling an attorney and life will get back to normal. Walker and I have been discussing things."

"What things? What does that mean?"

"Mason, honey," she said, hugging him tight. "Pulling a fire alarm in a hospital filled with sick patients isn't like pulling one at your school to get out of a math test. There are rougher consequences. But it's going to be okay. I just know it. We've been through worse."

Tears swelled in Mason's eyes, but he breathed deep and fought them back. He stared at the floor.

"I won't let you be in danger. Not again. Charlotte may have said she didn't kill the missing lady, but people lie. They do it all the time. Chief Walker is putting an officer on our street to watch the house, just in case she comes looking for you at home. But we don't want you there. So, you're staying at the station." She took the written statement from his hand and lead Mason into the hall.

Walker stood at the far end, talking on his cell phone while Jan handed him the legal pad. Mason didn't have the strength to eavesdrop on the chief's conversation, but unintentionally he heard Walker saying both "Mason" and "Evers" several times. All the relief he'd felt was now completely gone. He slid the hood over his head and stared down at the industrial carpet, wanting his mind to go numb. Instead, it ached. More specifically, his brain ached from overthinking, stress, and the lack of sleep.

"This way," Walker said.

They followed him down the back hall to the station's two small holding cells. They looked like they hadn't been used in a long time. Each one had painted cinderblock walls, a simple metal-frame bunk, a wall of bars, and not much else. Walker went to a nearby cabinet and brought over a stack of blankets and a pillow. Everything looked a bit dusty except for the bunks. Mason assumed the people who got arrested went to the bigger county jail instead, not this place, and he imagined it's only current use was most likely if Walker crashed on a bunk when he didn't go home.

"Are you sure about this, Jan?" Walker asked. "I can make

arrangements for you two somewhere in town. It's in the middle of the night, but I can wake people up. Hell, even my own house is going to be empty. You and Mason could come back in the morning."

She shook her head. "I want him in the safest place. That's here."

Mason looked at the cell, noticing how the interior had new paint but the rest was just as it was five years ago. "Mom, I'll be okay. Don't worry about me."

"Yes, you'll be fine. And so will I." She took the stack of blankets from Walker and handed half to Mason. "I'm staying in the other cell."

Walker shook his head. "Jan—"

"No, Terry. It's just till morning. That's only hours away, and I'm not leaving my son's side. End of discussion." She pointed to the metal bunk in the farthest cell. "Mason, go to sleep."

"Yes, Mom." He opened the blankets on the bunk and laid down. His mom went into the other cell without saying another word.

Walker took a step toward leaving then paused. "Bathrooms are down the hall," he said. "Come and go as you need."

Mason nodded, surprised Chief Walker wasn't locking him in. Maybe he deserved to be.

"Night." Walker turned away and flipped off the main lights as he left.

When he was alone, Mason rolled onto his side and stared at the painted cinderblock wall that he shared with his mom's cell. His emotions jumbled into a chaotic mess. Here he was, spending the night in the same jail cell he'd vowed to avoid the rest of his life. And because of his stupidity, his mom was in the next cell over.

Mason glanced at the ceiling in the dim light. Charlotte was right about one thing, maybe Mason and his mom *were* running away from someone who hurt them. Saying he left his father behind to serve a prison sentence didn't fix past events. Nor did it guarantee them a better life. Pretending to be normal was fake. He closed his eyes and swallowed against the lump forming in his throat. Despite his own efforts to fool himself, Mason knew the truth—he was still running.

27

BERTA

Berta drank her morning herbal tea a little quicker than usual. There wasn't time to preserve her routine, to let the amber liquid rest while she buttered toast and read the morning paper in the sunlight from the window. Most of the stories were drivel anyway. No, this time her fingers busied with the cup, ignoring the unopened newspaper on the chair, and she shuddered a little as the hot tea stung at her throat. *Normal* could wait till tomorrow.

During the night, she'd gotten very little sleep, a few hours at most. There, lying in the dark of her room, she'd replayed the same conversation over and over again in her mind—Charlotte's vague explanations, the deal, formulating a plan, and . . . the box of books. The young woman said Pearl had given the box freely. Berta had worked through her doubts and uneasiness for hours, wondering under what conditions Pearl would simply give them away to be sold second hand. What had Pearl Sanford been thinking?

She hurried to the sink and scrubbed the tea cup clean.

In the next room, Charlotte slept on Berta's living room sofa. Her breathing suggested the young woman wasn't quite awake. The sun wasn't up either, dawn being at least an hour away, but Berta didn't care. She needed time to get Charlotte back into town without any witnesses, and darkness helped with that plan more than sleep.

She stood by the sofa and tapped on Charlotte's foot. "Time to wake up," she said.

"Uh, huh," Charlotte mumbled, pressing her hand against her left collar bone as she sat up, a guttural moan escaping her lips. Clearly, the bruising on her shoulder hadn't subsided, even though the swelling under her eyes had improved. She looked less like a wounded prize-fighter. "I'm going, but I'm not sure I can move any faster."

"Sure you can. And today you have to drive, so sit up. Here, take these." Berta held out two pain pills and a glass of water.

"Are you drugging me?"

"Don't be silly. This is for the soreness. It's only over-the-counter stuff, but the strongest you can get without a prescription. I use them for my knee pain. It should take the edge off. Anything stronger would interfere with motor skills. Driving, remember?"

"Is that what you think 'motor skills' means?" Charlotte eyed the pills.

"Oh, for heaven's sake! You still don't trust me." Berta swallowed the pills herself. "See. The headache that you've given me will be nothing but a distant memory in about twenty minutes. Fine 'motor skills' preserved." She thumped the plastic pill bottle on the coffee table and sat the glass of water next to it.

"Thanks," Charlotte said. She eased into a sitting position. "I'll be ready in a minute."

"Perfect. I made you some breakfast. It's in the kitchen. The drug store opens in an hour and a half. We have a little time, but I want to get you inside the bookstore before sun-up."

"That's not a good plan." Charlotte swallowed a few pills from the bottle then drank the entire glass of water.

"What do you mean? I've thought this plan through. We go to the bookstore before light. You dye your hair, take my car, and leave from there. I conduct business as usual. Nothing will appear out of the ordinary."

Charlotte followed Berta into the kitchen. They sat at the table. "And how do you get home tonight? Are you going to walk the couple miles back to this house? Going to call for a ride? I bet Chief Walker can give you a lift since there aren't any cabs in Harding. Like I said, it's a bad plan."

Berta huffed, annoyed. "Since you're such an expert, what do you have in mind?"

"Actually," Charlotte said, her voice softening. "I am an expert on this stuff. I've been doing it for a long time."

"Doing what?"

"Staying on the move. Avoiding complication."

"So, you're running from someone. Like from the police?" Berta hoped she would learn something more.

But Charlotte simply rubbed her eyelids and didn't answer, staring down at the lace table cloth. When she looked up again, her glossy gaze rested on the curtain covering the kitchen window. She didn't say anything more, simply stared, obviously lost in thought for a moment. Berta knew Charlotte wasn't concentrating on the country-apple print on the fabric, and she resisted the urge to snap her fingers to get the young woman's attention.

"From the police?" Berta asked a little louder, studying Charlotte's face.

"No, not if I can help it."

"Then from whom?"

Charlotte stared at the table again. "It's complicated."

"Of course, it is," Berta snapped. A second later she regretted her slip of hostility. This whole mess was getting to her, knocking her off the even scale of predictability that dominated her life. Instead, she felt as if that scale was teetering her over a cliff while she hung on with one hand.

Berta cleaned her reading glasses with the soft side of her sweater. She needed to keep this situation under control. For the sake of her bookstore. And for the sake of her parents, who probably watched her financial struggles from the grave, and were likely disappointed.

"Okay, deary. Let me know when you've decided what to do." Berta busied herself in the kitchen, dishing up the extra breakfast so Charlotte could eat. As she brushed through the mundane task, an odd feeling found its way into her heart, one that was quick, unexpected, and subtle. It was nice fixing food for two—a bit of a hassle, but not too bad. The feeling surprised her. She'd lived alone for so long. No children. Never married. Although, she came close once and changed her mind. Instead, she'd taken care of herself and her aging parents until they both passed away. Then, as she'd done for decades, she took care of their bookstore. That was her life.

Charlotte sipped from her tea and downed the scrambled eggs. For several minutes, they sat in silence. Then Berta picked up the morning paper and thumbed over the headlines.

"Okay," Charlotte said finally. "Here's my plan. I'm staying put. You're getting the supplies we need, including cold medicine, which you will casually mention to the drug store clerk is for your sudden illness. Since you've caught a winter cold, the bookstore will be closed today and tomorrow. Bring the items back here. I'll get ready and drive away. If I'm caught, you'll claim your car was stolen, but being sick in bed, you didn't notice it missing. Therefore, no police report. But since I won't be caught, the car will be returned in a timely manner. At which time, your unfortunate winter cold will clear up nicely. You'll go back to the bookstore, and life will be back to normal. Only Berta Sheppard will be several thousand dollars richer. This plan has no threat to you. Are you ready?"

Berta bit her lip. Charlotte was right, she did have extensive experience with subterfuge. The young woman couldn't have been much older than her early twenties, but the somber in her eyes couldn't be hidden by plastered smiles. Berta wondered how much of Charlotte's soul was aged far beyond the youth of her body. The girl's mouth lied, time and again, but her eyes didn't. They had a painful weight behind them.

"I said, are you ready?" Charlotte asked again.

"Yes. Your plan is fine. I'll leave at dawn."

THE DRUG STORE was two doors down from Sheppard's Used Books and Gifts. Berta waited in her back office, glancing at her watch for the hundredth time and counting down the seconds until Bill Fuller opened his store. She killed time by checking the St. George Community forum. *FamilyIsLife* hadn't responded to her last message. Perhaps Berta's post about finding the next-of-kin on her own had fizzled any interest. It was just as well. Loose ends were unnecessary.

While her computer screen fell asleep, she glanced at the box of books she'd purchased from Charlotte, feeling a sudden need to protect them while she was "out sick." Harding didn't have a lot of crime, but she knew Terry Walker probably wouldn't care if anything happened to her valuables anyway. He and his friends used to egg the place as teenagers. Her parents would get so irate that Berta had often cleaned up the mess before they noticed. She was about twenty years older than Terry, and felt pretty old now in her seventies, but her memory was still sharper than his aim back in high school. Both memories and grudges lasted a long time in Harding. Still, she also knew he wasn't the same person from back then. He was fifty now. Time had aged both of them. Plus, she knew he'd had a hard time ever since his wife died. It was easier just to avoid talking about the past.

Berta turned her thoughts back to the box. There wasn't much room in her small floor safe in the office closet, but perhaps enough space for the *Gilly Heel* series. They were the most valuable. She gathered the ten-book collection, knelt by the closet doors, and slid the stack inside the safe.

When it was locked again, she felt a little better.

Berta hurried to the front of the store, made sure the *closed* sign displayed through the window, and left through the back alley door. It felt odd to leave the store locked up and dark for days. She hadn't taken a sick day, ever. Maybe no one would notice her absence. That thought troubled her more than missing work.

Berta buttoned her coat and shuffled across the back parking lot until she reached the tight alley between her store and the sewing shop next door. She headed for the Main Street storefronts and paused on the front sidewalk. The road was predictably empty. A few cars were parked along main street, mostly employees opening up their stores. Someone had shoveled the walkway and poured out a layer of salt, the blue crystals crunching under her boots.

"Good morning, Bill," Berta said when she entered the drug store.

"You're here bright and early," Bill said. He scratched at his long gray beard as he yawned. "Don't have the register turned on yet."

Berta fiddled with the handles of her handbag. She didn't make eye contact. "No one oversleeps at our age, Bill. I need a few things."

"Right. Help yourself."

She hurried along the small aisles, grabbing dark brown eye shadow and thick powder, gray hair dye spray left over from the Halloween clearance sale, two boxes of granola bars, a prepaid cell phone, and a bottle of over-the-counter cold medicine. She'd about gotten everything in her small basket when the store's front bell chimed. Berta stretched tall, glancing over the shelf of diapers. A man entered the store, someone she'd never seen before. His face was clean shaven, and his expression surprisingly alert for such an early hour. The man wore a heavy coat that looked as if he was about to traverse Everest—an obvious new clothing purchase by someone who lived in a warmer climate. His knit, winter cap and matching gloves had *Spokane International Airport* embroidered in the fabric. She guessed he was in his late forties and that this *outsider* had just driven over an hour and a half to get to a little town in the middle of nowhere.

The man approached the clerk.

"Do you know who owns the bookstore?" he asked.

Berta sank down behind the diapers.

"Uh, yeah," Bill said. "Hey, Berta. This guy is looking for you."

A heat flushed over her face. *Bill Fuller, you twit.* Berta peeked over the shelf. "Who wants to know?"

The man stared at her and squinted. "Do you own Sheppard's Used Books and Gifts?"

"Yes."

"Are you the only owner?"

"What do you need?" She gripped the basket handle with both hands and raised her chin. "I'm a respectable figurehead in this town. And I deserve to be treated as such, not questioned by strangers. I don't like surprises. Who are you?"

The man searched in his numerous coat pockets until he found his cell phone. "Are you . . . Alberta Sheppard?"

Bill snorted. "Of course, she is. Who else would she be?"

"Bill! I can answer for myself, thank you," Berta said, coming around the aisle. "What is it that you want?"

"Um." The man swiped the screen of his phone. "I just came from St. George, Utah. I have a few questions for you." He pulled out a small notepad from his back pocket.

As he moved, Berta noticed the flash of a police badge on the side of his belt. Her heartbeat shot up so fast she could hear a pounding sound in her ears. The man was from St. George? Asking questions. She racked her brain until she recalled the words written on the police status report she'd seen at the station. The summery had been written by a Detective Peterson. Berta's name was in that report, along with the name of her business and the books she'd bought from Charlotte. Apparently, loss of anonymity was her punishment for doing business with a criminal. Now Peterson would discover Charlotte hiding at Berta's house and haul them both away to prison. Berta couldn't go to prison. The only book she'd be allowed to read would be Crime and Punishment. *How dreary.*

"Ma'am?" he asked. "Are you alright?"

"Look," she said in a pseudo-casual tone. "You must be Detective Peterson from St. George. I already told Chief Walker that I didn't know anything about Charlotte Evers when I bought the books from her. I haven't spoken with the young woman since. I could have answered these questions on the phone."

He stared at her for a moment, then slowly nodded and quickly wrote something on his notepad. "Yes, ma'am. But I haven't been able to speak to the chief yet, and I wanted to start my own investigation in the meantime."

"Well, I don't know anything. Now, if you'll excuse me, I need to make my purchase." She handed her basket to Bill.

"Is this about the woman who's loose up here somewhere?" Bill asked. "I hear they can't find her? I hear she murdered someone."

"How do you know that?" Peterson asked.

Bill started ringing up Berta's items. "It's a small town. We talk. Since that lady crashed her car in the river the other day, we've had more excitement in Harding than the last fifty years combined."

"Detective," Berta said, turning her back to the register. "I'm sure Chief Walker is at the station by now. You should check in with him."

"I will. But one more thing, did one of the books have an inscription to a woman named Pearl?"

Berta's mouth went dry. She couldn't keep track of when she needed to tell the truth and when she needed to lie. Her face flushed. "One of them might have . . . possibly . . . contained some kind of . . . something like that. Unfortunately, I really don't remember. I can't help you."

"Okay," he said. "I'll be by the bookstore later to ask more questions."

She stammered, trying to remember Charlotte's instructions. "Sorry, I won't be there. Sick day. Might be out all week, actually. I have a cold." She fake-coughed and held up the bottle of over-the-counter cold medicine.

"You have a cold?"

"Yes. It's a small town. When one person gets sick, everyone does. Better to nip that beast in the bud before an epidemic sweeps through Harding. Isolation is the only responsible option. It's just a mild cold now, but in a week the entire town could be under the weather."

"That many people, huh?" he said.

"Are you making fun of our population size?" She raised an eyebrow at him.

Peterson held up his hands. "No, no, ma'am. You misunderstand me. I'm just surprised that in a town this small, a woman, who crashed her car and injured herself, can disappear within the city limits and no one knows where she's hiding."

Berta shrugged. "I'm as concerned as you are. If I see her, I'll let someone know. Beyond that, I'm afraid I can't help you."

"Well, for what it's worth. Thank you for your cooperation," he said. With that, Peterson glanced at the items in Berta's basket and then headed out the door.

She stood at the counter for a moment, breathing deep as her adrenaline levels returned to normal. "Bill, I'm in a hurry."

"Sure thing, Berta. But what's with the Halloween dye spray? You're already that color." He snickered while pointing to her short gray curls.

She sighed. "It's for my cat. We want to match."

"No, really?" Bill grinned until he noticed her serious expression. "Your total is on the screen."

"Perfect." Berta handed him her credit card without a second thought. "Bag it up for me. I think my cold is getting worse." At least that wasn't a total lie. Her headache was back.

28

WALKER

WALKER DOWNED two over-the-counter pain pills with a swallow of his morning Diet Coke. In truth, the dose of caffeinated beverage wasn't his first can in the last five hours, and it wasn't even his second. There had been one can right after he'd arrived with Mason Trent at the station. Without sleep, two o'clock in the morning seemed like days ago, not hours. Caffeine was his necessary friend. He never liked the taste of coffee, so Diet Coke was the winner.

Morning light filtered in through his office window. He glanced at his watch and then at his silent cell phone for the twentieth time in the last hour. Despite the night's freezing temperatures, the Harding police officers hadn't spotted Charlotte Evers passed out in a snow bank somewhere. Nor had the assisting county sheriff's deputies or highway patrol officers come across her frozen body. So far, she hadn't been spotted in a stolen vehicle along the highway or hitchhiking in a semi-truck. Walker expected them to find some indication that an individual was wandering around the city limits, but he'd received no new information.

The caffeine kept him awake, but it was the nerves and frustration that kept him jumpy.

"Chief?" Deputy Franklin leaned against the door frame of Walker's office.

"Yep?"

"I know you hate surprises, but that detective from St. George just walked in the station."

Walker rubbed his temples. "Why is Peterson here? That's a long way to come fetch a POI."

"Especially one who's missin' from custody," Franklin said.

Walker groaned. "Does he know she's missing?"

"Oh, yeah. And he's askin' a lot of questions. Thought I'd route things to you."

"Right," Walker said. He stood and headed down the hall toward the front lobby.

Jed slouched in the office chair behind the desk, his head lying on the counter with a puddle of drool below his mouth. When Walker and Franklin reached him, Jed snorted in his sleep.

"Detective Peterson?" Walker said, addressing the man standing near the waiting room chairs. He noticed how puffy and new-purchase the guy's unzipped coat and beanie hat looked. Obviously, Peterson wasn't accustomed to Northern Idaho winter weather. Outsiders from warmer climates tended to overcompensate with ridiculous clothing choices. The detective pulled his hand from his pocket, briefly exposing the law enforcement badge attached to his belt.

"Yes, Chief. Nice to meet you," Peterson said. He reached out to shake the chief's hand.

"I'm surprised to see you in person, Detective. I was expecting a phone call."

"Well, things changed yesterday. We found her."

"Who?" The word nearly stuck in Walker's mouth.

"Pearl Sanford."

Walker glanced at the ceiling. "She's alive?"

"No." Peterson shook his head. "She's not. We need to take Charlotte Evers down to St. George immediately."

"Are you sure it's Sanford?" he asked.

"Very certain."

Walker nodded and tightened his jaw. In two simple words, Mason Trent's statement and ultimately Charlotte's story about Pearl's ashes had unraveled.

"I'm here to collect Evers right away," Peterson said. "She's wanted for questioning. I've got the paperwork to bring her back."

Franklin snorted. "There's a problem with that."

"But there won't be a problem forever," Walker said. "We'll find her. The surrounding area is large, that's for certain, but it's all farmland until you get to the mountains. There's a handful of other small towns in the county, but mostly Evers will stay on a road if she's going to keep alive in the elements. It's only December, not peak winter yet, but Northern Idaho isn't a good place to trudge around on foot. She wouldn't last long."

"So you think she'll hitch or steal a ride?" Peterson asked.

"Yep." Walker checked his cell phone again for any new texts, hoping for a well-timed message that Evers had been found and was in custody. He willed the dumb thing to ring, but nothing happened.

"Hitch or steal if she hasn't already," Franklin added. "She had a good head start."

Walker side-glanced at his deputy chief. The last thing he needed was Detective Peterson and St. George P.D. on his case about losing a person of interest. "Franklin, go check on Jan Trent and her son, please."

Franklin rolled his eyes. "Yes, Chief." He left the room.

"How long till you find her? I can't wait forever. There's stuff to do back in Utah," Peterson said.

Walker tightened his brow at the question. Apparently in St. George, they did things at a faster, more unrealistic pace than a small town like Harding. He contemplated letting loose a joke about homicides on the golf course and senior-citizen speeding tickets, but thought the better of it. Bad stereotypes weren't helpful in a police investigation, nor were they accurate.

"We'll find her soon," Walker said.

"Perfect. Here's my cell number for when you do." He handed

over a torn notebook sheet with a phone number scribbled on the page.

Walker stared at the numbers, wondering how long it would take before he could end this mess and get things back to normal. "Good," he said.

"Great. I need to finish interviewing the bookstore owner this morning. Do you know where she lives?"

"Berta? She lives in the bookstore."

"No, really." Peterson checked his watch. "She's home sick today. A cold, but I get the impression she doesn't want to talk to me."

"A cold?" Walker checked his own watch. "She's not afraid to talk to anyone. People are afraid to talk to her. Berta's always in the store. Every day."

"I guess not today. Text me her address, please." Peterson headed for the glass door, placing his gloves on his hands, zipping his coat to his chin, and tightening down his beanie before exiting. The guy bundled himself as if he was leaving to hunt a Yeti.

"Wait," Walker said. "What about all the rest of the evidence? We need to make arrangements?"

Peterson gripped the door handle. "Yes, that's right. You have your officers prepare it all, and I'll check back soon. I'm going to Berta Sheppard's house."

"Don't you want to see the car?"

He hesitated, then glanced at his watch. "Right, the car. Um, okay. Where is it?"

"In the garage. Follow me." Walker led the detective down the hallway to the last stall in the garage bay. Pearl Sanford's Oldsmobile hadn't been moved from its place against the wall—the doors, hood, and truck still sealed with police tape. There was an aroma of mildew wafting in the air, the inner contents failing to dry properly in the cold temperatures of the garage.

"It's smells," Peterson said, wrinkling his nose.

"It's been wet."

"I guess that smells better than the cinnamon stench in your hallway."

Walker nodded. "Pine cones. It's December."

"Right. Any evidence outside the car?"

Walker took him to the evidence closet in the back of the garage. It took him a minute to loosen the pad lock hanging on the metal door. He pulled a box from a shelf, one of many containers holding Evers' belongings, and motioned to the detective.

Peterson didn't look through all the items, there were so many, but instead browsed a few books and glanced at the urn for a full minute. He held up the black, soot-coated wrist watch, checking both the front and back of it in the light and glanced at the evidence tag. "Any IDs? Family photos? Records?"

"Just the fake IDs. The state crime lab should have the bag by now. We're using the FBI field office for the facial rec and fingerprint ID."

"So it'll take a while then," Peterson said.

"It always does. I don't know how you do it down south, but our in-house system runs IAFIS matches at a snail's pace. We outsource to the field offices." Walker stared at Peterson. "I explained all this to Chief Redding."

Peterson nodded. "I know. I've been updated. Just recapping. You know, Evers might come here to get this stuff."

"You think she'll still try to get it back?" Walker stared at the burned wrist watch in Peterson's hand, then shook his head as the detective held the bag over the open container and glanced through the other items. "You really think that's possible?"

"Yes, she might come back," Peterson said. "Obviously this stuff is significant. And if you think she's hiding in town somewhere, there must be a reason."

Walker folded his arms and huffed. "Mason Trent said she wanted a few things, but now that she's on the run, I can't see her coming for them. Too risky."

"Still, keep it all locked up. I'll need to talk to Mason Trent."

"Of course." Walker turned and slid the loose containers back onto the shelves. He took the last box from Peterson's hands and locked the door.

"I'll be in touch, Chief," Peterson said. He walked away.

Walker stood by the car and glanced at his cell phone again. Still no message. "Please," he said under his breath. "I need to clean this up. I just . . . need this to be done." He hoped Charlotte would get sloppy and turn up somewhere, and he certainly needed more caffeine to get through whatever the day brought with it. But first, there was something else he needed to do. Walker headed for his patrol vehicle.

29

CHARLOTTE

THE GUEST BATHROOM in Berta Sheppard's house was decorated in eighties floral wall paper with a matching rose pink fuzzy bathmat and toilet lid cover. Even the color-coordinated shower towels looked dated and a little dusty. Charlotte wondered if anyone ever used that room, or if the woman had ever entertained any houseguests. She saw Berta as more of a "requires isolation" type of person.

Charlotte finished taking a shower, wearing a cap to keep her hair dry, and redressed in the neutral dark clothing she'd taken from the hospital. The only thing left to add was the coat. She'd made a habit out of always being fully dressed and prepared to leave.

"Charlotte," Berta called into the bathroom.

"That was a quicker trip than I expected," Charlotte said, opening the door.

Berta handed her the bag of drug store supplies. "Not too many people on the road this early. Farmers are up, but not in town. Take this. I would've been here sooner, except I ran into an irritating man at the drug store. By the way, I'm notifying you that I've spotted Charlotte Evers."

"What?"

"I promised to notify someone, just didn't say whom. Now, I'm not a liar," she said, shrugging. "I've spotted you."

"Okay, I guess. Noted." Charlotte riffled through the shopping bag. "Granola bars?"

"You'll need food so you don't have to stop. I also filled the car with gas."

"Good. You can keep the cold medicine."

"Oh, I'll take that. No one really has a cold. That was for my cover." Berta grabbed the purple liquid but left the grocery bag near the sink. "I'll pack you a sandwich and some water bottles. And you should take the bottle of pain meds. Just in case."

"Thank you," Charlotte said in almost a whisper. She held still, listening to Berta walk down the hallway and open cupboards in the kitchen. The old woman's house slippers shuffled along the wood floor, filling Charlotte's mind with memories—Pearl wore house slippers. Pearl also packed Charlotte a sandwich lunch every time they needed to move houses or apartments as she grew up. They were good at the routine, packing up all of Pearl's collections in less than a day and stuffing the duffle bags into a small U-Haul as if packing a puzzle box. All the food in the fridge became their meals until the next city.

There were a lot of moves and sometimes running away meant packing up in the middle of the night. Even as an adult, Charlotte couldn't leave without her grandmother. Except, this last time she would. A hollow feeling tore at her chest. She couldn't go back for Pearl.

"There's hair-cutting scissors in the drawer," Berta said from the kitchen.

Charlotte brushed her long hair and glanced down at the Halloween spray dye on the counter. At least this kind wasn't permanent. Her hair had changed so many times in the past that she didn't remember what her original color was. Brown wasn't any different from red or blonde or black. And gray was simply the next in line. She gripped the scissors and sliced through the hair strands without much emotion, dropping chunks of brown into the sink.

She chopped the back short, but left the top and sides just a little longer. Each cut should have felt freeing, as if a heavy weight was falling, but Charlotte no longer expected such an endorphin rush from a new style. She wasn't like other women.

Within a few minutes, Charlotte's hair looked closer to Berta's short helmet. Curls would help with the rest. She followed the instructions on the aerosol can of gray dye, though she could've done the task from memory. After she'd emptied the whole can onto her head, Charlotte tried not to care about how she looked. Instead, she pulled the prepaid cell phone from the shopping bag. She stepped into the hallway, making sure Berta sounded busy in the kitchen. Near the backdoor, Berta's purse sat on a small entry table.

Charlotte retrieved the old woman's wallet in less than ten seconds and slipped the credit card into her pocket before heading back to the bathroom.

Berta riffled in the nearby refrigerator, glass condiment jars clinking together in her hands, but didn't turn around. She hummed to herself.

Once inside the bathroom, Charlotte quietly closed the door. She used the credit card to set up the pre-paid phone and load it with a max amount of minutes. Berta certainly wouldn't approve such a purchase, but under the circumstances, Charlotte decided she could send back the exact credit charge with the envelope of ten thousand dollars. That would soften the woman's heart.

Charlotte then turned on the sink, letting the water run at full blast. She dialed a memorized number into the phone. Her stomach churned from both sudden nerves and the putrid smell coming from the aerosol dye.

"Hello?" a man answered.

"It's me," she said.

He didn't respond.

"I mean . . . it's Persephone. I'm contacting Zeus." She slowed her breathing. It was a rookie mistake forgetting her assigned Greek mythology name. Such carelessness wasn't like her. But she was rushed and nervous.

"This is Zeus," the man said. "I was expecting you several days ago. Are you alright?"

"Yes," she said. "Plans to reach you have become complicated."

"What is your current status?"

"Physically . . . I'm injured, but only superficially—can still travel. But . . . I lost my anonymity."

Zeus let out a heavy breath into the phone. "Local authorities?"

"Yes. But I'm close to you. About a two or three hour drive from the Canadian border. And I'm guessing you're about thirty minutes shy of the line—"

"No mentioning locations over the phone."

"Sorry," she said. Another rookie mistake. "I'll need new documentation. Mine are gone."

"You mean, yours are in the system," he said.

She stared at the floor. "Yes."

"Persephone, you can't lead the authorities here. And I can't send someone to retrieve you in a compromised location. That would jeopardize every person I—"

"Yes, I know," she said, trying to control her tone. "But I need to get to you. If not, I'm in the system and trapped here."

"Okay." His voice softened. "Follow your instructions. Don't get caught."

"Of course." Charlotte hung up the phone and slipped it into her pocket.

She felt terrible. How could she have screwed up so royally? Pearl never would have made these many mistakes.

Charlotte wanted to cry, but wouldn't let herself.

It took her fifteen minutes to replicate Berta's stereotypical senior citizen look, then she began to work on her face. The cut on her nose had scabbed, and the swelling had gone down from under her two black eyes. She used thick concealer to hide the burns and bruising from the airbag. Brown eye shadow added liver and age spots, and the make-up powder mixed with cream from Berta's medicine cabinet created wrinkles on Charlotte's young face when applied with skill. The ingredients were simple, though not easy to work with. The change had to be light, so as not to appear artificial upon casual interaction, but she'd changed her overall look so many times before that Charlotte was a pro. And this time, "Berta" only had to fool others from a distance. Once she was on the freeway and safely to Zeus, he would take care of the rest.

When she finished adding age spots to her hands, Charlotte stared in the mirror. Only her eyes looked like herself. But then again, her eyes never looked young. Too much had gone on for there to be any innocence left.

"Ready?" Berta opened the bathroom door. "Oh, sweet heaven above! Do I look like that?" Her face contorted in horror.

"Not exactly. But close enough."

"Here. These will help." Berta handed over a pair of reading glasses with an attached chain.

"Thanks. They're perfect."

"I'll get your lunch," she said.

Charlotte waited for Berta to enter the kitchen before she slipped the credit card back into the purse, right inside its wallet slot. She put on her coat.

When Berta came back, she handed Charlotte a sack lunch and a few water bottles. "I put a quilt in the car, plus kicked the tires and checked the oil level. You should be fine."

"Thank you," she said, cradling the items in her arms.

"One last thing." Berta took her wallet from her purse and handed over a small amount of cash.

Charlotte stifled a twinge of guilt. Sandwiches and pocket money? Were they having a real human moment? "I can't take this cash."

"Don't be silly, deary. Take it." She put the bills in Charlotte's hand, then gripped the young woman's fist without letting go. Berta stared directly at her. "I've been thinking about you. About the car at the station. About the books you sold me. How you came from St. George and obviously Harding wasn't your final destination. A lot of thinking, deary."

Charlotte swallowed hard.

"And here's what I've figured out about you—you're running from something, but you won't tell me what. You don't have credit cards, only cash. If the police stop you, like Terry Walker did outside my store, and you happen to have thousands of dollars on your person, they tend to ask too many questions. But selling Pearl's belongings along the way is smart. You never have a large wad of cash in your wallet to arouse suspicion. You map out the used bookstores, thrift and pawn shops, and antique dealers along the route. Sell a few things. Only handle smallish bills, and no one is the wiser. Then . . . you get to your real money stash."

"You're very confident," Charlotte said, glancing down at her hand. Berta wasn't letting go. "Perhaps you've read too many spy novels in that bookstore of yours."

"Certainly not. Reading too much is impossible. Regardless, I've got you figured out. Well, all except for one thing."

Charlotte's pulse quickened. In a moment, she was going to need a threat assessment on Berta Sheppard. And perhaps an exit strategy.

"I think there was a detail in the plan that didn't play out correctly," Berta said.

"And what is that?"

"I think Pearl wasn't supposed to die. I think she was supposed to be on this little road trip of yours. So, what happened? Why is Pearl dead?"

A wave of raw heat flushed through Charlotte's face. Her lips tightened together, her mind calculating how to deal with the threat in front of her. Anger swelled in her chest.

"But I guess that doesn't matter now," Berta said suddenly, releasing her grip. "We can't always control every situation. Even if we want to. I'm sure her loss was heavy to bear."

Charlotte let out the breath she'd been holding in, loosening her tightened muscles. She forced her body to relax. "Berta, sometimes we have to rationalize our situation and proceed accordingly to survive. Even if that means changing our plan."

Berta's expression softened. "True. Now, let's get you on the road."

CHARLOTTE STARTED Berta's car and scanned the snow-coated neighborhood. She glanced back at Berta, who stood inside near the kitchen window, and thought it odd that the old woman waved *goodbye*. As if Charlotte was a grandchild leaving after a holiday visit. But there wasn't time to analyze the oddity. She pulled onto the street. This was the moment—the test to see if Berta Sheppard could keep her word and not involve the police. But after glancing at Berta's hand draw map to the northbound freeway entrance, she decided the old woman deserved a bit of her trust.

But only a tiny bit. She flexed her fingers where Berta had gripped Charlotte's hand in a tight fist.

Charlotte followed the driving instructions out of the neighborhood and turned onto the south end of Main Street, keeping the car under the speed limit. She passed a handful of cars on the way, but no one seemed interested in "Berta" driving up the road.

As she neared the line of connected historic storefronts in Harding's old-town proper, Charlotte noticed a parked police truck outside the bookstore. She slowed in reaction and pulled off onto a narrow side road, parking beside a group of pine trees. For about twenty seconds, she weighed her options and analyzed threat levels. According to Berta's map, there wasn't a direct route through the side neighborhoods. The nearby street signs had word names for the roads instead of sequential numbers, which added confusion for an outsider. And the drawn map was incomplete. Berta had only sketched and labeled the roads in her planned route. There were no back roads listed.

Charlotte got out and walked to the last pine tree near the curb. She glanced between the branches and focused on the bookstore. Chief Walker stood at the front display window, looking into the dark shop while he talked into his cell phone. He didn't seem concerned about Main Street, merely stared inside the building.

It wasn't optimal, but possible that she could drive passed him without drawing attention. But . . . it was risky. The threat level didn't support the action. Instead, Charlotte opted to find another route through the neighborhoods. It would take more time to clear the town, but she deemed the deviation acceptable. And necessary.

She got back into Berta's Buick and continued down the side road, studying the curving residential streets.

Several minutes passed before she felt confident that she'd bypassed the bookstore. After a few more minutes, Charlotte spotted a connecting road that led her back onto Main Street. At the stop sign, she gripped the steering wheel while she scanned around. The connecting street had put her at a corner north of the gas station. A couple cars were parked at the pumps, but she didn't see Mason's truck. Charlotte wondered if he was alright, though she'd never know the answer.

Refocusing. She turned right, heading north. Landmarks started to look familiar. Although, the first time she traveled that stretch of Harding, she was going more than seventy miles per hour with a cop in pursuit. Most of the town had been a blur. She steadied her nerves, unsure which time she felt more threatened. Then or now. It was a toss-up.

When she spotted the bridge up ahead, a surge of panic caused her bruised body to ache. Three police vehicles were parked at the far end, creating a road block and check point. A pickup truck and a dark sedan waited in line.

Charlotte pulled over near a snow bank. In the distance, a Harding officer stood near his patrol car, leaning toward the stopped pick-up truck. He gestured his hands, as if speaking with the driver.

Behind his police car, a state trooper exited her SUV and headed for the dark sedan. Nearby, a county sheriff's vehicle had parked to the side—a K-9 unit. The deputy stood near the back bumper and held the leash of his dog. Charlotte couldn't guess the breed from the distance, but that didn't matter. Police dogs were trained to find people.

She glanced in the rearview mirror and studied her make-up. It was good, but enough to stand up to close conversation? Fooling a stranger was doable, but a Harding officer who may or may not have known Berta all his life? She noticed the twisted metal where her

Oldsmobile had crashed through the guardrail. Her ribs and bruised collar bone ached at the mere sight of the gaping hole. Once on the bridge, that escape route wasn't an option.

Charlotte pulled back onto the road, just as the Harding officer waved the pickup truck along then. He turned toward Berta's car. She released the gas pedal, letting the tires roll.

The officer kept staring, studying her from a distance.

Charlotte tightened her grip on the steering wheel until her knuckles turned white. Muscle and veins in her body seemed to tightened with adrenaline, her breathing speeding up until each intake of air became rapid and shallow.

The Harding officer tilted his head to speak into his shoulder radio mic, all the while keeping his gaze fixed on Berta's car. His mouth moved fast, the words urgent and distinct. Then he took a few steps toward her direction and motioned for her to stop.

Charlotte made a u-turn in the snow.

Plan A—one hundred percent a threat. Altering strategy to begin Plan B.

According to Berta's map, there was another freeway entrance in the south end of town beyond several farm properties. The spot was secluded, rural, in theory ideal, but with its own set of drawbacks. Still, plan's change.

She drove away from the bridge, glancing back in her mirror. This time around, she didn't see red and blue flashing lights in pursuit. Just to be safe, Charlotte turned into a side road. She retraced her path through the outlying neighborhoods, careful to avoid Main Street. If more roadblocks hindered her escape, she'd need a Plan C.

Charlotte's mind raced with calculations.

30

WALKER

THE PHONE CALL went straight to voicemail for the third time. Walker listened to Berta's full message again, holding the phone slightly away from his ear. Her voice sounded artificial and loud in the recording: "Hello, caller. This is Alberta Sheppard's cell phone. I'm not answering right now. Please leave a detailed message, and I'll get back to you when I'm willing. If you're one of those pesky telemarketers, don't call back. You should be ashamed of yourself."

Beep.

"Berta, this is Terry. I just stopped by your store. Surprised you took a sick day. Making sure you're not on your death bed. Give me a call. Detective Peterson from St. George P.D. wants to interview you."

He ended the call and stepped back from the bookstore window. There were a few people shoveling sidewalks and an occasional car would pass, but for the most part, the town of Harding was barely into the work day. He glanced at his watch. Maybe he'd stop by Berta's house after he checked on Stewart at the bridge. That would give Peterson time to interview Mason Trent and perhaps meet him at Berta's house.

Walker drove his truck north on Main Street. He glanced along the side roads as he passed by each stop sign.

His cell phone rang. It was Stewart. "Chief, the county K-9 unit is at the north check-point and waiting to coordinate with you. SAR just got here too."

"Ok. I'm about five minutes out. Apologize to them for the delay. I needed to do a welfare check on a resident."

"A welfare check?" Stewart asked. "Which resident?"

"Berta Sheppard. Bookstore's closed. She's ill if you can believe that."

"Huh. That's weird."

"I know. That woman never takes a day off. She'd have to be on her death bed."

"No, Chief. I mean, I'm looking at her car right now. On the bridge."

"Berta's car?" Walker said.

"I think so. Old Buick LaSabre. Dark red. Berta in the driver's seat."

"Hold her at the check point. I'll be there in a minute." Walker sped up.

"Negative, Chief. I can't. She flipped around. Headed back into town. Do you want me to pull her over?"

"No. She'll hate that. I'll catch her en route." Walker tightened his upper lip, convinced Alberta Sheppard was put on Earth solely to complicate his job. And she probably liked it that way.

As he neared the bridge, he glanced around for Berta's red sedan. When he didn't see her, he parked next to the other police vehicles. He grabbed his tablet before getting out.

"Didn't you catch her?" Stewart asked, meeting him in the middle of the road. "She took a left into a side street."

"No. Must've just missed her car. Which street?"

"First left off Main, onto Digby."

"Okay. I'll check at the bookstore on my way back," he said. Walker headed for the group waiting by the torn guardrail—a state trooper, a county sheriff's deputy with a K-9, and a few search and rescue members with their search dogs.

Stewart huffed. "I'm guessing Berta doesn't want to talk to the detective, does she?"

"I'm getting that impression. That lady . . ." Walker shook his head. "She's a stubborn one. Hard to change people who are set in their ways. They like how they are."

"Yep, you should know."

Walker stopped and stared at him.

Stewart's face flushed. "Not that you're stubborn . . . or set in your ways, Chief. I mean, there are people who . . . some people . . . who are older . . . but, wait, you're not old. What are you, in your sixties? No, I meant fifties. Fifty isn't old. Or set in any ways—"

"Stewart," Walker said.

"Yep."

"Focus."

"Right."

Walker greeted the other officers and apologized for making them wait. He pulled up a GIS map on his tablet, one which included a large satellite image of the surrounding area with a roads and trails overlay. "How are the trail searches going, Paul?" he asked.

The deputy stepped forward, motioning to the search and rescue crew behind him. "We're covering ground with the assistance of the K-9 handlers. But we can't haul the dogs up on snowmobiles, so that limits dog searches. SAR has a couple teams with five snowmobiles each. So we've run the trails through these mountains . . ." He pointed along the map. "Together, we've done a sweep up to several cabins, but no one's up there this time of year. Haven't seen a lot of vehicle tracks. You need a sled to get up to most places."

"So you're thinking she's not up in the East Hills," Walker said.

"Not unless she stole a snowmobile and a bunch of all-weather gear. If she took that route, we'll spot her eventually—barely alive or frozen to death."

Walker lowered his chin. He didn't like those options. "Okay. Keep me updated, Paul."

"No problem."

"Adams?" He glanced at the state trooper. "Still got all four road blocks up?"

"Yes," she said, motioning to the map as she explained. "One freeway entrance south bound, one north, and two more on the county highways. Here . . . and here. Not too many cars on those roads this morning. It's been manageable. And not too inconvenient for drivers. But we haven't spotted Evers or any stolen vehicles. The County Sheriff's office has extra shifts patrolling county roads."

"Okay. My officers will keep looking in town. Thanks, all of you. I appreciate the assistance." Walker headed back to his truck. His radio crackled.

"Bravo-One. Dispatch," Kim said.

"This is Bravo-One," he answered. "Go ahead."

"A store owner on Main is reporting unusual activity behind Sheppard's bookstore. He's requesting a police officer."

"Copy. Which owner?"

"Bill Fuller," she said.

"What did he see?"

"Something about the back alley door. It's not clear."

"Bravo-Four and I are responding." Walker motioned for Stewart, but his young officer was already hurrying to his patrol car. They headed for Main Street.

WALKER PULLED AROUND BACK, parking behind the row of store fronts near a group of dumpsters. Stewart pulled alongside him.

Bill Fuller stood near the farthest dumpster, waving at Walker with a cell phone in his hand.

"What's going on, Bill?" Walker asked.

"I came out to throw some trash bags away. Heard noise in the alley by Berta's place and saw this." He pointed at the back of the bookstore.

The steel fire door shifted in the breeze, the old hinges creaking as it moved. The door itself had been left ajar enough for Walker to see inside the dim-lit store all the way to the front cashier counter. He took a few steps toward the building to get a better look. The rear door's single glass window, a small square at eye level, was solid and the hardware was intact. But there were tiny scratch marks around the keyhole and a smudge of black dust, as if something besides the normal key had tampered with the mechanism. He suspected two metal lock picks, or perhaps some similar objects foreign enough to dislodge the old grease in the tumblers. Either way, the lock didn't look normal and Berta's car wasn't in the parking lot.

"You stayed outside, right?" Walker asked Bill.

"Of course. I ain't crazy. You guys are looking for a fugitive. I've seen movies. It's always the curious ones who die first."

"This isn't the movies," Walker said.

"True. But people in town are on edge. Things are weird. I tried to call Berta before calling you guys. She didn't answer. She's home sick, you know. Terrible cold going around town. Better stock up on cold meds. Just to be safe."

Walker motioned to Stewart.

Stewart nodded. "Hey, Bill," he said in a hushed voice. "Thanks for calling us. We'll check it out. Head back to your store, and we'll get a full statement from you later."

"Sure thing." Bill walked away.

When they were alone, Walker spoke softly into his shoulder mic. "Dispatch. Bravo-One. We are investigating a possible break-in at Sheppard's Bookstore. We're entering the building."

"Copy, Bravo-One," Kim responded.

Walker readied his sidearm. Stewart did the same.

"Maybe Berta just forgot to close the door," Stewart whispered.

"Maybe." Walker wanted that to be the case, but common sense and the sunken feeling in his gut didn't accept such a simple answer. He took in a steadying breath, raised his arms into position, then let his training take over.

They took positions on either side of the opening. Stewart reached his free hand to the handle, waited for Walker's nod, then pulled open the door all the way. Walker entered first.

Inside, he scanned around the aisles, keeping his sweeping focus on clearing the room while maintaining a fix on Stewart. It was dim, even with the oversized display windows, shadows loomed in his periphery. They shifted down the aisle ways, stepping over dumped piles of books, then swept the front area, behind the counter, and checked the private restroom. All the while, Walker listened for rustling and watched for movement as he checked each area.

The main room was empty. He sucked in a quick breath, realizing he'd been shallowing his breathing. Stewart motioned toward the back office. The door was open about a foot, and the office light had been turned on. He waited a few seconds for Stewart to position himself. Then they entered.

Walker scanned the small office at rapid pace, checking both sides of the desk and in a small closet.

The office was empty.

"It's clear," he said, both relieved and frustrated at the same time. He didn't expect to find Charlotte Evers so easily, but he had hoped as much.

Stewart nodded, using his free hand to wipe a layer of sweat from his forehead.

"But someone's been here," Walker added. He motioned to the box of books tipped over in the center of the room. The computer monitor was on, the screen open to the search page. Several of the desk drawers had been riffled through and left ajar. Papers and books littered the floor, and a microwave-sized firesafe had been pulled forward from the closet.

Berta had a reputation of keeping her bookstore in proper order. Everything had its place, even if she was the only one who could find anything. The mess couldn't have belonged to her.

"Go check the front door," Walker said, securing his sidearm. "See if it's locked. And check for other signs of a break in."

"Yes, Chief." Stewart left the office for a moment while Walker studied the computer monitor and keyboard. He couldn't tell if anything was missing.

"Front door is still locked up," Stewart said when he returned.

"Ok. Dispatch. Bravo-One," he said into his radio.

"Go ahead, Bravo-One," Kim answered.

"The store is clear. But there's signs of a break-in. Send Bravo-Two to this location, please. And did you reach the individual I asked you to contact?" He'd asked Kim to keep trying Berta by phone.

"There was no answer."

"That lady!" He said under his breath and grit his teeth. He needed Franklin here and Kemp could do the welfare check. "Dispatch, Bravo-One. Is Bravo-Three available for a welfare check?"

"Bravo-Three's at the south check point. Do you want him to leave it?" she asked.

"Hang on. I'll get back to you." Walker headed into the main part of the store. He retraced his steps back to the alley, glancing outside for a moment. Bill Fuller stood by the dumpsters again. This time, Bill held his cell phone high while recording a video of the commotion. Walker turned away, hoping the video didn't capture his frustration. He pulled out his own cell and called Berta one more time. No matter how old they got, that woman never seemed to forgive him for his teenage pranks. Even trying to give her a fix-it ticket for her old car was a nightmare. People in Harding had selective memories and long-lasting grudges.

His lips tightened together as he listened to her loud voicemail message for the millionth time that day. "Berta," he said. "Stewart saw you driving your car. I know you're not sick. Maybe you're avoiding us. Giving me the silent treatment . . . whatever this nonsense is, I don't have time for it. Instead, I'm standing inside your bookstore. Looks like someone broke in. And they made a mess. So if by some miracle you care about that, call me back now. Or I'll have to assume you're either in danger or being stubborn. Either way, I swear I will search the entire town for you myself."

He ended the call and waited, staring at his phone. Less than twenty seconds later, it rang.

"Berta," he answered. "You better have a damn good reason why you're avoiding my calls."

"Now just a minute," Berta snapped. "I'm not justifying anything until you tell me about my store. What in the world are you talking about?"

"Someone broke in. I need you to come here and tell us if things are missing."

"Wait, it's been what?" she said.

"Broken in to. Possibly burglarized."

There was a moment of quiet. Walker could hear Berta taking in a series of deep breaths, sounding as if she was holding back her emotions. He imagined her eyes were watering about then, and didn't want Berta to cry. Maybe she'd choose to snap at him some more. That would be easier to handle. Anything but tears.

Berta choked up. Then muffled sobs escaped through her attempt to stay composed.

Hearing her cry made him feel worse than being angry. His momentary frustration instantly melted away. "Look, Berta—"

"Why would someone break into my bookstore?" she said, then sniffled through another weighted sob. "That place is all I have."

He softened his tone. "Can you come down here? Or I can send someone to pick you up if it's too hard. I don't want you distracted while you drive. I'll send a car."

"Um, no," she said. "Wait. I can come down. Just . . . I need a minute. But I'll be there."

"Good. My officers are going to start documenting the scene."

"My bookstore is a crime scene!" She sobbed into the phone.

"Whoa, Berta. Calm down. Just a small one. Not big. Just small. We'll problem-solve through this. Figure things out. One step at a time. The good thing is you're safe. It'll be okay."

"I hope so. Just wait for me." She hung up.

Walker closed his eyes and touched the phone to his forehead. He just wanted things to calm down. To be over. When he looked up again, Bill Fuller was gone. Probably off to post the video online.

Just past the dumpsters, Deputy Franklin pulled up next to Walker's truck, and Detective Peterson followed behind him in his red, compact rental car. Franklin headed over carrying a digital camera in his hand.

"Franklin, start taking pictures," Walker said.

"Yep." Franklin began snapping images of the back alley.

"I'm guessing Evers wasn't hiding inside." Peterson leaned low to examine the fire door lock.

Walker shook his head. "If she had been, you'd know by now. Looks like someone entered and riffled through things. Could've been Evers. But not sure. Mason Trent said Evers wanted stuff from the station, not Berta's store. It's odd. By the way, was Mason helpful when you interviewed him?"

Peterson pulled his notebook from his coat, then cleared his throat. "Uh, I haven't talked to him yet."

"Why not?" he asked.

Peterson scribbled something in his notepad then glanced at his cell phone. "The kid wasn't at the station. I looked around. Waited. Couldn't find him. Still don't have Berta Sheppard's home address, but she probably wasn't really at home since one of your officers spotted her car. If I were to guess, I'd say your people are avoiding me."

Walker rubbed his temples. Charlotte, Berta, and Mason were all missing. The whole mess reminded him of a deadly game of hide and seek, and he was the unlucky player stuck searching for everyone else. Only this wasn't a game. And no one was going to show up at home base.

"Walker," Peterson said, squaring his shoulders. He held up his index finger. "This mess is small-town nonsense. Get your people in line. Charlotte Evers should be in custody right now, not loose in your town. Mistakes are being made."

Chief Walker stared at the detective, tightening his grip on his duty belt until the leather stretched under the pressure.

Peterson folded his arms. "You don't have the situation under control. Not even close. Charlotte Evers should be located immediately. If you can't do that, I'll persuade a higher agency to lead the search. Then you're free to focus on a small-time bookstore break-in."

Heat flushed Walker's face. "I don't have time for your ultimatums. Now excuse me, I have things to do."

He turned his back to Peterson and walked inside the bookstore.

31

BERTA

BERTA GRIPPED her cell phone in her hand, staring at the home screen photo—an image of her bookstore's *Open* sign from the front window. She shed several more tears as she blinked. The store was always open, every day, until today. Guilt and regret poured into her heart like a bucket of loose sand. She wiped away the tears.

Berta dialed the number for Charlotte's prepaid cell phone, squinting at the numbers on the bright yellow sticky note that she was supposed to hide.

"Berta?" Charlotte answered.

"Where are you?"

"Still in Harding. Do you know any more connecting back roads? I've tried both freeway entrances and state highways, and now I'm on some dirt lane called Plummer that looks like it goes into the Mountains."

"Toward the East Hills?"

"I think so."

"My car can't make it up there without chains," Berta said.

"Chains?"

"You know, on the tires. Where have you been living, child? How do you not know what snow chains are? You'd need chains or a snowmobile to get through the canyons during winter. I don't have time to get either ready for you."

"Just help me figure this out," Charlotte said.

"We've got a bigger problem. Someone broke into the bookstore. The police want me to come down there. And they saw you driving around in the Buick. Don't worry, your makeup worked. They think it was me, and we might be alright. But I need to go to the bookstore right away or they'll pick me up. So come back here. You can stay and figure out the roads. I have more maps."

Charlotte groaned.

"Look, deary. You don't have a lot of options. The roads are tricky. You can't go on foot because you'd never make it anywhere in the snow. Just come back. We'll make a new plan."

"Fine. I'll be there soon."

"Good." Berta slipped her cell phone in her purse. She put on her purple overcoat before briefly checking her hair in the bathroom mirror. Then she gripped her handbag and waited by the front window.

Time passed slowly while she stood there, watching neighbors drive up the street as if the day were a normal one. She successfully held back her worry, focusing on being a blank slate. There wasn't room for emotions right then. She had a job to do and a store to check on.

When Charlotte pulled into the garage, Berta was ready to switch over as the driver. She nodded to Charlotte as they passed each other.

"There's sandwich fixings in the fridge," Berta said. "I'll be right back."

Without a word, Charlotte hurried inside the house.

Berta felt the sudden impulse to glance at the front living room window as she pulled out onto the street, expecting Charlotte to be standing there waving. But she stifled the thought without looking at the house and shook her head at her own ridiculousness. Charlotte wasn't her granddaughter. And this wasn't a family visit.

OUT OF HABIT, Berta aimed for her normal parking spot behind the building, but the slot was filled with a police vehicle. Due to the additional cop cars, a small red car, and the dumpsters, there wasn't any room for her to park. She stopped her Buick behind the drug store, right next to Bill's 1970's VW Beetle. Normally she would've been annoyed by such a ridiculous vehicle choice, but Bill had owned that thing since his teens. One justification she understood well was sentimentality. Plus, it was Bill. She didn't expect him to be more complicated than a bright yellow Bug.

A minute later, she walked up toward the bookstore, gripping her handbag tight against the crick of her elbow. The back alley fire door had been left wide open against the building, and a cinderblock propped it in place. There was no glass on the ground, no twisted metal, or broken hinges—nothing visually typical for a break-in. Except for all the expensive heat the police were letting escape, the store looked fine. Berta kicked the cinderblock until the door closed behind her. She glanced toward the front counter.

"Terry," she called.

Chief Walker hurried from the office and stood at her side. "Thanks for coming, Berta. Are you doing alright?"

"Well, I don't know, Terry," she said with force. "Someone violated my bookstore and the police are letting all my heat escape. I've been better."

Walker nodded, and for a second, she could have sworn she caught him smirking.

"Are you taking this seriously?" she asked.

He straightened up. "Of course. Now, will you come in the office? I want to show you something."

Berta followed Walker past the aisles. She tried to hold her emotions together while glancing at the mess of scattered books. Most of the titles were still safe on their shelves, but even one tossed and discarded hardback was enough to made the heat rise in her head. Books didn't belong on the floor.

They entered the back office. Deputy Franklin and Detective Peterson stood by the small closet. Franklin snapped a few pictures as she entered the room, mostly of the desk and one pointed at Berta's bewildered face. She held back a snappy, reactionary remark. Even though he deserved one. The room felt claustrophobic with four people inside at once, and she decided Franklin would soon be the first one expelled.

"Berta, I need you to look around without touching much," Walker said. "Let me know if anything's missing."

"Alright." She glanced at the papers littering the floor, then at the open drawers and the box of books spilled over in the center of the room. She hid a surge of panic as she stared at the upturned box. Charlotte's books were scattered everywhere—hundreds of potential dollars, if not thousands, tossed on the floor like junk. Berta couldn't help but feel betrayed and violated. An uninvited stranger had been in her office, the one place guarded as her safe haven. If the burglar had ripped her heart out and lit it on fire, they'd have done the same amount of damage. Why did it have to be the bookstore?

She ran her fingertips along the desk, fighting the impulse to tidy up. Her parents' chamber of commerce desk clock, the one she'd wound only the night before, had been tossed aside and left face-down on the tile. She stared at it in disbelief.

"How about the safe?" Walker asked. "It's been touched. Anything valuable inside to steal?"

Berta glanced at the microwave-sized fire safe near the closet door. The safe itself had been dragged away from its normal place by about two feet and had left dust streaks on the tile, but the heavy door was still closed and hinges intact. It looked normal. She leaned closer and examine the combination code pad and key lock. No one could have guessed her code—1398—the birth year of Johannes Gutenberg, the man who invented and then first used removable type for a printing press, and who made mass printing books possible. She was confident no one in Harding would have that date memorized. Plus, the accompanying metal key never left her car key ring. Which never left her side. Never, except . . .

She put her hand inside her pocket, gripping the Buick's key next to the one for her house and bookstore, and realized she'd forgotten to remove them before Charlotte took the car. Still, there was no chance Charlotte could have known her safe combination or wanted to open it. Even if she's figured out Pearl's collection of *Gilly Heel* was inside. Which she wouldn't take. Berta was holding them as collateral payment. That was their deal.

"Berta?" Walker asked.

"Yes?"

"Are you going to check it?"

"No need. I don't think it's been opened," she said.

Franklin snapped a picture of the safe. "Open it anyway. Let's see."

"No, thank you. I know what's inside. Dusty old books. No use stealing those." She stood tall, ready to rip the camera from Franklin's hand if he tried to take her picture again.

"If they're not valuable," Peterson said. "Then why keep them locked up? Why not keep them on the shelf like the rest? Why are they so different?"

Berta's face flushed and her jaw tightened. She glanced at Walker, but he didn't say anything. "Because, Detective, that's the way I want it. A lady is entitled to her own organizational system in her own business. In other words, it's none of yours."

Franklin snapped her picture.

"That's enough," Walker said, waving Franklin out of the room. "Let's move on. Berta, I thought you gave me all of Charlotte Evers' books. Is it possible that you . . . kept some?" He stared at her without flinching.

Berta's stomach churned with nerves. "I . . . may have kept a few."

"How many do you consider 'a few'?" he asked.

She glanced at the scattered books on the tile. "Um . . . about that many."

Walker groaned, not even trying to hide his disappointment. "So, Berta, is it possible . . . that Charlotte Evers may have come back to get something from you? One of her books?"

"No. Not possible."

"How do you know that?" Peterson asked.

"Because, I just do," she said.

Walker rubbed his temples then wrung his hands. "Okay. Detective Peterson, can you give me and Berta a minute?"

"I'll have to," he said. "Until she cooperates."

After Peterson left the room, Berta began picking up the loose papers. Crime scene or no crime scene, this was her office and her business and under no circumstances was she going to let it remain a shambles. "He's a terribly impatient man," she said, tipping the box upright.

Walker leaned down to help her gather the books. "Berta, here's the deal. This burglary is small time. No chance of getting the CSI team to come out here to sweep this place. We took photos, made a police report. But whoever did this, didn't steal anything from what I can tell. Your safe is unopened, and your computer is here. They even woke up your screen and browsed the internet. The whole situation is weird."

She studied the computer screen. The browser was up and a small handful of webpages had been left open—namely, the St. George community pages including the forum where she'd communicated with *FamilyIsLife*.

Walker stood to his feet. "I had Stewart glance at it. He said the open pages came from your browser history."

"That's a bit nosy, Terry. Don't you think?"

"Ah, relax," Walker said. "Stewart could tell without fiddling with the thing. Says so right there . . ." Walker pointed to one of the open desktop windows. "We needed to check the scene before you came in. But Berta, I know there's more going on than what you're telling me. You've been talking to someone online about Pearl Sanford. Why? And why drive around this morning instead of coming to the store?"

She stood and scooted the box near the desk. "All I can say is, it's a good thing I wasn't here. I might have been in great danger."

He picked up her clock, setting it on the desk next to the computer. "Maybe you still are. Keeping secrets is risky."

"Don't be silly. I don't have any secrets. A lot of bad things have happened in town recently. But they're just that, a string of bad luck. It'll change. Now, if you'll excuse me, I have a store to clean up." She glanced into the main room at Peterson and Franklin, who both stood near the front counter. The mess would take her a while to reorganize.

"Berta?" Walker said.

She turned around. "Yes?"

"At some point you need to talk to me."

"I'm talking to you now." She picked up a three volume mystery series from off the floor.

"No," he said. "I mean, *really* talk to me. What's going on with you?"

She brushed the front covers, choosing her words. "Terry, you know me. If I have something to say, I'll say it. No holding back. If I don't have anything to share, then I keep to myself."

"I know. That's the problem," he said. "I need you to trust me."

Berta stared at the floor. "It's a giant mess right now. What I need to do is clean up. Let me know if you figure out who did this."

He nodded.

"Until then," she said. "I want some help tidying the bookstore." She pointed at Franklin. "That guy isn't doing anything helpful right now. Can you put him to work?"

"Sure."

Berta turned away from Walker and busied herself in the nearest aisle, hurrying so she could get back to Charlotte. She could only guess what that girl was doing back at her house.

32

MASON

MASON COULDN'T DECIDE if his mild headache was caused by a lack of sleep or the constant stench of heavy-dowsed cinnamon pinecones. He leaned on the dispatch office doorway, listening to Kim's responses as she spoke with the officers through her headset. Several police procedure booklets were open on her counter, the pages marked and highlighted. Pink sticky notes littered her computer console.

She didn't pay much attention to him. Chief Walker and the others were still investigating the bookstore break in, leaving the station nearly empty. A couple other dispatchers came in and out for their shifts, but it was easy for Mason to move around without anyone bothering him. Still, he wanted to listen and catch every detail of their investigation on the incoming radio chatter. Mason had stood there since Walker's 'all clear' check in—about fifteen minutes worth of eavesdropping and listening to Kim respond.

He checked his cell phone. His mom would be back soon. She'd gone to work for a couple hours after arranging for another nurse to cover her shift. Problem was, the replacement couldn't report to the ER until two hours after shift change. Before Jan left, she made

Mason promise to stay safe and stay put. So far, he'd done just that, although he'd wandered a little.

"Do you want some Christmas candy?" Kim asked. She held out a dish filled with red and green peppermints.

"Thanks." Mason took a couple for his pocket. "How long will they be at the bookstore?"

"Not sure," she said. "Depends on Berta, I think."

He nodded.

"Do you need something to do?" she asked.

"Oh, no. I'm good. I've . . . kept myself busy."

"Good." Kim put the candy dish on the counter next to her miniature Christmas tree and baskets of pinecones. "If you change your mind, there's always paper to photocopy and file."

Mason picked up a small pinecone from the nearest basket, absent-mindedly fiddling with it. "As tempting as office grunt work sounds, I'll pass. Don't want to take over Jed's fake job. Then what would he do all day?"

"Right."

"But still . . ." He tossed the pinecone back into the basket and wrinkled his nose at the cinnamon stench and silver glitter left on his skin. "I'm good."

"Okay," she said, turning away.

Mason wandered down the hallway to where Jed sat at the front desk. That morning, when he first passed the front counter, Jed had been asleep in his chair. Probably slept there all night. But now Jed sat upright while downing a can of heavily caffeinated energy drink—the kind with a high probability of dissolving away stomach lining. Jed swigged a full gulp without looking down and while riffling through a pile of paperwork near an open laptop.

"Hey, man. What ya doin'?" Mason asked.

Jed sat the can near the keyboard. "Data entry. It's important, I guess."

"Data entry?"

"Yep. The cops sometimes fill out police reports on actual paper. Old school, right? They have like, new tablets and laptops, but I think they get a kick out of making me enter their scribbles into the database. At least, Franklin does. Such a jerk."

Mason pulled a chair next to Jed, placing himself over the stack of papers. There were police reports and files of case notes. Some of the files contained ripped notebook pages and number lists relating to digital photos.

"You're a volunteer, right? Why are ya willing to do all this grunt work?" Mason asked.

"Because, I can," Jed said, thumbing a new sheet from the stack. "Don't you ever, like, do anything or help anybody because you know it just needs to be done?"

Mason stared at the carpet for a moment. Jed had just described Mason's entire Harding life in one sentence. To be accurate, his life with his mom. She needed him. And he needed to be responsible. That's all he ever did was do stuff because it needed to be done. He was stuck in survival mode. "Maybe," he said.

"Besides," Jed added. "I'm going to be a criminal justice student. And, like, this place looks good on my resume, and I get to read all their police reports and stuff. See . . ." He opened a file that contained a number of loose legal pad pages, two of which Mason instantly recognized.

"You're reading my statement?" Mason said.

Jed grinned. "Yep, 'cause I'm data entering it."

"Chief Walker let you handle that?" Mason held the file in his lap and stared down at his handwriting. "But it's too—"

"Important? Yeah, it is. But this time, I think he, like, really didn't have time to do it himself. Told me to, you know, put it into the computer right away. Front of the line. And same with the rest of the stuff."

Behind Mason's statement pages, he found notes from the Oldsmobile search—lists of belongings found in the car and a USB taped to the file folder.

Jed grabbed the drive and slid it into the laptop's side port. "Pretty sure the photos are already in the system. Just need to double check."

Sure enough, the image numbers matched ones already attached to a case file named *Charlotte Evers 07852-01.* Jed began clicking one by one through the images. "Some of these are from the CSI team, but most are from Franklin's camera. That guy needs photography lessons. I see his big fat thumb a lot."

Mason glanced at each image as Jed swiped through them—the interior of the car, the duffle bags and their contents, and the crumpled front end where the car had slid into the river. The next group of images were items from the trunk. They stopped momentarily on a picture of a plastic bag and loose items spread across a table, as if the bag had been emptied then photographed. Mason stared at the images of a burned, small metal wrist watch, then at the IDs with Charlotte's picture, and the urn. He swallowed hard, his heartrate quickening as he studied the exact items Charlotte asked him to retrieve for her.

"I wonder who's in the urn. It's creepy not knowing," Jed said, enlarging the image.

"You're kidding, right? You read my statement. It's Charlotte Evers' grandma—the missing Utah lady."

Jed chuckled. "I think you missed some stuff, man. The detective guy said they found that lady's body. She's dead. And *body* means, like, not in an urn." He pointed to the screen. "Those are mystery ashes."

Mason leaned back in his chair, a wave of nausea filling his stomach. "They found her body?"

"Yep. I was sitting right here when the guy said it. Well, they thought I was asleep but—"

"Her actual body?"

"No, her fake one," Jed smirked. "She keeps a spare in case she wants to fake her own death. Like, how many different kinds of bodies do you think there are?"

Mason rolled his eyes, his insides roasting. "If I say anything other than 'just the one,' are you going to have a witty comeback that's worth the effort?"

Jed held up his hands. "Dude, why are you so defensive? Throwing shade isn't the answer."

"Then what is? This whole mess got a little dark."

"Is that what you've seen?" Jed asked, squinting. "Darkness?"

Mason stood up. "Okay . . . data entry and therapy. Jed, you've got skills. Thanks, man, but I'm good. No psychoanalyzing needed. At least not today. You could do me a favor, though."

"Sure."

"I'm going to take a walk. Not too far, just need some fresh air like I did earlier. Can we keep that between us? If someone asks for me, just say I'm in the bathroom or something."

"Yeah, man. No problem. Bob leaves work all the time and tells me to say he's in the bathroom. Kim thinks he has irritable bowel syndrome or something."

Mason took a few steps toward the hallway. "That's . . . funny and disturbing."

Jed simply grinned and nodded his head.

"Okay. Thanks, man." Mason headed to the old holding cells in the back of the building and grabbed his coat. It took him less than a minute to walk out the front door with only Jed noticing his exit.

Outside, weak sunlight filtered through the December cloud cover, leaving a gray hue over Harding. It was snowing again. Mason zipped up his coat, flipped on his hood, and shoved both hands inside his pockets. Where was he going this time? Uneasiness filled his chest and he felt the impulse to walk a little farther than the breather he took after his vending machine breakfast. Without purpose, he headed toward the center of town.

The photos lingered in his mind—the wrecked Oldsmobile, the bag of IDs, and what Charlotte told him about needing to leave. The whole thing was so messed up. Mason understood that feeling. He suddenly remembered the psychologist his mother took him to see as an eleven-year-old, right after he was released from the Portland hospital. He didn't see the psychologist for very long, and Mason hadn't thought about therapy since. The few sessions he attended were all the same. The woman would ask questions, and Mason had to reply. He hated answering questions. The answers were too complicated to express in a few words, and the psychologist always wanted more words than he could give.

His mother decided to moved him back to Harding after that. She figured her home town would do him good. A change of scenery. A chance to relax.

But, as Mason walked toward Main Street, he kept feeling lost. There were so many questions, and Charlotte's answers were complicated. So, she was lying about the ashes, but . . . his instinct told him there was more evidence to consider. More details. Last night at the hospital, Charlotte's eyes didn't match her words. They were full of fear. But she sounded normal. That, he recognized. He was an expert in *I'm fine* on the outside, while hiding *I'm not fine* on the inside. Charlotte had been devastated to leave the ashes and wrist watch behind, even more than the IDs and the cash. They meant something to her. But what?

Mason walked faster.

How could he prove to Chief Walker and the others that Charlotte needed their help? Maybe Jed was right, maybe she was a murderer. But . . . his instincts told him otherwise, and he didn't feel threatened by her at all. The police needed more information. They needed Charlotte to come forward, and she needed a chance to stop running and explain herself. To clean up the mess of crap she left behind.

Mason decided to help, at least in the only way that his stressed-out, sleep-deprived, slept-in-jail-cell mind could formulate while speed walking in the snow—human bait.

And he was the worm.

Mason couldn't find Charlotte, but she could find him. Both Walker and his mom feared as much. That's why he'd spent the night in jail.

Jed was right. It was time to do something that simply needed to be done—not sit aside and watch while bad things happened. He could do something good for someone else, even if his father chose not to. Mason wasn't like his dad.

Walker would reject the idea, and his mom would hate everything about it. So, he'd become the bait alone.

Mason broke into a run, reaching Main Street.

33

CHARLOTTE

CHARLOTTE PACED BACK and forth in Berta's kitchen. She wrung her hands, glancing at the drawn curtains above the sink. Between the mid-morning sunlight reflecting on the exterior glass and the unlikelihood that a neighbor would be lurking in Berta's fenced backyard, no one would see her through the window. Still, she felt safer with the curtains drawn. It hadn't taken long for Charlotte to cover all the windows on the main floor.

She waited for Berta, just as instructed, but her nerves made eating impossible. So she paced, counting the steps, and analyzed strategy in her head. The road blocks increased threat levels for vehicle travel. There had to be other options.

The clothes she'd taken from the hospital were warm, but not enough. Charlotte searched Berta's hall closet. There were gloves and a pair of fur-lined rubber boots. Most of the coats looked fit for Sunday church but not trudging in December drifts along the roadside. None looked water-proof. Charlotte riffled through all the clothes until she found a long coat made of thick wool. She dropped it onto the floor along with the boots, gloves, and a knitted beanie hat.

Then Charlotte headed for the garage. She checked again for

winter equipment—perhaps snow shoes, all-weather gear, or flashlights. Mostly what she found was consistent for a person who only drove back and forth to a bookstore. There was a shovel and a bag of salt by the large metal garage door, a snow blower that looked at least fifteen years old, a lawn mower, and a single tennis racket hanging from a nail on the far wall. But no more. She glanced at the racket, unsure why Berta Sheppard would care about tennis. Something small and metallic caught the light—a keychain. Charlotte hurried over and reached for the nail, grabbing the item and untying it from the tennis racket. She examined the key. It looked small, square on the top, probably belonging to a padlock.

Her first impulse was to search the house for the lock, but her second thought saved her precious time. People didn't keep padlocks on interior belongings. They were for outside. Charlotte opened the rear door and walked through the backyard.

No shed. No padlock on the fence. Berta must have owned something else.

She went back inside and straight to the roll-top desk in Berta's spare room. The small shelves were filled with files, each one with carefully placed and meticulously printed labels on the top flap. Charlotte thumbed through them. There were financial records, taxes for the bookstore, and household bills. It looked like Berta was behind in her property taxes. Very behind. Then, Charlotte saw it—a file labeled *Storage Unit*. Inside, she found an invoice for a small storage business located near the south end of town. From what she could tell looking at the paper's photo, the building was an old barn that had been converted into four storage sections.

Berta had handwritten a line at the bottom of the page. *Slot #3. Item list: water barrels, Uncle Kent's work pickup—not running, Cousin Frank's snowmobile, bookstore A-frames, Dad's milk bottle collection . . .*

Charlotte stared at the words, tracing a single item with her finger. *Cousin Frank's snowmobile.* She gripped the page and the padlock key in her hand, then headed back to the garage where the snow blower sat against the wall. Directly behind it, she found a full gas can.

She then retrieved the roads and trails map that she'd ripped from Berta's ten-year-old county phone book.

Analyzing: Plan success probability—sixty-five percent. Charlotte pulled the cell phone from her pocket and dialed.

"Hello?" a man answered.

"This is Persephone. I'm contacting Zeus."

"This is Zeus. Go ahead, Persephone."

"I'm still in the same location," she said. "More complications, but I have an alternative plan. I need a pick up after exiting through mountainous terrain."

"Mountainous? As in, a back roads trail?"

"Yes."

Zeus huffed into the phone. "Based on our last call, I figured out your current location. And I'm aware of the 'mountainous terrain' you're referring to, at least an estimate. I can't send someone to track you through snow trails. It's too dangerous. The money isn't worth risking the life of one of my guys."

"It'll work," she said.

"Look. You get through whatever mountainous terrain you're brave enough to cross, then call me from the next town you come to. I'll arrange a pick-up from there. Not from some mountain peak."

"Fine." Charlotte picked up the gas can from the garage floor. "I'll get through to the next town. Then come get me. I'll have your money. You have my new IDs and a way into Canada. Same deal. Nothing's changed."

"Sounds good." He hung up.

The statement was almost true, nothing had changed. Nothing except the authorities now held her thirty thousand dollars intended for Zeus, and there was no way for her to get it back. But he didn't need to know that. Maybe he'd forgive her later when she finally accessed Pearl's other accounts and sent him the money . . . plus a bonus. Until then, she needed him. And she needed Berta. She hoped Pearl had enough reserves for both their fees.

Charlotte entered Berta's number into the cell phone.

"Hello?" Berta answered.

"Good day, Ma'am," Charlotte said. "This is *Knit and Crochet Magazine*, and we're conducting random satisfaction surveys to better serve our customers. Your name came up on our list. Do you have time to answer a quick survey?"

"Oh, deary. I don't have time for a survey right now. But if you call me in about fifteen minutes, I'll be back home and free to talk then."

"Thank you, Ma'am. You have a nice day." Charlotte ended the call and slipped the phone inside her pocket. Fifteen minutes. Just enough time to touch up her Berta makeup and gather the gear she'd need. She placed the gas can near the garage door and headed inside the house.

34

BERTA

BERTA WAITED in her car for Chief Walker and his law enforcement entourage to drive away before she headed back inside the building. She'd agreed to take the rest of the day off. Not only because of her "cold," but because they wanted her to stay away from the store. At least for one day. Just to be safe. Their report was finished, and the police helped her straighten up before they left, but she'd managed most of the mess clean-up on her own.

She reentered the office and knelt in front of the safe, the heavy thing now returned to its normal place in the closet. Berta used the code and key to open the lid, relieved to find the collection of *Gilly Heel* books still safe in their hideaway. The first book, the one with Pearl's inscription, was at the top of the pile. She brushed her fingers over the front cover. The plan could still work. Yes, there were tricky spots. But she'd make it pay off. Anything to keep the store open.

After relocking the building, Berta drove her car out of the parking lot. She spotted Mason Trent walking up the far end of Main Street. As she passed by, he didn't look up and instead kept his gaze on the sidewalk, watching his steps. It was odd to see him there during the day. She wondered why he wasn't at school, but Berta dismissed her curiosity. There wasn't time to worry about Mason

Trent's whereabouts. When she finally pulled into her garage, she scanned the street for nosy onlookers before closing the big metal door.

"What have you been doing?" Berta stopped at the pile of clothing near her hall closet. "And why is it so dark in here?"

Charlotte leaned out from the kitchen doorway. "I'm not taking any chances."

"You can turn on a light or two, you know," Berta said, squinting in the dim light. She'd forgotten how odd Charlotte looked in her "Berta" makeup, and in disgust, flipped a nearby wall switch. The pale, overhead light didn't help. It was like looking into a mirror with a twisted sense of humor. The mirror, not Berta. *She* didn't think any of this was funny.

"I have a new plan," Charlotte said. She held up the storage unit key. "I'll fill you in."

"Oh, gravy," Berta said. "There's an old truck in there that doesn't work. Blown engine. And a snowmobile that's been sitting there for years. Not sure if it'll even run anymore. It'll need at least a tank of gas and a battery. At least."

"Then let's get it some."

Berta glanced down at her handbag. "You realize, deary, that I'm keeping tabs on your extra expenditures. Purchases are adding up."

"I know. I'm keeping track, too." Charlotte smiled through her powdered wrinkles.

Berta's expression softened. "Well, okay then. Glad we understand each other. Now, let's figure this out." Berta took the key from Charlotte's hand. "You'll need a few things."

Just as they headed for the garage, Berta's phone rang. She glanced at it. Chief Walker was calling her.

"Who is it?" Charlotte asked.

Berta shook her head. "Someone who worries too much. It's fine. Voicemail will get it." She didn't have any answers for him anyway. "Let's go."

35

MASON

HE STOOD, awkward and unsure of himself, on the corner near Fuller's Drug Store, mainly because Mason didn't know where else to go. Drawing out a person of interest from hiding wasn't his normal routine. Nor did he possess any clue how to accomplish the task, except it probably wasn't as easy as wearing a sandwich board stating: *Hey, Charlotte Evers. Turn yourself in. Not sure how? Ask me.* He mentally filed that plan away under *desperate measures*.

There was always social media, and he could post and tag his location. Sure, he'd end up saying something stupid like, *Hey, people. Right now. Human bait at the drug store.* But, in reality, that kind of post would blend in with the rest of the online incoherent junk. Plus, Charlotte didn't seem like the kind of person to check a feed.

Mason walked past the drug store, not bothering to glance through the window at Bill Fuller. He assumed eccentric Bill knew how to get attention, but it was better not to ask. Bill would suggest running up and down the street screaming like a madman while waving his arms. That would attract a few odd looks. But not much else. And Bill would most likely video it for his vlog, the whole time amused at Mason's expense.

Maybe Charlotte would simply approach him seeking help, and

he needed to be patient. Like when a person gets lost in the woods and experts say it's best to hold still, wait it out. Let the rescuers find you.

But *waiting* sounded harder than being "the bait."

Mason wandered up the street to the bookstore, noticing how dark and empty it looked. By now, the police were back at the station—all concentrating on a burglary and a man hunt, and they were unlikely to notice his absence. He kicked at the snow near the curb and plopped himself down on the red-painted line. If he was lucky, Charlotte would show up before his jeans froze to the cement.

Fifteen minutes passed. The snow plow drove by. Then a few cars and a utility truck.

Mason rested his head against his fist, propping his elbow up by his knee. After a few more minutes, his butt felt numb. He stared down at his sneakers, listening to the mundane sounds of Harding, and groaned. Epic fail. He had no idea what he was doing.

A block north, someone pulled into the gas station. Out of habit, he glanced at the faded Buick parked near the pump. Berta Sheppard stepped out of the driver's seat and headed into the building.

Mason squinted to get a better look, puzzled to see her outside the bookstore. He glanced behind him at the *closed* sign hanging in the display window, then he studied her car again. Maybe, the shock of a burglary was too much for her. Selling books was now a dangerous occupation.

Moments later, Berta emerged from the building carrying her purse in one hand and something black and heavy in the other. She opened the front passenger door and placed the heavy item on the seat, buckling it in with the shoulder strap. Then she hurried to the driver's side and started the engine.

Mason knew Berta Sheppard was an odd lady, but buckling an object into a seat as if a person? That was a first. He wondered why she didn't set the dumb thing on her backseat, or on a floor mat, or even in the trunk. What was she up to? *Weird old lady.*

He stood from the curb.

Berta drove south from the gas station, passing Mason without looking at him or her bookstore. Another oddity. She drove by too quick for him to recognize the black object in the front, and instead he noticed a pile of soft, dark fabric covering the back seat—blankets or coats or something big.

The car headed down the street at a casual speed. About a block away, a second person popped up from under the fabric, glanced around, then laid down again. Mason squinted, unsure what just happened. For a moment, he thought there were two gray haired women in the car. To be specific—two Berta Sheppards.

He rubbed his eyes and stared, hoping to catch another glimpse before she was too far away, but the Buick turned onto a side road. His instincts kicked in. Mason half-sprinted, half-slid across the street, heading for the gas station.

Without slowing, he whipped open the glass door.

"Whoa! Mason, what the hell?" Ed stood by the soda machine, filling himself a forty-two-ounce mug.

"What did Berta buy?" Mason asked. He searched behind the counter for the tow truck keys.

"A battery."

"For what?"

"A snowmobile. She asked me what kind of battery she needed to make an old one work. If I remember right, she has one at the barn storage place. I got her a battery from the back and the right oil. She'd forgotten that part. People always forget to check the oil. See, I tried to explain to Berta the proper maintenance required for a—"

"Thanks," Mason said. "I'm using the truck. Someone needs a tow."

"Wait, what?" Ed's soda overflowed down his hand. "Craphead!"

"I'll be right back." Mason bolted for the door while his boss juggled against the spill. He ran for the truck and climbed inside the cab before Ed could do anything.

He pulled away from the gas station and drove toward the old barn. The place wasn't too far, about five miles out between two large potato farms, and he'd been there a few times with the tow truck. It was plain, not much to look at. And this time of year, the whole southern side of Harding was nothing but scattered farm houses, pine trees near the road, and white-coated fields stretching to bordering mountains.

He followed Berta's fresh tire marks in the snow—no one had plowed the road since the last storm—and spotted the old brown barn with its warped wood slats and metal roof. Berta's car had been parked near the third bolted door, the second to last storage slot away from the road, and she was walking the hinges open until the door propped against a snow pile.

Mason parked next to her car and hopped out.

"What are you doing here?" she asked.

He expected Berta to be irritated, since that was her normal state, but she surprised him. Her tone asked the question soft and shaky, as if she wasn't expecting to see anyone and unsure how to handle Mason's presence. She sounded . . . panicked.

"I . . ."

"Did you follow me?" she asked.

His words caught in his throat. Why *did* he follow her? *Worst human bait ever.*

She glanced behind him at the tow truck. "What's your business here, Mason?"

"Who's with you?" he asked.

"What makes you think I brought someone?" Berta stepped closer to the barn and positioned herself between Mason and the opening. "I'm just checking on my belongings."

"And going for a ride? On your old snowmobile? That's weird."

"Why?" she asked.

"The timing. Because of the break-in at your store."

"How did you—"

"I've been at the police station. I heard stuff." He leaned left to peer over her shoulder, toward the dark interior of the barn. She mimicked his lean to block him.

"Or you were the one who broke in," she said. "Do you have an alibi for every second of this morning?"

He squinted at her, tightening his jaw. "Where is she?"

"Who?" Berta asked.

"The other *you*."

"That makes no sense."

"It does." He maneuvered past her and entered the unit. A far window lit the interior, lighting the scattered items that were covered in dust and cobwebs. In the middle, crouching low near a snowmobile was the other "Berta." The woman's hair was short, gray, and helmet-like, and she wore heavy, out-of-style winter clothing that could have come from Berta's closet. But even with the thick layer of smudged age-makeup on her face, he knew her name.

"Charlotte," Mason said.

The woman looked up from installing the fresh battery. "Mason."

"Why are you still here?"

She stood, grimacing a little as she straightened. "Leaving proved complicated. I'm still working on it."

"But I gave you time. I gave you a chance," he said.

"And I'm grateful."

"They don't believe me." He moved next to her. Berta slipped in behind him.

"The police?" Charlotte asked.

"Yeah. This detective came from St. George. They found Pearl Sanford's body down there. I believed you about the ashes in the urn. But now, Walker doesn't believe me. So, explain it. How can your dead grandma be in two places at once?"

Charlotte sat down on the snowmobile. "That can't be." She shook her head. "A St. George detective said he found her body? That's not possible."

"Of course, it's not possible," Berta said, pointing at Mason. "Because Pearl Sanford is in an urn in Idaho. And Charlotte didn't kill her. And apparently, you were helping Charlotte earlier. And I'm helping Charlotte now. And the detective is an irritating man. So there, for once, we're all caught up and telling the full truth." She straightened up. "At least, most of the truth . . . to the people in this barn . . . which . . . such omissions should probably stay in this barn. Outsiders wouldn't understand."

Mason glanced at both of them and wrinkled his nose. "Like a circle of trust?"

"Exactly," Berta said.

Charlotte didn't respond. She simply leaned forward over her knees, bracing one hand on her sore left side and stared at the dirt floor.

"Look," Mason said, crouching low to be at Charlotte's level. "This whole thing is crappy. We tried it your way and it didn't work. Now let's try mine. I know you're tired of running. Even though that's all you know how to do. I get it. When I told you that I left someone behind, I did—my dad. He's in prison. And I nearly died as a kid because of his stupid choices. So, I understand wanting to run away. But . . . sometimes things are bigger than we can handle on our own. And I can't believe I'm saying this, but we don't need to hold back secrets. Not right now. We've tried that already, and we suck at it. Charlotte, you need to turn yourself in. Go to Chief Walker and tell him everything. All of it. Talking will feel like hell at first, but he'll help you. It'll get better."

"It's not that simple," Charlotte said.

"Why not? Berta has helped you. So have I. I've even seen photos of the urn and wrist watch you wanted me to collect. The watch is old and falling apart. But I think it's worth more to you than the money and IDs. Why? There has to be a reason. Tell them. They'll understand." Mason hoped he was getting through to her.

She glanced at him, then at Berta.

"Please, Charlotte," Mason said. "If it comes down to forming a circle of trust in this barn, then we will. But let Chief Walker in on it."

Berta waved her hands. "Wait, wait. Slow down. Mason, you might be right. But let's not be too hasty." She turned to Charlotte. "Let's get you out of town first, deary. You can leave a statement behind. We'll make sure Walker gets it."

Mason stood. "No. She needs to turn herself in."

"But we have a deal," Berta said, fisting her hands against her hips. "She needs to leave Harding. Look, kid. I'm concerned for Charlotte too, but I also need to keep my bookstore open and our arrangement will help me do that. You're not the only one with worries."

"What's your arrangement?" he asked.

Berta folded her arms. "It's complicated."

"Things don't have to be! We can fix this whole mess," he said, then turned to Charlotte. "Say something!"

Charlotte shifted over the snowmobile, taking a riding position. She put a backpack over her wool coat and adjusted her gloves and hood. "Mason, we are not the same. I wish my mess was fixable," she said. "But if there's a detective up from St. George to find me, then it's nothing but complicated. Berta, I'll still honor our deal. And Mason, as soon as I'm gone, it'll get back to the way it was before. You'll be okay."

She turned the key on the snowmobile. The engine sputtered and shook, taking several seconds to rev into life.

"No more running!" Mason shouted over the noise, a warmth of anger flushing into his chilled face. "I didn't go through all this for nothing!"

"I'm sorry!" she said.

The snowmobile drove sluggish over the dirt floor. Mason tried to block her path, but Charlotte jolted passed him before he could do much. Once the sled caught the snow, it took off. Mason chased after it for a few steps, but he slid to a halt. There was no way to stop her. Frustration, anger, and panic all roasted inside him at once.

"She'll be fine, I know it," Berta said. "Right? I mean . . . it's dangerous, but . . . she'll be fine . . . I hope." Worry lines formed above her eyes.

"No, she won't. And she's too stubborn to know it." Mason headed for the tow truck. He jumped in just as Berta reached the passenger door.

"Wait . . . I'm coming, too!" she said, hoisting herself onto the seat. "Does this beast handle off-road? We'll make sure she finds the trails. Put your seat belt on, kid."

"I'm stopping her."

"Now, hang on just a—"

Mason put the truck in reverse and floored the gas pedal. The tow truck lurched back and slid out onto the road in one fast jolt. Next to him, Berta grabbed the dashboard. He shifted again and cranked the steering wheel hard, fighting to keep control as the truck's tires spun forward in the snow.

"You'll never catch her," she said.

"I have to." Mason speed along the road. He kept glancing across the potato fields at Charlotte's dark outline against the white backdrop, tracking her movements. She turned right toward the East Hills, heading away from them. He spotted the markings for a side road and cranked the wheel.

"Too fast!" Berta shouted.

Mason pressed the brake and corrected the turn, but the truck slid sideways into a fishtail.

"Hang on!" he said, turning the front wheels to counter the slide. They shifted wide in a one-eighty, just as Mason pressed the gas. He pounded the wheel, his hands moving fast in full panic.

"You're going to kill us!" Berta said, flailing around to brace herself.

In that second, Mason believed her. The truck spun loose in the snow—full control gone.

Berta released a gut-wrenching scream. "The ditch!"

The truck sailed wildly, the tires reeling over the side of a hidden borrow pit and up a slight incline. They tilted quick on the edge, then crashed nose-first into a five-foot-deep drainage ditch on the other side. Mason jostled like a bobble head, bouncing forward inside the cab until he felt the truck's tires crack into the ice layer under the snow. Then the truck stopped dead. Mason fell against the steering wheel. His knees and hands jammed against the dashboard. Pain pounded into his joints.

Everything went quiet.

Mason pushed himself back onto the seat, breathing hard. A wave of motion sickness invaded his stomach and spun his view.

"Oh . . . good nothings," Berta said under her breath.

"Are you okay?" Mason asked. He glanced over at her.

She blank-stared out the front window while knuckling the dashboard in a death grip, her seatbelt still holding her tight.

"Berta?" he repeated. "Are you freaking out on the inside?"

"Freaking out? Maybe," she mumbled. "Teenagers drive too fast."

"Uh-huh," he said and nodded.

"You should have buckled up. I remember saying it."

Mason's hands and knees ached. "Yeah."

This time, she nodded in agreement.

They fumbled with the door handles. Mason leaned out the opening and fell into the snow, flopping onto his back. He stared at the sky and tried to catch his breath. Above him, the truck's loose tow cable swung back and forth. Sudden panic replaced his motion sickness. He'd just wedged Harding's only tow truck into a ditch. Ed was going to kill him.

36

WALKER

"Berta! Can you hear me?" Walker said. He rang Berta's doorbell for the third time, pressing the button into a long, drawn-out buzz. The house's dark interior wasn't promising, and her cell phone went straight to voicemail, again. Berta had been so tight-lipped inside the bookstore that he'd regretted letting her go without an explanation for her odd behavior. Something was wrong. Red flags were going off in his mind like firecrackers. He headed for the garage and peered into a side window. The car was gone.

"Dispatch, Bravo-One," he said into his shoulder mic. "Will you give me a 10-21."

"Copy," Kim responded.

His cell phone rang.

"Kim?"

"Yes, Chief. How can I help you?"

"Let everybody know the make and color of Berta Sheppard's car. We're looking for her . . . again. Welfare check."

"Sure."

"Anyone spot Mason Trent yet?"

"No, Franklin's still on it. Jan found Mason's cell phone at the front desk. Franklin talked to Ed at the gas station. Apparently, Mason took the tow truck right after he asked about Berta's recent purchase. Turns out, Berta bought a snowmobile battery."

Walker ran for his truck. "Do you still have that list of snowmobile owners?"

"Most of it."

"Is Berta on it?" Walker got inside and pulled out of Berta's driveway.

"Yep, Chief. One was registered to her about ten years ago, but the tags lapsed."

He peeled away in the snow. "Understood. I'm heading out. Tell Franklin to meet me at the old barn."

"Copy, Chief." Kim hung up.

Walker steadied his nerves, his mind racing. Berta didn't have a sled in her garage. That left one place for storage. And there was only one reason why she needed to get an old junk snowmobile working on the same day he wrote up a police report for her store. Berta and Charlotte were probably together. He'd had his suspicions. But what wasn't clear, and what worried him the most, was whether Berta was helping Charlotte voluntarily or against her will.

"Bravo-Three, Bravo-One," he said into his radio.

"This is Bravo-Three," Kemp answered.

"Are you still knocking on doors?"

"Yes," Kemp said.

"You and Stewart go to Berta Sheppard's house for a welfare check and clear it."

"Do you have reason to believe she's in distress?" he asked.

"Today, I do."

"On our way."

Walker left the main part of town and headed south on the side road, passing several snow-coated farm fields. He tunnel-visioned on the old barn in the distance. His knuckles tightened on the steering wheel, questions and demands and frustration feeding his anger.

About a half mile away from the barn, he noticed the dark outline in a nearby field. Metal beams stuck up over the edge of a drainage ditch. Walker slowed when he reached the side road and recognized the dark shape perched in the snow—the back end of Ed's tow truck. Dread pitted in his stomach.

He parked next to the ditch, then bolted from his vehicle and ran to the edge. Mason lay on his back in the snow, just past the front end of the truck.

"Mason!" Walker yelled, sliding down the side. He jumped through the snow and stood over the kid, trying to assess his injuries.

"Chief?" Mason sat up.

"Are you okay, kid?"

"He's fine," Berta said, shooing her hand at Mason as she reclined against the truck. "Now, if he'd been wearing his seatbelt like me, he wouldn't be in pain right now. Or sick to his stomach."

Walker stood between them, glancing at Mason before turning to Berta in disbelief. He rubbed his fingers over his forehead and spoke fast. "Berta, how in the world did you end up in a ditch with Mason? And both of you . . . how did the truck end up in the ditch in the first place? And how in the hell am I supposed to get this thing out of here without a working tow truck? The next wrecker is hours away. And where is the snowmobile? And where is Charlotte Evers? Tell me what's going on right now!"

Mason stared down at the ground.

"Terry, are you alright?" Berta asked. "You seemed freaked out."

"What?" he said, shaking his head.

She glanced at Mason. "Was that the correct usage of 'freaked'?"

Mason nodded. "Yeah, but I think we're all a little freaked out. Not just him."

"Everybody . . . just . . . stop." Walker glanced up at the red and blue flashing lights in the distance. He spoke into his radio to Franklin. "Bravo-Two, down-grade your lights. Slow down before you wreck in the snow. Keep going to the barn and check it out."

"Copy," Franklin responded, his voice sharp.

Walker helped both Mason and Berta to their feet. "First off, are you both okay? Any injuries? Do you need EMS?"

"No," Mason said.

"Clarify, kid."

"I mean, yes, we're okay. No, we don't need EMS. And if you could wait to tell Ed and my mom about this, that would be—"

"Mason," Walker said. "You're not in a position to ask for favors. In fact, I'm giving you one last chance, right this second, to tell me where Charlotte Evers is. And if either of you say the words *I don't know*, we have a problem. It's called interfering with a police investigation, and you've already crossed that line with me."

Berta stared at Mason, then looked back at Walker. "What if we say we're freezing and hungry? What does that get us?"

Walker's anger swelled. "Berta!"

"She's on a snowmobile heading for the East Hills," Mason said.

"Oh, Mason!" Berta swatted him with her glove. "Now he's thinking all kinds of bad things about our actions. There's so much more to the story than that, Terry. We've been helping, not hurting things. And if you could only talk to Charlotte, you'd see—"

"I'm trying to talk to her!" Walker yelled. "I'm trying to get her back into custody. And we don't have time to discuss my job objectives right now."

"But, Terry!"

Walker gripped his duty belt. "You two go sit in the backseat of my truck. We'll worry about the tow truck later . . . *if* we ever find a moment of sanity in this town."

"Yes, sir," Mason said, reaching out to help Berta climb the snow piles.

Walker grabbed his mic and leaned on the tow truck to steady himself. "Dispatch, Bravo-One."

Kim's voice crackled over the radio. "Go ahead."

"The POI is reported to be on a snowmobile heading northeast across the southern farm fields. She may be aiming for the trails. Dispatch, I want you to coordinate with the sled riders in Search and Rescue, and those assisting from other agencies. We're focusing our efforts on the East Hills."

"Copy," Kim said.

Walker let go of the tow truck, inhaling deep. The refill of cold air stung at his lungs, but he welcomed the release. He needed it to calm down.

His cell phone rang.

"Go ahead," Walker answered.

"Chief?" Franklin said. "Berta's car is at the barn, and it's obvious someone worked on a snowmobile. But no one's here."

"Thanks, lock it up." He adjusted his coat and climbed the ditch wall. Berta and Mason sat in the backseat of his police truck, both staring forward at the plastic partition that separated them from the front. They didn't make eye contact as he approached.

Walker opened the supply pack under his front passenger seat and grabbed two small pouches, each containing a folded, silver emergency blanket. He handed them to Berta and Mason before closing their rear doors. By the time he sat in the driver's seat and started the engine, they had wrapped themselves in the blankets and looked like two oversized tin foil-wrapped baked potatoes.

Berta's bottom lip shivered. "Are we being arrested?"

"Should you be?" Walker said, cranking up the heater. "Tell me what you've been up to the last couple days and I'll let you know."

"Don't joke with me, Terry," she said. "I was in a tow truck accident."

He noticed that Mason was just staring out the window.

"Berta." Walker spoke quick and sharp. "Let's get something clear. I've been worried about the two of you, thinking you were in danger and that I'd find you lying in a ditch somewhere. Turns out, I literally just did. We've hit rock bottom. If you keep secrets from me, I can't help you. We're on the same side here. Berta, I've been coming to your bookstore since I was barely able to read. We both have Harding blood. Our families have been here for generations. You know me. And Mason, your mom and I were kids together. So, let me help you. Both of you. Stop assuming I'm your enemy."

They sat in silence for a moment. He hoped his plea was sinking in.

"You used to prank my store," Berta said, her voice sounding calm but serious.

Walker felt like someone had just thrown a rock at his chest.

"Or have you forgotten that part of your *nostalgic childhood*? Maybe you wanted to impress your friends, or maybe be part of the group, I don't know. But I do know it was to annoy my parents. Be mean to them for your own fun. You didn't care about them at all. The problem went on for years. Yes, we are both Harding people. But that doesn't mean I trust you to help me."

He sighed, hard. "That was a long time ago."

"Not to me."

Walker shook his head.

"What did he do?" Mason asked.

They both stared at him.

"Uh," Berta shrugged. "Well, egged us mostly. But there were the bags of dog poo, the spray paint, the stolen flower pots, and a lot of things that I had to clean up." She looked at Walker. "You never got in trouble because your dad was the mayor. And let's not forget the time you stole a book. A book, Terry! How could you!"

"Now hang on, Freddy Hollis stole the book."

"Still. You were with him. I remember we finally called Chief Bedford to get it to stop. But you never got in trouble."

Walker rubbed his face. This wasn't going the way he'd planned. "Berta, I *did* get in trouble. The Chief told me that I had to shape up. He made me do volunteer work at the police station for a year. Every weekday after school. Why do you think I became a police officer? I started to like being there. And the work."

She looked away.

"I was a teenager. I was young and stupid. I haven't been that person for a long time. But I am the same kind of person I was three days ago before Charlotte Evers came to Harding. I want things to go back to normal. Please, let me help you."

"You have to help her, too," Mason said.

"What?" Walker stared at him.

"Charlotte's an outsider. Well, so am I. I'm not from here. But who cares? She needs your help, too. And . . . no one in this car is the same kind of person they were three days ago. Charlotte's changed that."

Walker's thoughts came to a full stop. He turned forward in his chair, staring out the front windshield. "I have to follow the evidence, kid. I have a job to do."

"So do we," Berta said.

"That doesn't make any sense." Walker reversed his car in the snow, then shifted into drive and gave it some gas. "Your job is the bookstore. Always has been. I don't suppose you know who broke in this morning?"

"No," she said. "And why do we have to leave my car at the barn?"

"We'll get it later." In truth, he didn't want her to disappear again.

The radio crackled. "Bravo-One, Bravo-Three. Can you 10-21?"

"Affirmative."

Kemp called his cell phone. Walker put it on speaker while he drove. "We cleared Berta Sheppard's house. Didn't find her, but there was a bunch of odd stuff in her bathroom. Piles of hair. Strange make-up. Does Berta dye her hair gray?"

"What are they doing in my house!" Berta pounded on the partition.

"We had to make sure you weren't dead, Berta!" Walker yelled.

"I wasn't dead! I was lying in a ditch. And he put me there." She pointed at Mason.

"I didn't mean to!" Mason shouted.

Walker groaned. "Everyone, calm down. We're going to the station so I can coordinate with the search. And you both are going to make an official statement—about everything. Including how the accident happened. We're not done with that."

"Fine," Berta said in a huff.

Mason put up his hood. "Whatever."

"Perfect." Walker turned back to his phone. "Kemp and Stewart, do a sweep of the east side of town. Let's intercept Evers before she makes it to the hills."

"Copy, Chief," Kemp said.

Walker made another phone call. "Kim, let the assisting agencies know that Charlotte Evers may have altered her appearance. She may now resemble an elderly woman in her seventies—short hair, gray color, age makeup."

"Age makeup?" Kim said. "Copy, Chief, be on the lookout for helmet hair and wrinkles?"

"I wouldn't use those words, but yes. That's affirmative. But be aware, I've already found Berta Sheppard. I don't want confusion."

"I'll let them know," she said.

Walker glanced in his rearview mirror and caught Berta grumbling in the back seat.

37

MASON

MASON STARED out the window for the entire silent, and very awkward, drive back to the police station. He didn't know how to feel about Walker anymore. Turns out the guy had his own mailbox bashing past, and Mason couldn't decide if he was pissed off about it or if the guy seemed more normal.

The chief had spoken over his radio a handful of times, mostly checking-in with his officers and with the Search and Rescue snowmobilers. If it wasn't for the two citizens in his police truck, Mason was sure Walker would've been out leading the search himself. Instead, the chief was driving two wet, shivering, achy, and somewhat foolish accident victims back into town. In other words, he was babysitting them. He had to be annoyed. Keeping quiet seemed like the easiest way for Mason to handle the drive.

They turned the final corner toward the station, and Mason wondered if his mom was pacing inside the building. By now, she'd know something was wrong. No question. He checked his red and swollen palms and assumed that his kneecaps looked as raw. With his bad luck, there was probably a steering wheel mark embedded in his chest—a kind of stupidity branding. Everything ached. Especially his pride.

"Are you sure you're okay, deary?" Berta asked.

Mason glanced up, hiding his swollen hands inside his coat pockets. "I'm fine. Just . . . worried."

"About what?"

"Everything."

She nodded. "Me, too."

They pulled into the police station garage. Walker parked in an empty slot, then opened the rear door so Mason and Berta could climb out. The three of them didn't make eye contact.

"This way," he said.

Mason followed behind them, glancing at Jed as they headed down the hallway. Inside dispatch, his mom rushed forward, squeezing Mason in such a tight grip that he thought she'd never let go.

"I'm okay, Mom. Not hurt," he said, wincing a bit.

"When I heard about the tow truck, I just . . ." She hugged him even tighter.

"We're fine. But Ed's gonna be mad."

"You let me worry about him. Oh, sweetie. You're so cold." She examined his hands. "Are you sure you're alright?"

"Yeah."

"Have a seat," Walker said. He pointed to one of two folding chairs that had been placed near the dispatch desk and motioned for Berta and Mason to sit, waiting while both hung their soaked coats over the backs of the chairs.

"They need something warm to drink," Jan said. "Chief, do you have anything?"

"Nope, but I think Kim keeps some kind of herbal tea stuff in the break room. That might work. There's a couple emergency blankets in the closet next to the first aid supplies. Those'll be better than these silver things." He opened another folding chair.

"I'll get them," she said, hurrying into the other room.

Walker sat down across from Berta and Mason, then glanced at his phone.

Mason didn't know what to do. They were being . . . nice. Too nice.

He'd left the station without permission, failed to turn in Charlotte, and then crashed a tow truck. At what point was Walker going to put him back inside the jail cell, this time with the door closed and locked from the outside?

Chief Walker didn't look up, but simply typed on his phone and turned away to speak to Kim. Voices crackled over the dispatch line.

"Just play it cool, kid," Berta whispered.

"What?"

"Play it cool," she repeated. "Remember our barn circle of trust. We didn't get our story straight in the ditch, so follow my lead. Don't break under pressure. No squealing. You hear me?"

Mason shook his head, staring down at his knees. "This isn't a crime novel. You realize you're *outside* the bookstore, right, Berta?"

She huffed. "Of course. But . . . this is my first interrogation. The Harding police know to leave me alone. I live my life, they live theirs. And we all get along. I'm not sure what to do next. Remember, someone broke into my store today. I'm a little . . . *off my routine.*"

"It's not an interrogation. Besides, we're all off. Just be . . . Berta. Not Frankie the Squid."

"Is that a real person?"

"I have no idea."

Walker flipped around in his chair. "Okay, you two. We'll take a full official statement later today when I get back. I want it recorded. In the meantime, I want direct answers to the following questions."

They both nodded.

"Where has Charlotte Evers been since she left the hospital?" he asked.

"At my house," Berta said. "It's a long story. One that . . . uh, well, . . . I'll tell later during my recorded statement. Not till then."

"I see." Walker turned to Mason. "Why did you leave the police station and get the tow truck?"

"I was trying to be human bait . . . but it didn't work. Charlotte couldn't turn herself in. The tow truck part was an accident."

"Uh-huh."

Jan came in with two steaming mugs and a couple blankets.

"Oh, thank you," Berta said as she took the hot cup by the handle. "Terry, this has been a pleasant interrogation. Best one I've ever attended. Makes me want to tell the whole truth."

"Really?" he said, folding his arms.

"Yes. Which is why you should know that Charlotte is innocent. She didn't kill Pearl Sanford. And those ashes belong to Pearl."

Walker stood. "That's not possible."

"I agree," Mason said.

Berta glanced at him, squinting her eyes. "What?"

He felt a sudden chill race down his spine. "No, wait. I mean . . . I agree with Berta. Charlotte is innocent. She didn't kill Pearl. No way. And when Charlotte tells her side of things, you'll know the full story."

"Exactly," Berta said. "I don't care what that St. George detective said about finding Pearl's body. Charlotte is innocent. She couldn't hurt anyone."

"Fine. You need to hear it yourself, do you?" Walker turned to Kim. "Call Peterson's cell phone. Get him in here. Tell him there are two Harding citizens who need the hard facts explained to them."

"Yes, Chief," Kim said.

Walker returned to his chair, his expression stern. "Look," he said, leaning forward to rest his elbows on his knees. "There's something I need you both to understand. Whatever Charlotte Evers did or didn't do before she came to Harding are events that St. George P.D. are investigating. She's a person of interest in Pearl's death, and she was found in Pearl's car. In *our* town. That puts Harding in the middle of the mess. But it's St. George P.D.'s case. We're assisting them with their person of interest. So, we processed the car as requested, but my job is about what happened *after* she got here. Then getting her back to them. In Harding, Charlotte evaded police, escaped custody, and needs to be located for questioning in a homicide investigation. You're saying that she didn't kill anyone, and maybe that's true . . . but I don't get to decide that and neither do you. The county judge has just issued an arrest warrant for the charges she's facing in Harding."

"An arrest warrant?" Berta said.

"Charlotte has dug herself quite a sink hole."

Mason felt numb, and not from the cold left on his skin. He leaned back in his chair. "What about needing her belongings from the evidence closet? If she is so guilty, why did she want them so much?"

"I'm not sure," Walker said. "Peterson might have those answers."

Kim waved her hand to get their attention. "I've tried Peterson's cell phone five times. No answer."

Walker retrieved his own cell phone and walked out the doorway.

"This is all overwhelming," Jan said, examining Mason's hands again. "You both should be checked out in the ER. I can have you back before Walker needs to record the statements. Does it hurt anywhere?"

Mason shook his head. He was sore from the accident, but knew it wasn't an emergency. Berta seemed fine. If she was injured, no doubt they'd all hear about it.

"The tea helps. Not cold anymore," he said, forcing a smile.

"That's good," Jan said. "Tomorrow you'll have some bruising where your seatbelt held you in. So glad you were smart enough to wear it."

"Oh, wait a minute." Berta lowered her mug. "As his mother, there's something you should know about that."

38

WALKER

WALKER LEANED his back against the wall outside of dispatch, listening as the call went to Peterson's voicemail. Not to a recorded message, but to the factory automated recording saying the user's voicemail box hadn't been set up yet. He stared down at his phone. A heat radiated in his face and forehead. First Berta and now Peterson. Why didn't anyone answer their cell phone when he called? He couldn't even leave a voicemail this time.

Walker returned to the room. "Peterson isn't answering. Mason, he interviewed you this afternoon, correct?"

"No. I've never met him," he said.

"Be honest."

"I am. I've never met him."

"How is that possible? Peterson was at the station this morning to talk to you. You weren't here. After he left the bookstore scene, he was coming straight back to try to interview you again."

"Never saw him," Mason repeated, leaning forward in his chair. "And I was here until the afternoon. Then I left."

"You were here the whole time?"

Mason stared at the floor.

"Mason?" Walker said.

"Okay. I did leave for a little bit this morning. Your vending machine food is ancient. I know I was supposed to stay at the station, but after my mom left for the hospital, I went to Angel's Cafe for breakfast. I was gone for about fifteen minutes. No big deal."

"Mason!" Jan said. "I asked you to stay put. To stay safe."

Berta snorted. "Wait till he tells you about the human bait part of the story."

"We don't have time for this," Walker said, scrolling on his cell phone. "Kim, inform everybody that we're keeping an eye out for Detective Peterson. I need to speak with him."

"Yes, Chief," she replied.

Walker moved into the hallway again, tuning out as Jan lectured her son regarding instructions and questioning what "human bait" meant. He made another call.

"This is Chief Redding," a voice answered.

"Hey, this is Chief Walker from Harding. I'm trying to get a hold of Detective Peterson, but he's not answering. I keep missing him. He might not know his way around up here. I'm wondering if he's checked in with you today, and if you can answer a couple questions about the homicide investigation regarding Pearl Sanford."

"The homicide investigation?" Redding asked.

"Yes, I want Peterson to interview two Harding citizens, but I can't find him right now. I don't have time to wait. Can I verify a couple things with you? And when he checks in, will you ask Peterson if he'll meet me at the station?"

"In Harding? Chief Walker, I'm a little confused. Hang on a second," he said, speaking away from the phone without putting the line on hold.

Walker heard mumbles over the line, mostly Redding and another man discussing a matter in tones too low to catch.

"Chief Walker?" a new voice answered. "This is Detective Peterson. I want to apologize for not getting back to you earlier. We've been swamped. Now, tell me, what makes you think the Sanford disappearance is a homicide case? Has the person of interest in the hospital, let's see here . . ." The phone fumbled for a few seconds, ". . .

um . . . has . . . the woman using the name *Charlotte Evers* given any new information regarding the elderly woman's location?"

Walker's thoughts stopped, as if they hit a brick wall and plummeting into a huge pit in his stomach. His mouth dried up, his next words sticking in his throat. "Wait . . . I need . . . clarification."

"So do I," the detective said.

"You're Detective Peterson?"

"Yes."

"The person who's been handling Sanford's missing persons case?"

"Um, yes."

"And you are in St. George right now?"

"Yes. Chief," the detective said. "Like I stated, sorry about not calling you yet. We've been busy doing—"

"Wait, you're Peterson? Is there only one?"

"Chief, this isn't funny—"

"No. It isn't. Let me talk to Redding again, please." He waited while the phone shuffled in the room. Walker tried to steady his adrenaline, but he felt like punching the wall, or at least pacing and cursing and wishing it was professional to pound a sledge hammer into a fire door. He took a steadying breath.

"Chief," Redding said, coming back on the line. "What's going on up there?"

"Well, I've got a guy, showed up yesterday, says he's Detective Peterson from St. George P.D. and has a badge. Didn't see credentials, but didn't ask. He talked the talk—St. George P.D. all the way. Mentioned that you sent him up to us. Knew the case and particulars. Knew all about Charlotte Evers. Said you guys found Pearl Sanford's body and needed Evers returned to Utah. Only . . . he's not your guy. And he's loose in my town somewhere."

"That can't be," Redding said. "Peterson is standing right next to me. Why would someone impersonate him? And we never found a body. We wanted you to search the car under probable cause since she ran from your traffic stop, suspecting you might find one. I read through your update. Except for the urn on the item list, which has yet to be processed, we don't have human remains. I know Charlotte told you she 'burned' Pearl, but like you said, that omission was under the influence of pain meds and isn't usable. A State Crime Lab will take time to even identify the urn's ashes as human, but it's not likely they'll get an ID at all, let alone as Pearl Sanford. On our end, we're still looking for Pearl."

"Okay. Right." Walker held the top of the cell phone to his forehead for a few seconds, giving himself a moment to decompress.

"Chief Walker?"

"Yes?"

"Best we can do right now is have the car and belongings shipped back to St. George. Evers can be charged with fake IDs and we're investigating her involvement in the missing persons case. There's a reason she was driving the Oldsmobile. It's suspicious. We'll prep the paperwork so we can get an official statement from her. Don't worry, we're going to find out how she's involved. Plus, we're working with Washington County Search and Rescue and our local hospital, just in case Pearl Sanford turns up somewhere."

"Okay. I've got to run with this new information. Let me know if you find the missing woman."

"Of course," Redding said. "And you let me know when you find the guy pretending to be my detective. That pisses me off like nothing else."

"Me too. And, hey, Redding, how would a guy from down there find out Evers was in Harding or that Detective Peterson was assigned the case?"

"Not sure. We did issue a Silver Alert. We used a security camera shot of Pearl Sanford, one we got from a local gas station, since we found no ID at her house. No DMV photo on record. So, we put the screen shot on the local news and online, along with a police number to reach Peterson if anyone had info. But we never mentioned that her car was found in Harding, Idaho."

"Thanks." Walker ended the call and headed into dispatch. He paced over to Kim, tunnel-visioned on the computer monitors and forgetting about the others in the room. His thoughts spun in multiple directions, trying to decipher the next logical step. He needed more of everything—more time to think, more answers, more manpower—to do his job. There wasn't enough. His small-town resources were stretched too thin. He was stretched too thin.

"Chief?" Kim stared at him. "Is everything okay?"

"No."

"What should we do next?"

Walker stared down at his dark cell phone. He didn't know what to do. But Harding was his responsibility. He had to figure it out. "I . . . uh . . . I want you to pull up this morning's security footage for the whole station. Track everything that fake Peterson did in this building since he got here."

"*Fake* Peterson?" she said.

"Yes. The real detective in still in St. George. This guy isn't him. Discreetly contact my officers and the assisting agencies to take Peterson into custody."

"Whoa," Mason said. "He stole a detective's identity?"

Walker turned. The others were staring at him.

Berta leaned forward. "That's much worse than what Mason and I did. Terry, by comparison—"

"Berta, that's not helping," Walker said.

"Right. Another time. But, why did this fake Peterson guy come to our town?"

"He must be looking for Charlotte," Mason said.

Berta shook her head. "But how did he know she was in Harding? I know this young lady pretty well now, and Charlotte didn't tell anyone where she was going."

"That's right." Mason nodded. "Charlotte's on the run. A person doesn't advertise that."

Walker wrung his hands. "There's no time for discussion. Kim, pull up the footage. Send a screen shot of the guy's face to Chief Redding in St. George."

"That's a lot of time recorded on a bunch of different cameras," Kim said. "It'll take me hours to go through it all while I also answer 911 calls. Everyone else is busy."

"I know, but we don't have a tech department. You're the only one left. I've got no one to do this. So . . . use Jed and . . ." Walker glanced at Berta, Mason, and Jan. He sighed, feeling defeated and desperate. "Can you three handle looking at footage? Just watching it like boring television and taking notes?"

They nodded.

Mason stood, glancing around the room. "I can hook up a few extra monitors to your laptops. We can get this done faster."

"You know how to do that?" Berta asked.

"Yep, it's easy. Don't you?"

"Well, if I—"

"No," Walker interrupted, clicking his fingers in recognition. His mind raced. "She doesn't know how. And she only has the one computer at the bookstore that she can barely use."

Berta frowned. "Terry, I don't see how berating me has any—"

"At the bookstore today, your computer was open to your browser history. You've been on some St. George websites," he said.

"Yes. But I left my computer on sleep or whatever. The thief must have used it and—"

"And," Walker hurried over and sat in the chair across from Berta, taking a quick moment to calm his voice. His heart pounded. "The truth. Were you communicating with someone on a website?"

She stared forward, her face stiff and her lips clenched tight. Then her jaw dropped and remorse shown in her eyes. "I talked to someone called *FamilyIsLife* on the St. George community page. But it was innocent. The person was one of Pearl's neighbors. Real concerned about her. I said I had some of Pearl's belongings and was trying to get in touch with a family member. I was only trying to find out information, Terry."

"Did you say you were from Harding, Idaho?" Walker asked.

Berta shook her head. "I didn't think . . . oh, land. Maybe. I was talking to him? Is this fake guy here because of me? So, Charlotte is in trouble because I blew her cover." She used the blanket to wipe the sudden tears in her eyes.

"Blew her cover?" Mason said, staring at Berta. "She not a spy. Well, probably not."

Walker stood and put on his coat. "Charlotte is in trouble because of herself. Now, I gotta go find her and fake Peterson." He held up his hands. "Please, everyone, stay in this room. That's an order. I've searched for you all too many times for one day, and if I have to, I'll handcuff you to the chairs. Kim is in charge. Watch the security footage to help out, and find what Peterson did all morning."

"Yes, Chief," Kim said. She eyed Berta and Mason.

Walker moved toward the door. "Kim, did you get in touch with my officers? Do they know about fake Peterson?"

"Yep. Sent out a text message instead of using the radio. It's quieter that way."

"Perfect. I'm heading for the trails." He hurried down the hallway to the back closet that held his all-weather gear. A minute later, he headed for his truck.

39

CHARLOTTE

CHARLOTTE STOPPED the snowmobile behind a group of trees at the south base of the East Hills, strategically placing herself and the sled under the thick pine branches. As she scanned the area for movement, she determined the temporary hiding place as sixty percent a threat, but at that point, probabilities were harder to calculate. Too many variables. Sounds of motorized vehicles echoed through the canyons, making it difficult to determine their point of origin.

From a safe distance, she studied the first trailhead marker labeled *Devil's Whip,* and the multiple snowmobile tracks leading in between the pine trees. As long as it didn't snow, her tracks could blend in. She glanced at the setting sun. Another advantage in her favor—darkness—plus, she'd guided herself by moonlight before. This time would be no different. Charlotte tightened the string around her hood, the freezing temperatures stinging at her nose and cheeks. She used her glove and a handful of snow to wipe the smudged "Berta" makeup off her face, drying afterward with her sleeve. Covering her skin would be easier without the layers of grease and powder. She then adjusted her goggles and pulled up the top of her turtle neck shirt, the one she'd gotten from Berta, until it covered her nose. Charlotte wished there'd been time to collect proper gear, but Berta's winter coat and snow pants were close enough.

For a moment, she wondered if Berta and Mason had made it back to town, hoping they didn't run into problems. A slight ache formed in her chest, and this time not from her sore muscles, but from a feeling that hadn't crossed her mind since her final day with Pearl. The odd sensation first took the form of *concern*, maybe even *worry*. Did she actually care about what happened to Berta and Mason?

She shook her head and forced a refocus. There wasn't time for attachments. From her sleeve, she retrieved the folded map Berta kept in her desk—a map of trails, hunting cabins, and roadways that only locals used. She studied the markings. Two separate canyons led through the mountains. The first was a paved roadway labeled *East Brick Pass*. Although, according to Berta, they closed that canyon in the winter. Logic deemed the pass too obvious a choice. A wide roadway meant nowhere to hide. The threat level was too high.

That left the other canyon, the one with a snow-covered dirt road called Devil's Whip, or the number of hiking trails stretching over the hills themselves. The trails seemed to connect in a spider web of winding pathways, confusing without a printed guide. On the other side of nearly fifteen miles of mountain range, there was a small town on the map called Angleton. She'd need to contact Zeus from there and arrange for a secluded pick-up. Charlotte slipped the folded map inside her sleeve, and for peace of mind, double-checked her right front pocket for the cell phone.

A motorized hum echoed over the trail, light at first then the sound grew. Charlotte slouched behind the thickest pine branch, grateful for the dark shade of her clothing and the faded paint on the snowmobile. She was hidden, but out of habit raised the threat level to eighty percent. Her fingers tightened on the accelerator.

The hum spun into a high-pitched buzz. A rider sped from the trailhead and slid across the snow at full speed. Then a second sled followed. Both men wore red Search and Rescue mesh vests over their winter gear, but Charlotte barely caught sight of their official markings before both snowmobiles were gone. With any luck, the sunset was forcing Search and Rescue to step aside for the night.

As soon as they were gone, Charlotte edged her way into the clearing, paranoia filling her with anxiety. The old snowmobile lurched over the powder, fighting against the climb. She ignored how her heart pounded wild against her rib cage. Each breath became short and labored. Charlotte maxed the speed, calculating how fast she could comfortably travel while still maintaining control of the sled. Green pines raced past in her peripheral view. She centered on the brilliant white snow, tunneling her focus on the trail.

Each time she navigated a curve, Charlotte felt the rush of caution mixed with a sliver of freedom. Chilled air whipped her skin inside the small spaces around her goggles and seeped through the turtle neck. Her nose and lips stung.

Within minutes, shadows covered the trail, until the setting sunlight couldn't reach through the canyon any longer. Charlotte felt tempted to turn on her headlight but decided against it. She slowed to a more manageable pace and studied the branching side trails that forked south toward East Brick Pass. Each trailhead had been marked by a small reflective circle stapled to a pole.

In the dark, a distant headlight moved toward her. Charlotte darted into a side trail and pulled behind a group of snow-coated trees. She turned off the engine and waited.

The other rider's engine hum reached her first—high-pitched, mechanical, climbing up the trail to her location. Then she felt the subtle vibrations in the snow, sending pins and needles through her cold extremities.

The snowmobile stopped abruptly at the fork in the trail. Charlotte heard rustling and crinkling, caused by paper perhaps or a map, then subtle, low thumping sounds as if the person walked around in the snow. Someone sniffled and coughed.

She held perfectly still, breathing slow through her mouth.

A cell phone rang.

"Ah, what now?" a man said. "I don't have time for this."

The phone rang a few more times.

Charlotte's heart pounded. Something about that voice sounded familiar, but she couldn't place it. Intense fear overshadowed her mind, the treat level jumping to one hundred percent. She fought every instinct telling her to run, and gripped the sled handles.

"Hey, Chief," the man said in the phone. "Look, I know I've missed your calls . . . I've been searching . . . sorry 'bout that, but . . . I can barely hear you. I think the connection is bad out here . . . No, I can't come back to the station right now. I'm close . . . but, Chief . . . Evers is out here somewhere . . . I know that, but I have a job to do . . . but this is official St. George P.D. business . . . I understand that, but she's on a trail right now . . . Devil's Whip. I'm on Devil's Whip . . . Yes, I know for sure! I have a map!"

Charlotte grit her teeth and scrunched the bridge of her nose, estimating how long it would take to start her own snowmobile and gain distance down the side trail. *He's standing. Eleven or twelve seconds to react and start his engine . . . then perhaps another minute to catch an old sled at max speed . . . taking into account the trail turns and narrow stretches . . . the dark.* She could keep moving, but evading was impossible without going off trail, and that was risky by itself. Driving without a headlight didn't help.

She bit her lip. It was taking too long to formulate a plan. The man kept talking into his phone, his tone growing impatient as he yelled through the bad cellular connection. She searched her memory, trying to recall the familiarity of his voice.

"Yes, Chief, I could use your help . . . why do you want me to stay put? . . . can't you start searching at the trail entrance and . . . No! I said why do I have to stay put and wait for you? . . . I said I don't want to wait for you! . . . bad connection! . . . what? . . . are you heading this way? I can't hear over the sound of your motor!"

Charlotte moved her glove onto the ignition switch.

"Walker? . . . Walker?" The man let out a groan. Heavy boots padded into the snow, then there was a *thump*, as the man plopped down onto the sled. He started the engine.

Charlotte listened to the machine rumble and replayed the man's voice in her mind. She could almost picture his face without seeing him, imagining a person with dark hair and a rough expression. Something wasn't right. Instead of focusing on the pure white snow around her, Charlotte's mind saw fire and ash—black billows of smoke that filled her body with the memory of burning wood. She could almost smell heated cinders in her nostrils and hear embers popping and crackling, her hands silhouetted in black as they protected her face from the swell of a heat plume.

She jerked back on the sled, for a second feeling as if the memory had stung her fingers. Her glove snagged the ignition switch, and the engine sputtered to life.

Panic surged through Charlotte with so much pain, she thought her heart might stop. She sucked in a chilled breath.

"Hey!" the man yelled.

Charlotte flipped on her headlight and took off down the side trail, landing rough on the new snow pack. Behind her, the man's snowmobile buzzed into life. She glanced back for two seconds and saw him for the first time. He wore heavy winter gear and goggles, no way to see his face, but she knew who he was—one of *them*.

Pearl had told her all about those people, the ones wanting to separate the two of them and take her grandmother far away. They were the reason Pearl made Charlotte move cities in the middle of the night, the reason for every pseudo identity, and why Charlotte couldn't make friends or tell her past teachers about her home-life. *They* were the reason Pearl forced Charlotte to learn survival training and calculate every possible scenario while analyzing her environment—the need to hide from *them* or be vulnerable. *They* were the people who started fires and broke up families. Charlotte had hoped that without Pearl, maybe she'd have a chance on her own. But there was still a threat. It wasn't enough that Pearl was gone.

Another echoing buzz pierced her eardrums. She glanced back for only a moment and tracked a headlight from a third snowmobile trailing in the line, but Charlotte couldn't visualize the rider in the dark. She flipped forward and tipped her body to counter-balance the next curve. The engine sputtered, then a crack and grinding vibrated through her grip. The snowmobile slid in a tail spin.

Charlotte muffled a scream through the layers on fabric covering her mouth. The old snowmobile pelted through the pine trees, the dark branches whipping at her body as she spun wild.

Charlotte sailed off the seat.

She hit the snow and rolled to the base of a pine tree. When she glanced up, she couldn't see the snowmobile in the dark, but heard a deafening crunch as it made contact with a nearby trunk. Heavy packs of snow thumped to the ground. Charlotte crawled under the tree and laid in the frozen pine needles, pain in her ribs stabbing at her insides. She grit her teeth and stifled a trembling cry.

"Charlotte!" the man yelled as he slowed, his headlight shining on Berta's crumpled sled. He hopped off his seat and put both gloves round his mouth. "Charlotte! Where are you!"

She willed herself to leave but failed to move even an inch. Every instinct Pearl had ingrained into Charlotte's psyche told her to run. *Evaluating current situation—one hundred percent a threat.* But all she could do was lie still.

The man searched near Berta's sled, pointing his flashlight at the tree line. "You can't hide! Not anymore!" He stomped through the snow, whipping his light along the ground passed broken branches and sled tracks. "Don't run. I'll only keep looking!"

The beam brushed along Charlotte's tree, grazing her black boots with its tip then flashed away. She rolled onto her stomach, ignoring the pain in her ribs until she could pull herself onto her knees.

"Peterson! Harding P.D.! Let me see your hands!"

Charlotte looked up. The third snowmobile had reached them. The silhouette of another man shone in the headlights, his arms raised taut with a firearm, pointing near Berta's sled. This time, she didn't question the familiarity of this man's voice, but was surprised how relieved she was to hear it.

"Peterson!" Walker repeated. "Harding P.D. Drop the flashlight and put your hands on your head." He moved closer.

"Chief, what are you doing?" Peterson shouted. "She's here somewhere! In the snow. Don't stop me from finding Charlotte—"

"Place your hands on your head . . . now!"

Peterson let out a guttural moan. He dropped his flashlight, then touched both hands to his head and sank down on his knees. "She's here, Walker! It's your job to find her."

"But it's not yours," Walker said. "Don't move." He walked over to Peterson and handcuffed the man's wrists behind his back, stating firm instructions until Peterson was secured. "You're under arrest for impersonating an officer. Do you have a weapon on you?"

Peterson hesitated. "No."

Charlotte crawled on her hands and knees through the snow, taking advantage of their divided attention as Walker patted Peterson down. She scooted behind the pine tree, then quietly rose to her feet.

Radio static crackled. "Bravo-One, Bravo-Two. Where are you on Devil's Whip?"

"Down a side trail. You can see our headlights from the main road. I need county officers and SAR right now. Who do you have with you?"

"Copy. I see y'all. Got Stewart, Paul from the Sheriff's office, and two Search and Rescue sleds with me. We'll be there in just a minute."

"Yes. I've got one in custody. But it's not our POI," Walker said.

Charlotte followed the outer edge of the small clearing, stepping behind the trees to avoid being seen. She crouched low to get a better look at Berta's snowmobile. The front end was wedged against a tree, both skis had dislodged in the crash, one snapped clean in half, and the air smelled of leaking oil and gasoline. There was no hope. Berta's snowmobile was dead. She hid herself in the tree branches, defeated and without a plan.

A flashlight beam rested on the snowmobile for a brief moment then shined through the clearing in a sweeping pattern.

"Charlotte Evers!" Walker said. "You'll freeze out here! Call out!"

For a moment, she considered doing just that—to call out in exhaustion and pain, accepting help. To end the chaos. Charlotte thought of Berta and Mason, and the trust they'd surrendered in order to help her. Then she thought of Pearl and all the running and preparing and uncertainty. All the fear. Raw emotion surged in

Charlotte's core and overpowered her aching ribs. In that moment, she hated Pearl.

"Charlotte!" Peterson shouted. "Come out!"

His voice grated at her memory—a broken memory—one Charlotte still couldn't quite reach.

She stayed hidden in the darkness and stepped around the outside of the clearing. Five snowmobiles buzzed about a hundred feet away, their headlights flashing closer along the trail. There were two more labeled police officers in the group, plus those wearing Search and Rescue reflective vests.

Evaluating situation—one hundred percent a threat. She groaned. How were the threat levels helping her if she couldn't ever truly make them go away? Pearl never mentioned when the threat would end, as if it would go on forever. They were always running hoping to find peace. Pearl was so sure that Canada would be better. But, standing there—cold, hurting—Charlotte knew that now she was running on blind faith alone. Merely a small hope rooted in her grandmother's last plan.

She owed herself one more effort. One more surge of strength.

Charlotte took one solid step out of the tree line and noticed the two men were watching the sleds approach with their backs to her. The others would reach the clearing in a matter of fifteen or so seconds. Walker unzipped Peterson's coat and pulled it off his shoulders, better searching the man's back and inside the loose coat-lining, and then patted his pockets. Before they noticed her, Charlotte ran for Peterson's snowmobile. She plopped down on the seat, starting the ignition in the same movement.

Walker leapt forward, but reached for her too late. Charlotte coasted over the snow at full speed.

40

WALKER

WALKER BARELY CAUGHT HIS BALANCE, grasping thin air as Charlotte raced away from him. Exhaust fumes stung his nostrils.

"Wait!" Peterson shouted. He body-slammed Walker with his shoulder. "Stop!"

Walker took the force in his back and face-planted in the snow. Before he could roll over, Peterson darted after Charlotte.

"Stop!" Officer Stewart shouted. "Taser! Taser!" He leapt over Walker and shot two taser wires at Peterson's exposed back. Electrical pops sounded and tiny shock lights lit up the man's t-shirt where the wires attached to his skin through the fabric. Peterson groaned, flopped to his knees in an awkward slump, then fell headfirst onto untouched powder.

The electrical popping stopped after only a few seconds, just enough time for Walker to regain his footing and reach Peterson.

"Safety on!" Stewart said. He stepped aside.

Walker and Deputy Franklin rolled Peterson onto his back.

"You . . . tased me!" he mumbled, the words slurring.

Franklin hoisted him into a sitting position. "Calm down. You'll be fine."

"Next time, don't body-slam an officer," Stewart said.

Walker glanced back at the headlight from the additional riders. "Paul, where are you?" he shouted over his shoulder.

"Here, Chief." Paul came over and knelt down.

"Can you and your SAR team take this trail in the dark? See that headlight?" Walker pointed down the mountain side, steadying his finger despite the adrenaline surging through his veins. The slope descended into a canyon about a mile away, and the hillside was covered in pine trees. As Charlotte's sled curved the trail, an occasional flash from her headlight shined through the tree branches. She was moving quick, probably carelessly. Walker's panic spiked every time the light beam whipped wild, as if she was fighting a fishtail. "See right there," he said.

"Yep, I see it. Moving fast."

"That's Charlotte Evers. More deputies are coming to help apprehend her. Just track where she goes."

"Right. On our way."

"But be careful, Paul. Pull back if it gets too dangerous for your team."

"We know," Paul said, nodding as he climbed on his sled. "Is she armed?"

"Not sure. Don't think so. But we don't want her to freeze to death out there either. Keep your distance."

"Got it." Paul and the other two riders took off down the trail.

Franklin and Stewart removed the taser spikes from Peterson's back and hauled him to a snowmobile. They plopped him down on the seat.

He spat a chunk of slush from his mouth. "That was unnecessary," Peterson said.

Franklin snorted. "Relax. It was five seconds of pain and your clothing took most of it."

"But I didn't need to be tased in the first place!"

"You knocked over an officer," Stewart said, "This is the second time I've had to remind you. Is it going to take a third time?"

Walker patted Stewart on the shoulder. "He's got it. Let's move on." He spun around and watched the distant headlights move down the trail. As Search and Rescue whipped through the pine trees, it became difficult to track their position, and after a few more minutes, they disappeared in the woods leaving only a subtle glow in the night sky. The engine buzz faded in the distance.

Franklin motioned to them. "We can't sit here waiting. Let's get this guy out through the canyon. It's freezing."

"Franklin," Stewart said. "You've been in Idaho almost a year now. Aren't you used to the cold yet?"

"Yes, I'm used to it. Got winter all figured out—it's stupid-cold and frostbite is a real thing. Chief, we need to get this guy off the mountain and out of the wind. He's warm-blooded like me."

Stewart shook his head. "We're all warm-blooded. You know that, right?"

"That's enough," Walker said.

"Chief." Franklin moved to his side. "We can't wait out here, and you know it."

Walker hesitated to answer, staring at the quiet tree line. He knew Charlotte's fate was in the hands of county sheriffs and SAR. The East Hills were in county land and a number of agencies were assisting Harding in the search, but still. After all that had happened in the last few days, he hated sitting on the sidelines, unable to finish this mess.

"Chief?" Franklin repeated.

"Okay. Let's go. Figure out how to get him back on the sled while he's still handcuffed." Walker headed for his snowmobile.

"The handcuffs aren't necessary, Chief," Peterson said. "I'm not a threat."

Walker leaned forward, looking Peterson in the eyes. "At this moment, I don't know who or what you are." He started his engine.

WALKER LED his officers through the trailhead entrance of Devil's Whip and onto the plowed road where the Sheriff's department and Search and Rescue had parked their red-painted command trailer.

They pulled alongside the various police vehicles and unloaded Peterson.

"Take him inside," Walker said.

"I'll do it." Franklin gripped Peterson by the arm. "Inside's gotta be warmer than out here."

Walker helped Stewart line up the snowmobiles, and they headed toward the trailer. "Dispatch, Bravo-One," he said into his radio, noticing how his lungs fought against the cold air.

"Chief?" Kim responded.

He pulled off his goggles and cloth face mask. "Just checking in. I'm back at the SAR command truck. Bravo-Two and Four are with me."

"Copy."

"Any reports from other agencies? Tell them we've located the POI on the trails. Still trying to apprehend."

"Hang on, Chief."

Walker heard a series of crackles into the radio, along with a fumbling mess of static and squeals through the microphone headset.

"Dispatch?"

"Stop that!" Kim shouted, but she sounded distant. "You can't use it!"

There was a loud *thump.*

"One moment, Chief," Kim said quick into the radio. "I need to squash a mutiny!"

"What?" Walker repeated the word a few times, but Kim didn't respond. Instead, he heard muffled voices—one sounding like Berta Sheppard—then multiple microphone rumbles.

Walker let out a guttural moan in frustration. He dropped his hand from the radio and wiped the frozen sweat drops from his face. Frigid air bit at his skin. He could only imagine how Paul's team and Charlotte Evers felt out in the wind chill—a frozen hell. Walker stared at the dark mountains and second-guessed his decision, realization and rationality washing over him. Keeping anyone on the trails was foolish. He wanted to switch places with the riders and be out there himself to bring Charlotte back. To assume all the risk. But mostly, he wanted everyone to come back alive.

He pulled the borrowed SAR radio from his belt. "Search and Rescue, can you hear me?"

There was only static in response.

"Paul, this is Walker. Can you hear me?"

The radio static crackled, but the voices came through as garble.

"Paul?" Walker held the radio to his ear, listening to the silence. He closed his eyes, praying they didn't freeze to death.

41

MASON

MASON SLOUCHED CLOSER to the computer monitor and sped up the digital recording from that morning, watching security footage of the fake Peterson guy and Walker head toward the station garage. There wasn't audio in the recording, and the image was in black and white, but the movements were smoother than he expected from the station's five-year-old system. It wasn't too bad. Still, he rubbed his eyes and straightened the knot forming in his back.

"How do I make this tape go fast forward?" Berta asked him. "I can't handle watching Jed eat his entire cheeseburger. He still hasn't noticed that he's dripping ketchup on the front desk."

Jed flipped around in his chair and stared at her from across the dispatch room. "If you wait like, a minute, I wipe up the ketchup with a sticky note. I know how to eat and stuff."

Berta groaned. "I don't think I'll last a minute."

"Well," Mason said. "Could be worse. I just watched Jed take a nap for fifteen minutes while I waited for Peterson to show up this morning."

Jed acted like he didn't hear the comment.

Mason paused his own screen and stood from his folding chair, stretching his body in an awkward bend. Berta, Jed, and his mom had helped him screen footage for several hours, each taking a certain camera for a set time period. After a while, Jan left to pick up pizza for everyone, insisting they needed to maintain their blood sugar levels. Now, she sat somewhere in the station, discussing the tow truck incident with Ed over the phone. Mason owed her big for this one, well beyond anything he could ever repay in his lifetime. All he could do was finish his task quickly so she could go home. Mason kept his attention divided only between his monitor and listening for Chief Walker's radio reports. According to Kim's screens, they were on Devil's Whip.

"Help me, Mason. I'm dying here," Berta said.

"That's the button." He leaned down and instructed Berta in basic computer keyboard commands for the fourth time. Computers weren't her thing, but she was just as invested in Charlotte's case as himself. He didn't mind her questions.

"Fast forward the tape for me. Get to the part where Jed is done with lunch."

Mason scrolled through the time stamps. "Um, it's digital. Not a tape. And I don't think Peterson was near Jed at lunch anyway, so you're right. Let's skip ahead." He forwarded the images by ninety minutes.

"Thanks, deary." Berta rested her elbows on the counter.

He plopped down in his chair, staring at the paused image of Walker leading Peterson through the garage and pushed play to watch the video in real time. The two men stopped at the Oldsmobile. From their body language, they were talking about the car and Peterson glanced in the windows. Then Walker opened up the evidence closet. Mason slouched, frustrated at watching mundane television without the audio, and let his eyes glaze over like a doughnut. The two men kept talking, and motioning to the boxed items, and talking some more, and motioning again, and Walker turned back to the evidence closet several times. It all seemed boring.

He wondered if there were any slices of pizza left.

A subtle movement broke his stare. Mason paused the video and pulled back the timestamp by ten seconds. He leaned closer to the screen and squinted. In the footage, Walker once again turned his back to Peterson, placing a box into the evidence cabinet. And as before, Peterson stood with his back to the camera, holding the last remaining evidence box. Mason watched as Peterson held up an object in his hand, one too small for the camera to clearly identify, then he swiped over the back pocket of his jeans.

Mason watched the movement multiple times, studying the sleight of hand as if trying to capture the exact moment a magician makes a playing card disappear. After the seventh replay, he sat back, his thoughts heavy. In a hurry, he fast forwarded through the footage of Peterson leaving the garage. Then he scrolled back and replayed the loop at the evidence closet for the eighth time.

"Hey, look at this nonsense," Berta said.

Mason could barely pull his gaze away from his screen. "But, I found—"

"No. Look. That simpleton Bill Fuller posted a video of my bookstore on the Harding community page. He called it *Berta's Bookstore Blunder*. What a terrible alliteration! And he didn't bother to ask my permission. Now everyone in town knows about the break-in." She slapped her palms on the counter. "That self-serving beetle-bug of a man was filming the back alley before it even happened. Talking to himself the whole time while he took his trash to the dumpsters. Talking to the camera like he's some TV host. He could have prevented the crime if he'd been paying attention. Such a beetle-bug of a man."

Mason glanced at her screen. The others huddled over her shoulder. Berta had obviously abandoned the security footage and managed to pulled up the community page on the internet. They watched as Bill Fuller cheerfully narrated his actions while carrying a black garbage bag across the rear parking stalls.

"What's a daily vlog?" Berta pointed at the words under the video. "And why is there elevator music playing while he's carrying trash? And why are there more shots of his feet than anything else?"

"Wait! Stop." Jed pushed pause. "Dude, look."

They squinted at the blurred background.

"That's fake Peterson's rental car behind the bookstore. See?" Jed touched the screen where the front end of a compact, red car could be seen parked beyond the dumpsters.

They tilted their heads in unison.

"Are you sure?" Mason asked.

"Think so."

Berta's expression tightened. "He was at my store *before* it was burglarized?"

"And probably during it," Mason said.

"Why, that little sneaky, two-faced, fake, monkey bucket—"

Kim waved her hands. "Berta, hang on. There's no proof that it's his car or that he was there. Police like proof or at least probable cause. Jed has to be certain on the ID, not wishy-washy."

Jed nodded. "That's true. I read that somewhere."

"But I found Fake Peterson stealing an item from an evidence box," Mason said, motioning to his monitor.

They scooted over as a group, huddling around Mason's screen.

He replayed the loop, pointing to the moment Fake Peterson placed an object from the evidence box into his back pocket. "Whatever he took, he has it on him. Or at least he did this morning. We need to check that evidence box and see what's missing. Jed, don't you have a list of the items?"

"Sure do." Jed smiled wide. "Data entry is my superpower!"

"Oh, no," Kim said. "You bunch can't access evidence boxes. An officer has to do that. And they're all gone right now."

"Where's Officer Kemp?" Mason asked.

"He's home asleep. They're resting in shifts until this Evers mess is done." Kim sat back in her chair. "I'll report to Walker, but no one is looking in any closets."

"But I know where the spare key is," Jed said. "Just get the Chief's permission."

"No way." Kim folded her arms. "You guys are guessing. Walker hasn't checked in yet. I'm not sending him bad info. And you're not touching evidence. I'm in charge, and I have no plans to get fired!"

"Neither do I," Jed said, mimicking her arm-folding. "But I'm still willing to try."

"To get fired?" She shook her head in disbelief. "You're a volunteer!"

"No, I mean I'm willing to *try* to solve this case. And so are Mason and Berta. Those of us who care about, like, justice and the American way of life." He pointed at the others.

Mason leaned back. "Okay, people, let's be calm for a second. I want to double check the evidence box before we call Walker on the radio, just to be sure Peterson stole an item. That's it. Knowing what he took could help Walker right now. Let's check it out."

"I said no way," Kim repeated. "You guys aren't officers."

Berta rose from her chair, pointing to the red car on her computer screen. "But that fake dye-job of a criminal broke into my bookstore! He riffled through my books. Terry needs to arrest him and throw his butt in jail. I want justice! No one crosses Alberta Sheppard and gets away with such blatant—"

"Dispatch, Bravo-One." The Chief's voice crackled through the room. Kim had placed radio communications on loud-speaker so she wouldn't miss any incoming calls while they checked security footage.

Kim hurried to her chair. "Chief?" she said into her headset.

"Just checking in. I'm back at the SAR command truck. Bravo-Two and Four are with me."

"Copy," she responded, tying on her keyboard.

Mason, Berta, and Jed crowded over Kim's chair.

Walker continued. "Any reports from other agencies? Tell them we've located the POI on the trails. Still trying to apprehend."

"Tell him about my bookstore," Berta loud-whispered. "Tell him Fake Peterson is the burglar. Tell him I want that man arrested right away."

Kim shook her head. "Hang on, Chief." She covered the headset microphone with her hand. "Berta, I'll tell him what he needs to know, not you. My job isn't your business. So, step back."

"My bookstore *is* my business! He needs to know what

happened."

Kim turned away from her.

"Fine. I'll do it myself." Berta reached for Kim's headset, grabbing mostly hair in the process. "Mason, push the talk button!"

"Stop that!" Kim shouted. She fumbled from her chair, grabbing the headset in an attempt to pry Berta's fingers from her head. "You can't use it!"

They leaned over the counter, both locked in a death grip of head-set and bits of Kim's hair, Berta shouting, "Terry! Can you hear me?" into the microphone.

"Push the talk button, Mason!" Berta commanded.

He froze, watching in shock while Berta and Kim struggled for control.

"Let go!" Kim reeled back, ripping the headset from Berta's grasp. Her sweeping elbow made contact with the row of weaved baskets on the counter, sending dozens of cinnamon-dosed pinecones shooting across the floor.

Mason lifted his shoe as a cone rolled under his foot, a glitter trail in its wake. He glanced at Jed, then at Berta and Kim who now stood a few feet apart and both stared at the bent headset.

"Whoa. Weirdest cat fight ever," he mumbled under his breath.

"You mean, cat-lady fight," Jed whispered to him.

Berta stepped back, breathing hard, a scowl on her face. "Boys, I heard that. It wasn't respectful."

"Sorry," they said in unison.

She nodded.

Kim placed the headset over her disheveled hair and pressed her index finger to a button on the keyboard. "Just a moment, Chief," she said. "I need to squash a mutiny."

"What?" he answered. The connection crackled. Walker repeated himself a few more times, but the sound cut in and out.

Kim leaned down and picked up a pinecone. "There's a way to do things here," she said, " . . . and you guys don't get it. This is a police investigation, not a community pie-eating contest." She motioned to Berta and Mason. "If you two hadn't interfered, Charlotte Evers would still be in custody, probably booked in county jail, and I'd be home drinking peppermint hot chocolate right now with my family."

They stood in silence.

Mason didn't know what to say. He felt overwhelmed by everything.

Berta eventually sat down in her folding chair and locked her fingers together. "You don't know that."

"What?" Kim asked.

"You don't know what would have happened without our interference," she said.

Kim stared at her for a moment, then she slumped in her own chair. "I guess we'll never know."

Berta glanced around at the pinecone carnage then turned back to Kim. "I hear you aren't very good at your job. Is that true?"

"I hear you're a difficult old lady that nobody likes. Is *that* true?"

Berta sighed. "Well, I suppose it depends on whose opinion you believe. That's the thing about gossip. People say whatever they want in order to fuel their grudges and don't bother checking if it's real or not. It's worse in a small town."

Kim slouched and shrugged.

"Especially when you're new," Mason said. "When people don't know you, they fill in the blanks with whatever they want."

They stared at him. His face flushed.

"That's true, I guess," Berta said.

"Well, I kinda like you," Jed said to Berta. "You seem cool for a cat-lady."

Mason nodded. "Yeah. You're alright." He shrugged awkwardly and looked away.

Berta reached down and gathered the pinecones near her shoes. "Kim, I don't know if the gossip about you is true or not, but if you're doing your best, then I suppose you're doing something right." She handed Kim the handful. "And these things smell too strong. But it's good you celebrate the holiday. Even if no one appreciates your efforts."

Kim's expression softened a little. "Okay. Let's write down

everywhere Peterson went in the station today, then I'll report to Chief Walker when we're all done with the footage. But I'm sorry, I can't approve searching inside an evidence box."

"That's fair," Berta said. Her tone sounded diplomatic, but when Kim looked away, she glanced at Mason with a deceptively subtle expression, one implanted with a complex, non-verbal meaning.

Mason got the message.

He casually sat down in his chair and began texting on his cell phone behind the cover of his monitor. Berta was right. No one knew what would've happened to Charlotte without their interference. For better or worse, they changed the outcome. And the same applied to Walker, the other officers, Kim, and even Fake Peterson. They were making choices. All of them. Changing outcomes. Every day.

And he was making another choice.

Mason glanced at the sticky note on Kim's dispatch monitor, the bright pink paper with Chief Walker's cell number scribbled in Officer Stewart's handwriting. He typed in the number and wrote the first, longest, and probably most interfering text message to a man he'd successfully avoided for the last five years . . . until Charlotte Evers entered Harding.

Chief Walker, this is Mason. We looked at the security footage. Fake Peterson stole an item from an evidence box. Something small from Pearl's car. We don't know what it is. And we think he broke into the bookstore. Sending you a video screenshot of his rental car in the back alley before the break-in. He's a bad guy.

Before Mason pushed *send*, he shifted over to Berta's computer. The others were occupied picking up pinecones and moving chairs. He took a screen shot of Fuller's video, the moment revealing the red car near the dumpsters, and then sent the image to his phone over the WiFi. Mason did the same with the paused shot of Peterson stashing the item in his back pocket. A few seconds later, he texted the message and both images to Chief Walker.

"Are you going to help clean up this mess?" Kim asked.

He glanced at her before meeting Berta's gaze. "Yep," he said. "Trying to do just that."

42

WALKER

WALKER WAITED to hear SAR respond on the radio, but he wasn't getting a response from Paul. Neither could the sheriff's deputies on scene or dispatch. The messages should had been relayed through the repeater towers, but Walker wondered if Paul and his team couldn't hear their radios over the snowmobile engines. He listened again as the deputies kept trying to call the SAR team back to command.

Again, no response. But this time a little static.

Stewart approached. "Coming, Chief?" he asked, motioning to the Command trailer where they'd temporarily put Peterson. "We read him his rights. We're ready for you."

"Yes, just a minute. You go in." Walker took one last glance towards Devil's Whip. In the darkness, the snow-capped mountains retained an eerie glow, as if the white powder still hung on to the day's light. The hills and whipping wind filled him with a sense of isolation. He glanced at the snowmobiles, considering if he should reenter the trail himself.

His cell phone beeped.

Walker opened a text from Mason and enlarged the images, his cold fingers barely registering on the touch screen. He squinted at the pictures—one of a car and another of himself in the station garage—then he read the text. A second later, Walker hurried around the backside of the trailer. He squinted through the dark, using his phone as a light. When he'd passed the line of Harding police and county vehicles, he stopped in the snow and held up the flashlight from his duty belt, scanning. A petite red sedan had been parked near a snow drift. He'd seen the thing several times that day, but had dismissed it earlier. He crouched near the bumper, matching the partial plate in Fuller's screen shot to Peterson's rental vehicle.

Anger roasted through his core, his jaw tightening. Walker returned the text: *How sure are you that this image is from before the break-in?*

Mason responded: *Very.*

He stepped away from the car, his mind racing.

"Chief?" Franklin came over. "You need to come in. This guy wants to talk. But he says he'll only talk to you."

"Already on my way." He sprinted to the trailer and popped open the door.

Stewart stood on the left near the cabinets, a section of the trailer where SAR stored equipment. Peterson glanced up from his seat on the padded booth, his hands still handcuffed behind his back.

"Chief," Franklin said. "We found something interesting when we searched his pockets."

Walker looked down at the table—car keys, wallet, a law enforcement badge for Kansas City Police Department, a cell phone, and a small plastic bag with a dark item inside. "Well . . ." he said, looking at Peterson. "Now we know what you stole from the evidence box."

Deputy Franklin straightened up. "Wait. He did what?"

Walker held out his cell phone so Peterson could see the screen. "This is an image from our station security cameras. That's you and me this morning. Back when you were impersonating a St. George Detective. And that's you stealing a piece of evidence from a box. This evidence, most likely." He held up the bag and examined the small metal object inside the plastic. "But tell me, why is this wrist watch so important that you're willing to go to jail over it."

Peterson kept his head low, staring at the cell phone screen. His eyes tensed on a single point, as if lost in thought, then Peterson grimaced.

Walker wondered if the guy's head was going to explode. "Look," he said. "You'll only talk to me, right? Well, talk. I'm listening."

"You need to find Charlotte before she disappears again."

"I already know that."

"No. I think this incident in Harding is the last time she'll surface. If she makes it out of the mountains, she'll be gone. I'll never find her again. I will cooperate and tell you everything I know, but I need you to not let her disappear."

"Okay. We're already doing our best to find her," Walker said, sliding into the opposite side of the booth. He bit his bottom lip, stifling the frustration growing in his mind, and locked his fingers together on the tabletop. "I'm going to need more answers than that. Let's start with your real name. What is it?"

Peterson hesitated.

Walker leaned back. "Look, I don't have time for games. We're booking you into county lockup even without a name." He turned to Franklin. "Go start your car. Let's take him to county right now."

"Wait," Peterson said. "I need to stay here."

"Then give me helpful info."

"My name is Ruthan Pierce. I'm an officer with Kansas City P.D. in Missouri."

"Current, fired, or retired?"

"Current, but took a leave of absence after . . . insistence from the chief."

Walker picked up the Kansas City P.D. badge off the table, feeling the weight in his hand. "Well, Ruthan Pierce, we have probable cause to search your rental car. If you are a police officer, then you already know this."

"Yes, I do. My ID is in the center console."

"Is there a firearm in your car or other items I should be aware of?"

"No. But you can search it all the same."

Walker handed Franklin the car keys. "I hate to do this, but wake up Kemp. Get him out here to help you."

"Yes, Chief." Franklin took the keys and left the trailer.

Stewart moved over to Walker's side, taking out a small notebook from his coat pocket and jotting down Ruthan Pierce's name and badge number.

"Why are you looking for Charlotte?" Walker asked Pierce. "She's from St. George. What does Kansas City want with her?"

Pierce leaned back in the booth and braced himself against the cushion. "It's not Kansas City. It's me. I thought Charlotte was dead."

"How are you connected to her?" Walker studied Pierce's expression, analyzing his movements, his tone, whether or not the man's statements seemed genuine. In all their interactions throughout the day, fake "Peterson" had given him nothing but lies. He questioned every word the man said, right down to the guy's real name. What kind of a given name was *Ruthan* anyway? It had to be a family name. "I repeat," he said. "How are you connected to Charlotte Evers?"

"She's my daughter."

Walker unlocked his fingers. "Are you certain?"

"Almost one hundred percent."

"Almost?"

"I haven't seen or spoken with her since the day she died. Well, the day I was told she died. But then I figured out that might not be what happened. I've spent the last two years trying to find her."

A strange and blunt realization came over Walker—Charlotte *was* running from someone, and she was scared.

"I'll prove it. Look at the watch," Ruthan said.

Walker picked up the small bag, examining the tarnished metal through the plastic. "It's damaged. Looks burned."

"Read the back."

He flipped it over. On the back face, he noticed an inscription, one almost too scorched to decipher. "To my angel," he read aloud. "My Joy. Love, Ruthan."

"I gave that to my wife on our first anniversary," Pierce said, staring at the bag. "We were so poor, but I gave it to her anyway. She wore it every day and placed it on the dresser at night. She loved that thing."

"Where is she?" Walker asked.

"I lost her in a house fire a long time ago."

Walker set the watch down, shaking his head. "How does that connect you to Charlotte? Why do you think she's your daughter?"

"A year before the fire, my father passed away. That left my mother alone. Her name was Pearl Pierce, and she began behaving sporadically. Turns out, she'd been diagnosed with a delusional disorder, with paranoia. It was complicated. I didn't quite understand the diagnosis. And I didn't research it on my own when I found out. Too hard to think about. My parents hid it from the family for years. Pearl thought dangerous people were tracking her, trying to harm her and my family. They were just delusions, but to Pearl, they were real and scary. And worth running from. My wife and I made a room for her at our house. It was in a rural area outside the city. Thought she'd like it out there. She just needed medical care and patience and love. Things were rough, but okay. For a while."

"And what happened?" Walker asked.

"Mom got worse. Her paranoia was overwhelming . . . her theories. She didn't want to harm anyone. But I . . . stayed at work more. Then when Charlotte was seven, a candle started the carpet on fire. At least that's what the fire investigator suspected. I was working late, catching up on paper work at the station. I didn't know what was happening. But dispatch called me. The house was totally destroyed before anyone got there. My wife died. They found her body. But only her. They assumed my mother and child died, too, but weren't recoverable."

"How did you find out otherwise?" Walker asked.

"Two years ago, I finally opened my mother's storage unit. It had been locked up since she moved in with us. I loaded the unit myself.

Knew everything in it. But this time, there were some missing items, sentimental valuables that I know my mother would never abandon —her collectables, some jewelry, her grandfather's books, and our family history. There wasn't evidence of a burglary. That stuff was just . . . gone."

"And it seemed suspicious?"

"Yeah. The cop part of me knew it. The security cameras caught an older woman getting inside the unit. I couldn't see her face. It seemed like her, but I wasn't sure. For six months, I tracked possible places my mother might go. I had hope that she'd wandered away from the fire with Charlotte and that her condition was making her stay away. Took a while, but I found a jewelry shop in Florida selling some of her stuff." He shook his head. "Antique ruby necklace and some earrings. Pearl was on their security camera. They paid her well. The clerk remembered a young woman waiting outside. The two left together. That gave me more hope."

"Could you identify the woman waiting for Pearl? Did you see her face?"

"No," Pierce said. "Only my mother. But it has to be my daughter. The young woman's description puts her at the right age. And in St. George, they were both using their real first names—Pearl and Charlotte. That's too big of a coincidence."

"Possibly . . . or she could be con artist taking advantage of an old woman who has valuables to sell."

Pierce shook his head. "I don't believe that."

"Pearl is still missing and under suspicious circumstances. The woman driving Pearl's car came into Harding alone, which means something bad did happened. Do you believe that?"

Pierce hesitated, glancing at the ceiling. "I'm worried about my mother. And my daughter. But I know they lived through the fire. It must have been horrible and scary that night, but they lived! That young woman out there right now, on the trails, in the snow, that's my daughter. How would you feel if there was a chance your loved one lived instead of died? Would you stop looking for her?"

Walker leaned back against the seat cushion. An image of Marie's warm smiling face flashed in his mind. He would've done anything to bring his wife back. And for a second, Pierce's actions made sense to him. But, he had a job to do. This couldn't be about him.

"You took fingerprints from Charlotte in the hospital, right?" Pierce said.

"Yes. Still waiting for the crime lab to get back to us."

"Well, my daughter's prints are in IAFIS under a missing child case number. I found one of those papers they let kids fill out and stamp at police fairs. Her prints were old, but the ink was clean. I created the case number after I found the jewelry shop. So compare the two sets of prints. Please."

Walker stood from the booth, unable to sit still any longer. He wrung his hands for a moment, then popped open the trailer door. "I'll be back."

"Do you need something, Chief?" Stewart asked.

"Just . . . hang on." He shut the door behind him, letting himself stand in the December cold and suck in the deep, chilled air. His thoughts rattled with uncertainty. How could he believe anyone at this point?

When he collected himself, Walker scrolled through the contact list on his cell phone until he found the email address for Lee Parks, the field Crime Scene Investigator out of Coeur d'Alene. He knew she'd be off the clock at that late hour, but he needed confirmation.

Walker sent her an email: *Lee, I need an update on the fingerprints you collected from the car and the ones from Charlotte Evers in the hospital. Can you check with your contact at the FBI field office and ask them to compare those prints to unsolved missing child cases? There might be a case file under Charlotte Pierce. It's urgent. Thank you.*

After sending the email, Franklin hollered at him from across the row of cars. "I found his ID, Chief! Ruthan Pierce from Missouri. Driver's license and Kansas City P.D. identification."

Walker nodded before reentering the trailer. "Okay, Mr. Pierce," he said, sitting at the booth again. "Let's suppose for a moment that you're telling the truth about Charlotte being your daughter. And that Pearl was your mother. Why did you pretend to be a St. George detective and follow her to Harding? Why not just contact us? Ask for help?"

"Because," Pierce said, shaking his head. "The last time I had a good lead was in Tennessee. I contacted local agencies to help, but just having the police searching in Pearl's area scared her off. I think she'd developed a paranoia about police . . . and they wouldn't let me be active in the search since I was family. They thought she might be harmful instead of endangered. So they shut me out. Pearl and Charlotte fled in the night. I missed them by one day, Walker," he leaned forward, "I had to take a leave of absence from my job to keep looking for my family. When I saw my mother's picture on the news out of St. George, I had to locate Charlotte before she left forever. Please, let me find her."

"I can't let you go," Walker said. "How can I trust your story?"

"Because Charlotte needs you to trust me. Even if she doesn't know it."

"*If* she's your daughter . . ."

The door burst open. Paul stood in the doorway.

"Walker, we had to turn back," he said. "Tracked her toward East Brick Pass, but lost her headlight. The ground is too unstable out there. We'll have to try again in the morning, but it's bitter cold. Evers is on her own for survival."

"No," Pierce said, his voice hollowed.

Walker nodded and glanced at the floor. He felt helpless and sick. "Pierce, we're going to hold you in one of our cells at the station and start processing there." He glanced at his watch. "First thing in the morning, you're going to County."

"But, I need to—"

"We have you on impersonating a St. George detective. Interfering with an investigation. We haven't even discussed the burglary at the bookstore yet, or the stolen watch. I have no choice but to book you."

"Wait, I needed the watch to prove to Charlotte who I am. And same for the bookstore. It had Pearl's personalized collection of—"

"Stewart," Walker said. "Put Ruthan Pierce in your car."

"Yes, Chief." Stewart tucked his notebook away.

"I have to stay!" Pierce stumbled to his feet, but Stewart was already guiding him out of the trailer.

Walker didn't wait for Pierce's rebuttal. The guy was right about one thing, Tennessee law enforcement shut him out for a reason. Family complicated matters. Cop or not, Pierce had proven himself an unpredictability.

Come morning, the sun would change the mountainside, and Walker knew exactly what he'd be doing—searching for life in the snow. If there was any to find.

43

CHARLOTTE

CHARLOTTE GUIDED the snowmobile off the path and slid behind a group of pine trees. The engine hummed and popped, then died, taking her headlight with it. Sudden helplessness chilled her core more than the wind digging into the crevices of her clothing. Shivers surged through her body.

She tried the ignition switch, her fingers stiff, but the sled didn't sputter—perhaps a mechanical problem or more likely out of gas. Either reason was a death sentence.

From her backpack, Charlotte retrieved a flashlight and studied the trails map again. She listened for approaching snowmobiles. It had been a while since she'd seen any other headlights behind her. Plus, she'd taken numerous turns as the path crossed side-trails. Each time she counted, memorizing her path.

Second right, third left, three markers over from the end, down a half mile, first right . . . She traced her progress on the map, though her muscles trembled. She needed to keep moving. But she was freezing. Could she afford a detour? And did she have a choice? Hunting cabins had been marked on the paper. The nearest, labeled *Boyd's Place*, looked about a quarter mile from her position on the map, just off East Brick Pass. Charlotte leaned back, breathing hard. Her backpack included a compass and a flashlight, but the odds of finding the place in the dark weren't in her favor. *Reevaluating—travel on foot . . . night winds . . . snow . . . dropping temperatures . . . distance to Angleton by way of East Brick Pass . . . odds of dying in the elements during the night . . .*

Charlotte deemed staying on course as one hundred percent a *threat to life.* She started walking in the snow, heading for the cabin. There was no other choice.

Somewhere higher on the mountainside, snowmobiles buzzed over the trail, their engines echoing through the canyons. Charlotte attempted to run, but her boots kept sinking in the snow. Her bruised ribs ached at each breath. Without the sled, she decided to head straight through the forest and avoided the zigzagging trails, letting the compass, map, and flashlight guide her.

Each step got harder to take, and Charlotte's pace slowed to a stagger. She checked the map and compass multiple times.

Soon, the engine sounds faded in the distance. Charlotte prayed they were giving up for the night and wondered if her own frozen body was doing the same—giving up on her.

As she emerged through the trees, her flashlight beam swept across a clearing until she spotted the sweet tucked-away refuge of Boyd's Place. The small, single-floor structure had been built at the base of the hill and showed signs of abandonment during the winter months—like most of the hunting cabins. It bordered the forest on one side and the clearing on the other. In the near distance, she spotted the glistening, snow-coated roadway of East Brick Pass about a half mile or so away at the base of the canyon.

Charlotte reached the cabin just as it began to snow. Everything hurt, even her nose and lips under the layered turtle neck.

The door was locked. Understandable. Charlotte wondered why she'd expected to find it open. Perhaps exhaustion was getting to her judgment. She could handle the frailties of physicality, but not the slippage of her rational mind. Her brain couldn't betray her. She wouldn't allow it. Charlotte scanned the door. No deadbolt. She considered breaking the wood or a window, but decided against compromising the air flow of the structure. Heat was her saving grace.

Focus. Get the pins. She unzipped her coat and retrieved the two precious bobby pins from the small pocket in her sweater. It was an older doorknob and worth a try. She knelt down and shaped both pieces as needed—one into a pick and the other into a lever. It took two attempts with her teeth, but Charlotte managed to remove the coated tip from the "pick" bobby pin. Opening the old keyhole would be doable, as long as the pin and tumbler lock wasn't frozen shut. She leaned close to the knob and blew warm breath into the lock several times. Then, she positioned both pins inside the opening and worked the mechanism with her gloved hands until she heard distinct clicking, allowing the lock to turn.

The door creaked with aged hinges and weathered wood. She shone her flashlight beam through the interior—a main living space, a bulky couch with heavy upholstery, table and chairs, a bunk bed on the far wall, rough kitchen counter and sink, a potbelly stove, and one small, rudimentary bathroom. Well, sort of a bathroom. No electricity. No running water. The decor betrayed the building's age—built in the eighties—but the light coating of dust suggested someone used the place only rarely every season. It was old, but out of the wind.

She closed the door, relocked it, and headed for the potbelly stove. A nearby crate held a supply of chopped wood, and with the lighter from her backpack, she managed to start a small fire. Smoke filtered up through the flue. Flames popped and crackled, a sound that normally filled her with uneasiness. This time, she welcomed the small, radiating heat. Charlotte ate the stiff sandwich and a few rock-solid granola bars from her backpack, saying a silent thank you to Berta for forcing her to take them, and she placed her frozen water bottles near the stove to thaw. She held her hands near the warm fire until her arm muscles shook, then she stretched down on the woolen rug. The floor was stiff, but she was too exhausted to make it to the couch.

Charlotte wondered if the elements would overtake her tattered body before morning. Maybe Mason was right. Maybe she couldn't keep running. It was too hard to live at full pace forever, always escaping, always on guard and under threat. Perhaps death would win. It took Pearl out of spite. And at the moment, Charlotte felt just as fragile. Just as weak. She closed her eyes, trembling in her skin, and she waited to see if sleep or death won the battle during the night. Either way, she would be at peace.

44

WALKER

Nearly a foot of fresh snow had buried Charlotte's stolen snowmobile. Walker stood over the frozen machine, feeling lucky he'd noticed its abandoned outline among the surrounding pine trees. If it wasn't for the morning sunlight and the reflective neon stripe on the front end, he probably would've missed it.

He marked the GPS coordinates in the handheld unit he'd borrowed from Paul. There wasn't a cell phone signal in the canyons to call it in. The repeater tower and the SAR radios were their only communication, and any messages had to be relayed back to dispatch. It was easy to get lost if you weren't prepared. His hope at finding Charlotte alive was dwindling. But he still had some.

The deputies and Paul's team needed more searchers on the ground, and he knew the trails well. So, he'd volunteered. Plus, Walker couldn't wait in Harding. That felt helpless.

"Paul?" he radioed, wiping the fog from his goggles. "I found the sled."

"Copy. We'll head to your location."

Walker searched around in the snow, kicking mounds with his boots. His adrenaline spiked every time his boot tip made contact with a hard surface, though each one turned out to be a log or a rock.

Finding Charlotte's body would be like searching for a marble under a blanket.

"Terry!" Paul approached on his sled. Franklin and the other SAR members were behind him. "Is she with it?"

"Not that I can see," he said, scanning the ground. "She could have walked away. But the tracks are filled in."

"There's no tellin' which way she went next," Franklin said. "No way she made it on foot to Angleton or doubled back to Harding. Probably lying in a drift somewhere. We won't find her till spring. Best thing is to split up. Cover more ground."

Walker shook his head. "Not you, Franklin. Paul's team knows the area, trained on it, been working out here for years. You're a skilled officer, but this is your first search in this type of terrain. There are dangers. I want you to stick with a partner on the trails or head back. No crossing over wide open ground."

"But, Chief, Paul gave me the proper gear and instructions how to—"

"No exceptions," Walker said.

Franklin nodded. "Okay. I guess you're right." He sat on his sled.

Paul moved to Walker's side. "He's right about one thing, Terry. This might turn into a recovery."

"I know. I've already considered that possibility." He headed for his snowmobile. "But Berta Sheppard admitted to giving Evers a trail map. There's only one hunting cabin within two miles, and it's not listed on the County's plat."

"You're talking about Boyd's place," Paul said. "We checked it yesterday. Marked it on the GPS list. It's locked up."

"But that was yesterday."

"Right. We'll head over the trails toward that area."

"I'll go direct through the trees," Walker said.

Paul started his engine. "Be careful. That fresh foot of powder changed things during the night."

"Keep an eye on Franklin." Walker steered his snowmobile through the trees, using his handheld GPS unit to guide him.

He drove between pines at a cautious pace, checking the

landscape for unusual mounds in the snow. Several times he stopped to dig with his gloves, but after repeatedly finding nothing, he was both relieved and frustrated. Soon, Walker worried that the slight divots he was seeing weren't snow-filled footprints but actually false marks his brain was imaging. He compartmentalized his anxiety to stay focused.

When he emerged into a clearing, Boyd's hunting cabin looked undisturbed on the other side. He scanned up the hill to where the slope met the higher trail, the distance a bit longer than a football field. With care, he crossed the bottom of the clearing and slid to a stop near the cabin's front porch. He silenced the engine quickly, but there was no way to hide his approach. So, he decided to act fast.

The door looked intact. No light shown through the windows, but he smelled a hint of smoke. Walker retrieved his sidearm from under his coat and checked the door handle—locked. The cabin's frame and walls were sturdy, but the door jamb was simple.

Walker aimed and kicked the door just in the right spot. The jamb cracked and shifted. He landed a second, swift kick, snapping the lock out of the frame. Splinters flew in the air, the door popping wide on its hinges.

He raised his gun, scanning the small interior. "Police! Let me see your hands."

Charlotte lay in front of a couch, on the floor, her face tilted toward a cold potbelly stove. The room smelled of camp fire.

"Harding Police! Let me see your hands," he ordered, stepping closer.

She didn't move.

"Charlotte Evers!" For a few seconds, he stood still, unable to take his gaze off her pale face. *She's dead.* His throat choked up. *I didn't get here soon enough.* Walker crouched, stretching to check her pulse.

Charlotte opened her eyes.

He startled back.

She slowly rolled onto her side, struggling to pull herself into a sitting position.

"Uh . . . place your hands on your head," he repeated.

She simply stared at him. "You're that cop," she said, her words soft and weak, obviously in pain. She looked defeated. "The one from town."

He narrowed his gaze. "Yes. And in the hospital. You remember? You need to come with me back to Harding."

"I can't. Made a promise. Got to keep going." She stared down at the floor, her body swaying as if gravity was too much.

"But you'll die out here."

"I'll die if I go back," she said, leaning away.

"That won't happen. Place your hands on your head, right now." He lowered his aim, but watching her, she was too weak to fight him anyway.

"I'll die either way."

"What does that mean?" He reached his left hand back to retrieve his handcuffs. He'd sort out the details later.

Outside, snowmobile engines revved in the distance.

Charlotte glanced at the window. "Oh, no. He's with them," she mumbled.

"Who? Ruthan Pierce? Do you know that name?" He studied her face, watching her expression tighten and her eyelids squint together. All the answers were right there, in her mind, so close. He needed those answers before they faded away.

"Ruthan?" she repeated. "How can that be? He's dead."

"Who told you he was dead?"

The snowmobile engines grew louder, coming closer. She looked at the window again, her face rigid.

"Just follow my instructions," he said. "We'll get this all straightened out. Put your hands on your head. I'm going to cuff you."

She acted as though she didn't hear him.

Walker shot a side-glance through the window and spotted the other officers and Search and Rescue high on the trail. Deputy Franklin broke away from the leader, heading down the slope ahead of them. Instant panic filled Walker's core as he watched his new officer make a dire mistake, but there was nothing he could do.

The top of the slope shifted under Franklin's weight, breaking loose as if the fresh snow pack was made of fragile glass. The smooth, pristine white layer shattered in an instant. An avalanche billowed under Franklin, tossing him and his sled like a rag doll.

Walker lowered his weapon. They had only seconds. Through the window, he watched helplessly as the approaching wave of white headed for the cabin at freeway speeds, a loud roar echoing in his ears.

"Move!" He screamed at Charlotte. Walker dove for her, reaching to shield her body.

A deepening *thump* hit the building, and the wooden walls buckled under the pressure. Beams snapped. The foundation shifted. A river of snow pushed the small building and invaded the interior as it tore through the broken windows.

Cold and darkness instantly surrounded Walker's body. The snow pressed him against the floor, then rolled him as he tried to keep from being buried. Pain shot through his limbs, but he only registered raw panic.

In seconds, his torso slammed against the floor, and he pushed against it to force his head into an air pocket behind the broken tabletop, just as the avalanche slowed and the snow began to harden.

The sounds of destruction—snapping wood, roars, and buckling—subsided. Walker coughed and spit, trying to catch his breath. He was lying on his side, buried from the waist down. The table top had created an air pocket around him. Everything looked blue. He tried to move, but the snow pack now felt like cement.

"Hey!" he cried out. The effort was weak. He managed to reach for the zipper of his coat, noticing all his loose stuff—gloves, hat, SAR radio, and his gun—had been stripped from his body. His muscles ached, and his fingers shook in the cold.

Walker didn't know the fate of Franklin and the others, but he was alive. The avalanche beacon strapped to his chest was working. Maybe Franklin's tracker was, too. Minutes mattered.

He calmed himself and slowed his breathing, minimizing the carbon dioxide building up in his air pocket. To his left, he found the half-buried edge of a floorboard plank. He guessed the wooden floor must have been just underneath him, under a layer of snow. Walker stretched, trying to dig out his legs with the plank. His knuckles were raw and every muscle ached. He tasted blood on his lip.

Then he heard a moan.

Adrenaline shook his body. "Charlotte? Where are you?"

"It's cold," she said.

"I know. Where are you?" he repeated. She was close.

"Trapped. Under a couch. There's snow and wood. It's hard to breathe."

"Do you see daylight?"

"Yes."

"Head for it." He heard thumping sounds in the snow—shifting debris and an occasional groan. Then there was a long moment of silence.

"Charlotte?" he called again.

No response.

Walker rested his head on the ground, gripping the broken plank in his hands. At least she made it out alive. He thought she was dead many times in the last four days. Once was too many. That was enough dread for a lifetime. He was done.

A small hole burst through the wall of his air pocket. Charlotte's hands stretched through the opening. She began digging at the side walls and dragging the snow away in chunks. Then she poked her face into the hole and stared at him. Except for the dark circles under her eyes, her skin was almost as pale as the snow.

Beyond her, Walker spotted the cushion-less couch propped over her body like the protective roof of a tunnel. She could crawl out on her belly, if she had the strength for it. He stretched, but couldn't reach her.

Somewhere above him, a roof beam groaned under the weight.

"Charlotte, it's not stable here, and I'm stuck," he said. "Just crawl out to safety. I have air now. Go."

She kept digging, making the hole a couple feet in diameter. As she moved, Walker noticed a dark shape on the ground next to her elbow—his gun.

His heart rate sped up, pounding in his temples.

Charlotte paused, noticing it for the first time. She picked up the weapon with her shaking fingers.

He felt helpless.

She sighed. "Pearl never liked guns," she said in a detached monotone, staring down at the Glock. "But I see why other people do. They make you feel safer. Even if it's not always true." Charlotte gripped the handle. She rubbed her eyes with her free hand. "I'm so tired."

"Charlotte, put it down." He kept his voice as quiet and calm as his adrenaline would allow.

She didn't act like she heard him. "Pearl never felt safe. Never trusted anyone. People wanted to take her away. So, we hid from them. She said we could run forever and be safe. But it didn't matter. Death found her anyway. Can't hide from that."

Walker tunnel-visioned on the Glock's black tip, pointing in his direction—pointing at him. But Charlotte wasn't aiming. She was looking down at her hands. A chill of nerves stabbed at the back of his head, then his chest hollowed with each shallow breath. "Charlotte, put the gun down, please."

She rested her fists on the floor, but didn't let go of the gun.

He needed to keep her talking. "Charlotte, what really happened to Pearl? Please tell me the truth."

"She died. Didn't lie about that when Mason asked me. Can't seem to lie to him. He's running, too."

"And Pearl's in the urn, right?" he asked, the questions spilling out of him like beads of sweat. He needed to keep her in the moment.

She nodded.

"How did Pearl die?"

"On her own. Alone." Charlotte's voice cracked, tears welling in her eyes. "She was sick. Wouldn't let me help her. Didn't trust anyone. No one should die alone. Not Pearl. Not my mother. Not my father. But they did." She leaned forward on her elbows, raising her voice as she steadied the gun. "Someone should've been with them. Don't you want someone to be with you? To be with you right then—the moment just as important as your birth? Then to morn you when you're gone?"

Walker moved his gaze from the gun barrel to her strained and worn face, imagining the thoughts churning in Charlotte's head. He reached for her in desperation, but still couldn't get close enough.

Her blank-stare relaxed. "I'm not going to be alone." She shook her head. "That's not how I'm going to end."

"Charlotte," he said, desperately reaching for her and opening his hand. "You're not alone. Just . . . please, don't use that."

She didn't answer.

"Please," he repeated.

"I'm so tired."

"I know, but choose to trust me," Walker said. "Make the choice on your own. For you. Your choice. Not Pearl's."

Charlotte pulled back, hesitating for a long moment.

Walker kept his hand extended, waiting longer and forcing more patience in those seconds than he'd ever done in his life. Feeling the same uncertainty as the day Marie told him her cancer wasn't going away. That life was changing in an instant. That all control was out his hands.

"Please," he said again. "Choose to trust me."

She loosened her grip on the Glock's handle. "I'm tired of running away. Pearl was wrong, and I'm done with being alone. But . . ." she stared at his eyes, as if really seeing him and fully connecting with his presence for the first time since he'd entered the cabin. "I think we need to trust each other. Can you trust *me* for a moment?"

His mind raced. Then a sense of calm washed over him. "Yes."

Charlotte laid the gun on the snow and pushed it with her finger until he could reach the handle.

Walker quickly slid the Glock in his holster.

She held out her arm, stretching far into the air pocket. "Take my hand. I'll pull you out."

Walker took her grip.

45

CHARLOTTE

CHARLOTTE'S EARDRUMS beat with the whomping sound of the helicopter blades. She sat on a snow pile near the destroyed cabin remnants, squinting into the sunlight as the rotors whipped white powder in the air. Walker sat next to her on the pile, both of them shivering inside their wet snow gear, and both covered in scratches, bruises, and probably braving through a couple broken bones. But at that moment, there wasn't a way to fix those problems.

She felt numb and not simply from the melted snow throughout her clothing. From everything. Her mind was in a haze.

The rescue helicopter hovered over the others in the clearing, hoisting Franklin up in a stokes basket. His beacon had worked. The Search and Rescue team found him quickly, but he'd injured his back in the avalanche, and Charlotte and Walker insisted he be the first one airlifted to the hospital. It had taken them time to crawl out from the cabin remains, but there had been plenty of skilled rescuers on the outside, already combing the wreckage and ready to help them to their feet.

Neither said a word as they waited for the helicopter to return, but she didn't feel the moment required any. The questions would come on their own very soon, and she wasn't nervous. Instead,

Charlotte felt relieved. Despite the chaos and the swirling snow, she found herself feeling at peace for the first time since she was a kid. This time, she planned to let the truth spill from her—about the years she and her grandmother were afraid to stay still, about how Pearl said the same people who burned down Charlotte's house and killed her parents were looking for them in order to take Pearl away, and how she needed training to stay hidden.

She was feeling so strangely light, that she even considered telling Walker about Zeus—the contact she and Pearl arranged to meet before entering Canada. Zeus specialized in new identities and helping people get in and out of the United States the "non-traditional way." But he required a hefty fee and secrecy, though Pearl never explained how she found Zeus in the first place. Pearl kept secrets of her own.

When the helicopter returned, they were lifted one by one and flown towards County hospital. Charlotte listened to the engine noise, whipping wind, and the crew's muffled voices, savoring what freedom she could before they landed.

A short time later, Charlotte rode on a hospital gurney to the ER—this time fully alert and aware of her situation. They wheeled Walker into the slot on her left. She glanced over, mentally checking that the medical staff was taking care of him. It felt odd to her that she cared. But she did. Nurses and doctors hovered nearby, ordering things like heated blankets, IV's, and x-rays.

This time, Charlotte never wore handcuffs. Nor did Chief Walker order the other officers in the room to detain her, but that wouldn't have mattered. She didn't feel the need to run. No matter what came next, Charlotte was too worn and frayed to fight anymore. She just wanted peace.

46

BERTA

BERTA WAITED in the backseat of Officer Stewart's patrol car, a bit impatient, but she was trying her darnedest not to be. She was also determined to practice a new found sense of patience and empathy, however long it lasted. The memory of Christmas pinecones spilling across a tile floor would stick with her for a long time. As well as Kim's reaction when she learned Mason had sent a text to the chief despite her forbiddance. Berta groaned to herself. Those were two "rock-bottom" memories in a long line of "rock-bottom" moments during recent events. It was time to be sensible again.

Stewart hurried to the door and opened it for both Mason and herself. Jan climbed out of the front passenger seat.

"Thank you, deary," Berta said, glad she'd persuaded Stewart to bring them to the hospital since her car was still stuck at the barn. Plus, they were supposed to be supervised, and Kim sounded more than happy to pass that responsibility off to Stewart.

They entered the emergency room and followed Jan past the front admittance desk to where Walker and Charlotte were being treated. Stewart paused outside the curtains to talk to the doctor.

Berta refused to wait, pushing her way around the nurses and stood in the aisleway. She found Walker and Charlotte across from each other in the large room. "Are you two alright?" she asked, glancing between them.

They both nodded. Their faces were blotchy and red, with bits of dried blood stuck to their skin, but they were covered in heated blankets. Medical staff moved in and out of the area, checking on their needs. Berta had been told they were inside a cabin during an avalanche. All things considered, both were lucky to be alive.

"Good," she said, her tone all business. "I expect you're getting the best care."

Walker snickered. "Are you concerned about me, Berta?"

She tried to squash her smile. "Well, someone's got to give out speeding tickets."

"Would you like one?"

"You'd have to catch me first."

He tried to grin but winced a little. Berta's smile faded. Both he and Charlotte looked like they'd been battling over custody of the Gutenberg Bible. Well, maybe not that bad. More like fisty-cuffs over a first edition of *Old Man and the Sea*. "You both look . . ." she began, then thought twice and dismissed the comparison, unsure if either of them had ever read Hemingway. ". . . tired."

"Yes," Charlotte said. "But okay."

Mason stepped between them. "So, Charlotte, you're going to tell the chief everything, right? Clear this mess up?" He paused, glancing between Charlotte and Walker.

Berta leaned forward. "Wait, everything?" She raised an eyebrow, wishing Charlotte could read her mind. *Everything* coming to light wasn't in her best interest—problematic at best.

"Yes," Mason said. "Everything. It's easier that way."

Berta gripped her handbag, swallowing hard. She whispered to him, "I'm not sure if I like your new-found sensibility, kid. Maybe you should go back to being a hoodlum. Apparently, our circle of trust is null and void outside the barn."

"Yep," he said.

"Well, Charlotte will do whatever she needs to." She stood by Charlotte's bed.

"Berta." Charlotte reached out and touch her on the arm, then lowered her voice. "I'm sorry, but I can't keep our deal."

Berta pressed her lips shut, the wrinkles tightening where her smile should have been. Strangely, she felt okay. And actually, a little relieved it was all over. "Oh, deary, I figured that much already. And I'm not sure what to think about it all yet. I'm glad you didn't meet your demise, not tragic like a Shakespearean heroine and all, but maybe there's still a slight chance I could drive you out of here and—"

"Berta," Walker said.

She straightened up. "Oh, Terry. Be calm. I'm not serious."

"Wait," Charlotte said to her. "You can keep the books. Pearl would've wanted them in the hands of someone who appreciates finer things."

Berta nodded again, her face flushing after such a compliment. She cleared her throat and tried to keep her composure. Perhaps herself and Pearl, if the universe had ever made it possible, might have enjoyed a pleasant conversation or two about Hemingway.

Jan stood at the monitor tracking Walker's vitals. "Terry, they'll come get you for imaging soon. I'm going to check on Franklin's status. I'll be back." She touched him on the arm. "I'm so glad you're okay."

"Thanks," Walker said. "Me, too."

Jan then walked over to Mason. "You and Berta need to stay out of the way. There's a couple chairs by the nurse's station. Hang out there. I'll find you."

"Okay," he said before she left.

Berta glanced between Charlotte and Walker one last time. They both rested against their gurneys and looked in need of a nap. The chief kept hiding a grimace. She supposed all of them looked . . . *tired*. It had been four days since Charlotte entered her bookstore. Only four days, and yet . . .

"Come on, Mason," she said. "Let's go."

"Okay, I just need a sec." He talked to Charlotte for a moment, then went over to Walker.

Berta waited for him in the chairs.

He plopped down beside her. "I just needed to say good bye to Charlotte. I have a feeling I'm not going to see her again. But I'm glad she's okay."

"Me too, kid. I guess I'll need to find another way to keep my store going without Charlotte's money. But we Sheppards are survivors, so I'll be fine."

Mason gazed up from staring at the floor. "Oh, I know. Have you thought about creating a website and selling your books online? You know, then shipping them out?"

"I don't know the first thing about—"

"I can help you ... maybe be the store's tech support."

Berta didn't know what to think. Someone being this helpful had never happened before. "Well, I'm not sure if I even need that. The internet can be complicated and ..."

"It's not as hard as it sounds. And besides, I think Ed is going to fire me anyway. So, you'd be doing me a huge favor."

Berta perked up. "Oh, I suppose if you're destitute then I can take pity on you, help out the needy ... you're hired." She shook his hand. "But I can't pay you until we sell some books."

"Understood." He nodded. "Hey, what about the ones Charlotte sold you?"

"Um," she said, hesitating. "I think I might hang onto those."

"Okay. That makes sense."

"Oh, but the modern ones on my shelves. I'll part with them. No problem."

"Sounds good. How about we rename the business? *Sheppard and Trent Used Books.*"

Berta snorted, tilting her head away so he wouldn't see her smirk. "Don't press your luck, kid."

"Right. First things first. We'll start with the website. Then we'll work our way up to business partners."

In the next few minutes, Mason rambled on using phrases like "bandwidth" and "web hosting" and rattled through other terms she had no intention of remembering. Instead, she glossed over his words and focused on Mason's expression. He was smiling—wide, without care, free, and at pure ease—a look she'd never seen on the boy's face before. Mason was happy.

And she realized, much to her surprise, so was she.

47

WALKER

WALKER BREATHED deep through the oxygen tube in his nose, though the action made him a little light-headed. The extra air probably wasn't needed anymore. His head ached, but it felt better than the suspected fractures in his left wrist, broken nose, and the torn muscles throughout his body. He'd limp and moan like death itself tomorrow, but that was better than having actually died. So, he couldn't complain.

He glanced at Charlotte. She was staring at the medical staff, watching them attend to her and perhaps finding a weak spot in their routine in order to escape. But . . . he knew she wasn't really.

"Thanks, doc." Stewart nodded to the ER physician as she walked away, then he pulled out his phone. "Hey, Chief. I want to show you something. Hang on."

While he waited, Walker glanced across the aisle at Berta and Mason in the chairs. He couldn't hear their words, but they were both engrossed in conversation and seemed to be stress-free. He hoped their optimism would last. Perhaps with some doing, chats with the judge and attorneys about leniency, the kid might only get probation for pulling the fire alarm at the hospital. Mason had cooperated since then, and that would count for something positive. Berta, she was another problem. She harbored a person of interest who in turn had a warrant out for infractions in Harding. No one would want seventy-something year old Berta Sheppard arrested and prosecuted, including the judge. And an attorney could argue that she had been manipulated—swayed because of her age. She'd hate that implication, flat out deny it, but Walker would make sure from afar that she took whatever deal was on the table. He would watch after both of them.

But Charlotte . . . there was nothing he could do for her.

A heaviness churned in his stomach, one not subdued by the pain meds filtering through his I.V. line. If only her consequences would repair as easily as they unraveled. But she was still looking at some jail time.

"Here it is, Chief," Stewart said. He held up his cell phone so Walker could read the open email on the screen. "It's from Lee Parks. She sent it to me when you didn't return her voicemail."

"I lost my phone in the snow," he said.

"We'll get you another one. Sounds like I should start stocking up."

Walker rolled his eyes then glanced at the email.

Walker,

I checked with the FBI field office for you. They knew this case involved a missing person and put a rush on things. Facial rec on the false IDs isn't complete yet, but IAFIS ran the fingerprints against missing person cases like you suggested. The prints taken from the woman in the hospital, a.k.a. Charlotte Evers, match that of a recently-opened missing child case. That child, Charlotte Pierce, was suspected dead fifteen years ago, then added to the database as a missing person by her father—Officer Ruthan Pierce. An FBI field agent is planning to visit Harding and get things straightened out. They'll be in touch.

Hope that helps,

Lee Parks

Walker read the email through a second time, then handed it back. He motioned for Stewart to lean closer so he could speak quietly. "Did you call Kansas City P.D. yet?" he asked.

"Yep. Talked to the police chief. Double-checked Pierce's badge numbers, his photo, and his story. He's legit. The chief confirmed it. And he's surprised that his officer broke the law. Says Pierce is a good cop, otherwise. I guess, under the circumstances—"

"We can sympathize, but it's not our job to sort out that stuff. Ruthan Pierce is in for a bumpy ride."

"Right." Stewart straightened up. "It's just . . . sad. The whole thing."

"Agreed," he said. "Stewart, call the real Peterson in St. George. Let him know that Pearl Sanford is actually named *Pearl Pierce*, and that we believe she's in an urn in Harding, Idaho. Not missing. We just need to confirm that. And we'll get Charlotte's statement soon."

"Of course, but that's important news. Don't you want to handle the call yourself?"

"You'll be fine," he said. "Look after the station till I get back."

Stewart grinned. "No problem, Chief. Take all the time you need. I'll look after Harding."

"Thanks, now did you check on Franklin?"

"Yeah, I just spoke to him. He's still getting more scans. They think he ruptured some discs in his back. He's on pain meds. A lot of them. He called me Stewie."

"Be careful or that will stick. I'll go see him as soon as they let me leave."

"Okay, Chief." Stewart left.

Jan came over. "So the x-ray tech will be here soon. Hope you're photogenic."

"Always, but I need a minute first."

"Sure. You have one." She walked over to Mason and Berta.

Walker waited till no one was looking before he sat up. He groaned and shuttered under his breath, his traumatized muscles barely lifting his body off the gurney. Treatment had to wait. He had one last task. Walker pulled his IV stand with him and hobbled over to Charlotte, gripping one hand on her gurney's railing to steady himself.

She looked up, her expression tightening. "Is everything okay?"

"Not yet. And maybe not for a while. We have a very brief window before things get complicated. But eventually, those things will settle. In the meantime, I'm going to make arrangements for my officers to bring a guy to the hospital today to see you."

"Who is it?" she asked.

He relaxed, loosening his grip on the railing. "Someone you need to meet. Well, someone you need to meet again."

48

CHARLOTTE. LATER.

SUNLIGHT STREAMED through the truck's open window and warmed Charlotte's face, a bead of sweat forming on her temple as her hair whipped in the wind. The drive from Kansas City to Northern Idaho had been long, especially in the old truck, but she didn't mind. Taking an urn on a plane would've been difficult to explain to security, and Charlotte had decided that she preferred simple.

She glanced at her dad in the driver's seat. He hummed along with the radio. Having him in her life again was surreal, and perhaps would take years to become normal. But that too, she didn't mind.

Ruthan noticed her stare and gave her a smile. "Almost there," he said.

"Good." She adjusted her sunglasses and stared out the window. The first time she'd traveled those roads, she'd been too preoccupied to notice the view. This time, it moved and breathed with rich color, as if she were witnessing a living thing for the first time. Antique barns and farm houses dotted the picturesque summer landscape. Fields of green and gold lined the freeway on both sides, adding perfectly outlined rows of symmetry and order. In the north, mountains and thick pine trees bordered the fields. Even when the land was wild, it was a peaceful and lulling drive. She'd forgotten how beautiful Idaho was.

Too much had kept her occupied in the last few years—statements and testimonies. Federal investigators wanted to know all about Zeus and his operation. Turns out, they'd been suspicious for a while. They knew an American citizen in that area was not only providing false identities for individuals leaving and entering the country illegally, but that he was also assisting foreign nationals on the government's watch list to enter the United States from Canada. Pearl had contacted Zeus on a grape-vine fluke—a contact through a contact through another contact. Apparently, Pearl promised to pay his fee in the hundreds of thousands of dollars. A sum she didn't have. Pearl stowed cash and sold the last of her antique jewelry until she'd stashed away thirty thousand. And lied to Charlotte, again, saying her family fortune was accessible when they reached Canada. But that part wasn't real. Only in her mind.

Charlotte didn't blame Pearl for any of it. Nor did Ruthan. And they didn't feel anger or betrayal or hatred. They carried sadness instead, and grief, and a long-lingering heartbreak. Pearl wasn't herself back then. She didn't see the world as they did, nor as she saw it when she was younger. She was ill. That wasn't her fault. And they loved her, and couldn't change the past, only steer the future.

She leaned forward and turned up the radio, humming a little to herself and returning to the car window. Her dad didn't notice. More than once in the last three years, he'd broken down and asked for Charlotte's forgiveness, wishing he had taken better care of his mother. Regret would stick with him for life, and Charlotte witnessed that emotion every time she looked in his eyes. But perhaps that, too, would ease with time. Therapy was helping both of them.

Plus, their focus had been occupied. Federal investigators made her a deal in exchange for contacting Zeus, setting up a meeting, and then later testifying against him. The deal included pages of conditions regarding forgiveness of the criminal charges she faced in Harding, the confusion in St. George, and also her father's charges. As part of the deal, there was "probation" for her instead of jail time. She assumed the FBI simply wanted to keep tabs on her location until the trial was over. And the U.S. Marshal's watchful eye kept her safe. Ruthan was told to "retire" from law enforcement, but he did it gladly and stayed at her side. The last few years had been long, complicated, but she didn't face them alone. And now, they were free.

"Well, we're here. Harding, Idaho," Ruthan said. "Stop on Main Street, right?"

"Yep."

He exited the freeway and drove the car toward the center of town, parking in front of the used bookstore. "I'm supposed to text Walker when we get here. The four-wheelers should be waiting by the trailhead. He'll be along soon."

"Sounds good. And text Berta, too. She's coming." Charlotte glanced toward the back seat, double checking that the box containing Pearl's ashes was still safe in the seatbelt. She planned to carry them herself, even if that meant riding slowly all the way along Devil's Whip to the remnants of the cabin. She'd been told most of the structure was gone and the owner didn't plan to rebuild, but it wasn't the floor boards or the potbelly stove that made Charlotte return there to spread Pearl's ashes. That place marked a memory— the moment she made the decision to stop running. The same ground would serve as Pearl's place of rest. Then they'd both be at peace.

Charlotte got out of the car and stood on the curb, staring down at the parking slot. Ruthan had illegally parked against the red line. She touched the paint with her sneaker and chuckled to herself. Perhaps Walker would overlook their bad parking job, even though this was the second time she'd broken Harding's parking ordinance, and apparently, she never learned.

"Perfect. Here he comes," Ruthan said.

Charlotte glanced up. Chief Walker's police truck headed toward them. Jan and Mason were inside.

Ruthan glanced at her. "Are you ready for the last step? To get to the right place?"

Charlotte tucked her hands in her pockets, waiting while Chief

Walker pulled in behind their car. She felt a sense of ease wash over her, a sensation that she was still trying to get used to despite the three years since leaving Harding. She used to crave peace, and now she had it in such abundance that Charlotte wondered if at times she would burst from its strange normalcy. Being at ease was foreign, though she loved the thought of getting used to it.

"Yes," she said. "I'm ready."

49

ST. GEORGE. BEFORE.

CHARLOTTE COVERED her head with a baseball cap, shielding her face from more than the December rain as she stepped out of the Oldsmobile. She'd dyed her hair from blonde to brunette that morning, done the job in a rush. There wasn't a lot of time to waste. Charlotte adjusted her sunglasses, an item not being used to block the sun, and simultaneously scanned the pharmacy parking lot for odd human behavior. There was plenty of that in St. George, and in just about every city she and Pearl had stayed in during the last fifteen years. But the kind of behavior she tracked wasn't common oddness. As she approached, she analyzed how long it took for the others in the parking lot to enter the building, studying them through side glances and tracking their focal points.

But this time she got lucky. No one paid attention to anything but their own selves. Her out-of-style "laundry day" clothing helped blend with the mundane. It always did. *Evaluating—Ninety-five percent harmless, five percent a threat.*

Charlotte bypassed the main counter where the pharmacist dispensed prescriptions. She didn't have one of those anyway, and visiting a doctor wasn't an option. Doctors asked too many questions.

She glanced up from the far aisle. Overhead cameras faced the counter—pointing straight down with a line of sight to the "pick-up" window—and in addition, the older building hadn't installed plex dividers near the register. She wondered how often the pharmacy was robbed for narcotics. The aged set up seemed like an easy mark. They were too trusting.

Charlotte headed down the aisles, stopping at the over-the-counter cold medicines. She grabbed pain killers/fever reducers, cough syrup in various strengths and brands, an ear temperature thermometer, and a consumer stethoscope. Within three minutes, she'd paid cash, while keeping her chin too low for the camera, and headed back to the car.

Ten minutes later, Charlotte pulled against an entry curb on Pearl's street, scanning the houses and cars for neighbors. A man walked his dog to the community mailboxes. She'd seen him many times before. *Harmless.* A woman who lived across from Pearl's rental house climbed into her truck. Charlotte recognized her as well—Mary Doone, a busy-body type Pearl tried to avoid. She waited while the woman backed out of her driveway and exited the street at the far end. After another thirty seconds, Charlotte approached Pearl's house and pulled into the garage. She left her jacket, hat, and sunglasses in the car. They would be leaving soon anyway.

"Grandma?" Charlotte called out. She took the medicine into the kitchen. "I'm back."

There was no answer.

"I brought medicine." She headed toward the master bedroom, stepping around the packed duffle bags and boxes piled through the living room. Packing would have to wait. Pearl's fever was the priority.

She found Pearl lying in the same position as when she'd left twenty-five minutes earlier. Her grandmother slept under a thin blanket, the linen up to her shoulders. Pearl's face was pale and thin, mostly from not eating much in the last week, and she strained a little with each breath.

Charlotte sat on the bed. "I have something for your headache and the fever. You'll feel better soon. I know it."

Pearl moaned in a soft exhale.

"Let's take your temperature." She used the ear thermometer, holding the device gently against Pearl's head. "103.9." A heavy feeling sank into her stomach, hollowing her insides even more than the past week's worry had already done. "That's too high. You need the emergency room."

Pearl shifted. She reached her hand outside the blanket and rested it on Charlotte's knee, her fingers trembling. "No. Can't go there. You know why."

"But I think you have pneumonia. Or maybe bronchitis or something pulmonary. It's bad, Grandma. And it's been over a week. Getting worse."

"I'll be better tomorrow. We'll make it to Zeus."

"Are you sure about him?"

"Yes. Promise me you'll stick to the plan. Follow his instructions."

"Of course, I will," Charlotte said, putting a cool cloth on Pearl's head. Sweat beaded in her gray curls.

Pearl's hands trembled. "This will be the last move, honey. I promise. Canada will be different. They can't find you there. Just get to Zeus."

Charlotte leaned back, shaking her head. "You mean, they can't find *us*. Why do you keep talking like you're not coming with me?"

"Nonsense. I'll be there. Just remember, they may have killed your parents, but we'll be safer in Canada. And they won't be able to take me away from you—" she said, a coughing spell interrupting her sentence. Her wheezing sounded wet.

Charlotte helped Pearl sit. "You have fluid in your lungs. Please, take some medicine."

"Just put it on the table next to my glasses. I'll take it. You get things ready to go. Pack. Wipe the fingerprints. Don't forget to let the dog go free. We'll get a new security dog in Canada. Such a shame. This one lasted three moves."

"Packing can wait. I'm worried about you."

"I'm . . . fine." Pearl choked on her words, gagged, then tried to catch her breath.

"You're not."

"I will be. We always are." She smiled at Charlotte. "Now. Go, dear."

Charlotte hesitated, staring at Pearl's pale face. Anxiety churned inside her, clouding her mind with awful scenarios. They had a deadline to meet Zeus, to cross the Canadian border and start a new life once and for all. He had new identities for them. No more running. But could Pearl handle the trip with probable pneumonia and a 104-degree temperature? She analyzed options, just as Pearl had taught her to do since age seven—risks at the emergency room, a doctor's office, and medical care along the route from Utah to Idaho. She calculated, ran probabilities, the outcomes stacking in her mind at a manic pace. Her cheap fake IDs wouldn't hold.

Pearl squeezed her hand. "We'll be fine—one hundred percent."

Charlotte set the medicine down and quietly left the room. She finished stashing their sellable valuables in the boxes, including the collection of books from Pearl's grandfather. Some things couldn't be sold at any price . . . too treasured.

She then placed her mother's wrist watch, her only keepsake since age seven, into a bag. For a moment, she stared at the fire-blackened metal through the plastic. Even soon after the house burned and her parents died, Charlotte couldn't focus on that night. Pearl saved her—rescued her from the fire. That much she knew. The rest of her memories came and went, always in pieces. She remembered digging through the charred remains of her house, crawling through the soot until her body was covered in black ash and finding nothing recognizable but the watch her mother left on the dresser. Soon after, Pearl took Charlotte by the hand and kept her safe.

She placed the watch inside a larger bag and double checked the seven thousand American dollars they planned to change into Canadian money, another thirty thousand in cash meant for Zeus' fee, then stashed both bundles with their back up IDs—three for her, three for Pearl. And they'd each carry one on them. Zeus would supply the new Canadian identities and residency contacts.

The plan was in place. They'd sell valuables to predetermined stores and pawn shops along the route, keeping on the move. The final stop in a small town called Harding, Idaho.

Charlotte busied herself organizing the bags until the living room pile became a single grouping. The rest would have to stay— furniture, dishes, various simple living items they'd purchased in St. George. Those types of objects never moved with Charlotte and Pearl. Plus, most of the furniture belonged to the landlord. To them, *leaving* had long become a perfected task.

She put on a pair of rubber gloves and used disinfectant wipes to clean the door frames and handles, as well as the cupboards in the kitchen. At one point, when they lived in Tennessee, Pearl had decided that they couldn't realistically eliminate all their DNA from a safe house, but they could at least wipe clean the fingerprints—make it harder to process the scene. Police had entered their Tennessee apartment right after they left it. Charlotte remembered noticing their patrol cars in her rearview mirror as they parked outside the apartment, just as they drove out of the neighborhood.

Charlotte and Pearl didn't breathe easy until they crossed state lines. Then Pearl smiled again, and Charlotte did as she was told. It was easier when Pearl felt safe.

Thirty minutes passed while she wiped down the St. George rental house. Cleaning surfaces required an entire package of wipes. When she finished, Charlotte let the brown-speckled mutt, a dog they'd never bothered to name, outside in the front yard. He'd have to survive on his own.

She then headed to the back patio and pulled out the small portable fire pit they'd purchased on their first day in St. George. She dumped the dirty wad of disinfectant wipes onto the existing pile of sticks. Lighting the fire pit would be last. Now, all she needed to do was pack the car and get Pearl out of bed. Cleaning and wiping down the bedroom wouldn't take very long. They could leave within the hour, and she'd stop often so Pearl could rest on the way.

Charlotte entered the master bedroom. "It's time to go, Grandma," she said, waiting for an answer while busing herself with the cold medicine. "You spilled the meds."

"Grandma?" she said again. Charlotte glanced at her grandmother and reached for her hand. Pearl's touch felt different—hollow—and a vacant paleness shone on her face. Reactionary fear, instinctual and raw, surged through Charlotte's fingers until every part of her core shook with adrenaline and panic.

She pulled back.

"Pearl?" she said louder.

The woman didn't move.

Charlotte reached down to Pearl's sternum and placed her hand over her grandmother's heart. There was no movement, no heartbeat, no breathing, or signs of life. She frantically felt her grandma's neck and wrist, searching for a pulse . . . and found nothing.

Pearl was dead.

Charlotte grabbed the stethoscope from the pharmacy bag and held it to Pearl's chest, praying in desperation that this nightmarish moment wasn't real.

Still nothing. The pneumonia must have taken over.

Charlotte ripped back the blankets and lifted Pearl onto the floor, positioning herself for CPR. In haste, she began chest compressions the best she could and contemplated calling 911. But she knew Pearl wouldn't want that. A memorized phase ran through her mind, one that had been drilled into her since the house fire, and recited in Pearl's voice: *Anonymity is everything. We can only trust each other.* Charlotte had been taught to avoid helplessness, even in an emergency.

Minutes passed in which Charlotte didn't count the seconds. She didn't analyze her movements, calculate options, solve any problems, she simply fought for Pearl to come back to life until her own body ached. Her panic seized every rational thought, creating a jumbled mess in her mind. Then, Charlotte stopped CPR. It wasn't working.

She felt numb.

Nothing seemed to exist beyond her tunneled view of Pearl's face. She leaned against the wall, tears invading the shock. Pearl wasn't coming back. Death had won.

Charlotte sat on the floor for hours, unable to move, until the sunlight was gone from the room. Every memory, every uncertainty, every fear from the last fifteen years on the run with Pearl flooded back to her in a wave, burying her in unwanted grief. Pearl's words kept haunting her. *We'll be fine—one hundred percent.*

That wasn't true anymore.

Charlotte dried her tears and made a plan, keeping her promise to leave. But she couldn't abandon Pearl. Her grandmother died alone. And probably died scared. Charlotte also couldn't let Pearl's body be left unwanted until the landlord found it. It wasn't right.

Twenty-seven minutes later, Charlotte studied a young man from afar, an obvious twenty-something college student and mortuary tech, as he locked the back door to a local funeral home's crematorium. She slipped the spare seven thousand dollars into her jacket—it had taken years to save it—and glanced at the rear seat where a quilt covered Pearl's body.

Evaluating mortuary tech—fifty percent harmless, fifty percent a threat. The need outweighs the uncertainty.

Charlotte pulled her car near the young man, scanning for security lights and cameras, and parked in the dark, just outside the wall's floodlight beam. The young man stood still, watching her.

The transaction was simpler than an "off the books" human cremation should have been, but then again, there was money involved. He'd get half now and half when he finished. Charlotte stifled her feelings as she arranged the bribe, demanded full discretion, and they moved Pearl's body inside.

He told her to come back in a few hours.

Charlotte drove to the rental house, scanned the street, and closed the garage door behind her car. She then packed the Oldsmobile, stuffed Zeus' thirty grand and the plastic bag under the car jack, and left room for the final box she'd add at the funeral home. The master bedroom wiped down easy. Some of Pearl's things would have to be left behind. And Charlotte couldn't take all of her keepsakes. She placed the over-the-counter medicines, Pearl's reading glasses, and her grandma's IDs into the fire pit. Then, in her final task, Charlotte placed one last item on the pile—the bound pages of Pearl's family history. It was more of a journal than an official record, but Pearl kept the homemade book every time they moved cities. Charlotte never read any of it. Not one page. Pearl insisted that their family's past needed to stay secret, for Charlotte's protection, and she asked for trust and loyalty on the matter.

The flexible book rested in the fire pit as if it fit naturally, waiting to be burned. She studied the cover one last time, but knew she couldn't read a word. She trusted Pearl's judgment. Always did.

In the dark, surrounded by cinderblock walls, no one witnessed the fire. Charlotte stood in the open sliding glass door for several minutes, watching the flames burn holes through the pages. When all the contents turned black, she walked away from the smoldering pit.

Charlotte waited in Pearl's car for forty-five minutes, parked in the dark and staring at the funeral home. The young man met her at the crematorium's back door.

They exchanged money and a box.

Charlotte checked inside the foam interior, touching her fingertips to the urn, before placing the box inside the Oldsmobile's trunk. She tucked the quilt around the sides. A sense of relief washed over her despite the heaviness in her heart. She wasn't leaving Pearl behind.

Charlotte started the engine and pulled away from St. George, heading north. She tamed her emotions and concentrated on fulfilling her promise to Pearl—to keep going until she didn't need to run anymore. Until then, she would stick to her plan and keep to herself. Trusting no one until she could walk slow again, like she did before any of this happened—to find the safety that was her early life before her house burned to the ground. She owed that to Pearl . . . to find a restful, normal sort of place where life was harmless.

A place where both she and Pearl could rest.

ACKNOWLEDGMENTS

Harding Proper would not exist without support from the precious family, friends, and writing community in my life. First and foremost, I need to humbly thank my husband and kids, who support and encourage my passion for writing stories even when I ramble on about characters like they're real people. Without you guys, I wouldn't be me. You are my world.

Thank you to my parents and brothers, who understand that creativity and craziness are sometimes the same thing. You will always make me laugh.

Many thanks to my writing groups and the numerous writers who have given me feedback on this novel over the years: author E.B. Wheeler and author Betti Avari (There are not enough cookies in the world to pay back how much I owe you both), the members of BCW, author McKel Jensen, and author S.L. Clarke.

Although Harding itself is a fictional town, I tried to have the police/CSI/first responder procedure in this book be as realistic as possible, while also accounting for the flexibility that exists in a small town. Thank you to those who helped with my research: David Cowsert, members of my local police department, and forensic investigator Ashlee Moline. Any procedure mistakes or plot accommodations in the book are mine, not theirs. I want to thank them for the service they give their communities.

Also, thank you to Josi Kilpack, who took me to my first writers conference, started me off in the right direction, and has given me so many words of encouragement over the years.

Lastly, thank you to M.D., an individual who encouraged me to do more than I ever thought possible, and to "fake it till I make it."

M.D., I'm doing fine. No, really, I'm good.

ABOUT THE AUTHOR

K.G. Montgomery is an award-winning short story author, with published works under her full name in numerous collections and anthologies. As an ambitious learner with a wandering attention span, she's gained a variety of random life-experiences that have impacted her writing for the better (by giving her a bunch of wacky story material). K.G. has been a museum manager, children's storyteller, volunteer ESL teacher, impulsive traveler, photographer, college graduate, planning commissioner, writer, indie editor, board member, firefighter/AEMT, graduate student, and mom to the best bunch of brilliant and rowdy kids. When not writing fiction, K.G. enjoys extreme sports such as raising teenagers, rage cleaning, and eating ice cream while being lactose-intolerant. She lives along the Rocky Mountains and owns a chicken. Harding Proper is her debut novel.